FIVE SUMMERS

ROBERT SHINFIELD

Grosvenor House
Publishing Limited

This book is published by
Grosvenor House Publishing Ltd
Link House
140 The Broadway, Tolworth, Surrey, KT6 7HT.
www.grosvenorhousepublishing.co.uk

This book is a work of fiction. Any resemblance to
people or events, past or present, is purely coincidental.

A CIP record for this book
is available from the British Library

ISBN 978-1-80381-255-7

1974 - 1975

OUR GANG

1976

THE LONGEST SUMMER

1977

PUNKS

1978

LET'S TALK ABOUT GIRLS

1979

THE VACATION

1980

THEN LIFE BECAME COMPLICATED

1974 - 1975

OUR GANG

CONTENTS

3

SNIDE

If you were asked to describe your personality in ten words or less, what would you say?

How would you best summarise yourself physically? Intellectually? Emotionally?

How about if someone asked you to sum up yourself socially. Would you be outgoing? Generous? Shy? Complicated?

Me? Well, I would describe myself as physically disappointing, intellectually outstanding (and that is a burden - believe me!) and emotionally fragile. And socially? Well, that would certainly fall into the category of complicated.

Let me explain. I have always seen myself as standing on the outside of any social circle looking in, rather than vice versa - critically observing the behaviour of others rather than putting myself in the limelight. Friends that have drifted in and out of my life, have always been managed at arm's length - cultivated in order for me to feel part of the crowd rather than as lifelong emotional ties with all the baggage that that entails.

Much of this I can trace back to my early childhood. A febrile convulsion that lasted far longer than medics would have liked, left one side of my face limp, most notably with a 'lopsided' right eye and mouth. I think it may even have been some type of a stroke. It didn't worry me at all though. When you are that age you just accept things like that and adapt. It wasn't until I started school and found myself subject to jibes from my peers that I began to feel that my facial disfigurement (for that was how I once heard a doctor describe it as to my mother) was something to be ashamed of. There is nobody so cruel (and so honest) as children. Nature dictates that those who stand out for all the wrong reasons should be isolated and put on trial. Only the strongest survive. That is the way of nature, or Darwinism, or whatever belief you choose to follow. Those who can stand up in defiance of their perceived disabilities may, given the right circumstances flourish, even become dominant.

In my case it was nothing like that. I found that, despite my facial handicap, I had a talent for making others laugh. My own life experiences meant that the choice of humour I employed was what some might consider to be offensive. But, when you are in a vulnerable position, there isn't always a choice. For me I felt it was a case of destroy or be destroyed. And my acerbic tongue was finely tuned enough to ensure that I always got a laugh at the expense of some other unfortunate when it was deemed absolutely necessary.

Luckily for me, as I grew older, my brain repaired itself, grew new neurological pathways (or something like that) and as the years unfolded, the muscles in my face re-established themselves. By the age of ten, nobody could ever tell of my childhood impediment.

My method of establishing friends by being the class 'Snide' though was by now hard wired into my brain. I knew of no other way. And besides, when you're ten years old you don't care what it takes to make people laugh - just so long as they laugh.

My reputation also seemed to have established itself with most of my teachers who, although never hostile, didn't seem to have much time for me despite the fact that academically I excelled in most subjects. I guess they thought I turned my abilities in the wrong direction. With hindsight I could have put that right and been the class swot. But that just wasn't me. I was 'Snide' and that was just the way it was.

The mental scars remained though. When you've been teased, you never forget that feeling. But I guess when I saw others being bullied (even took part in the bullying myself) my attitude was one of, 'Well I was strong enough to survive it so, if they can't, then that's their own fault. Isn't it?'

CRAIG

My friendship with Craig came about quite by accident. He was new to the area and arrived in my class one Wednesday morning midway through the Autumn Term.

I can still clearly remember our headmaster, Mr Darrel bringing him into the classroom just after registration and presenting him to our supply teacher for the day.

My first impression of Craig was one of a scruffily dressed urchin with uncombed hair and the look of someone who generally didn't want to be there.

"Oh, Miss errr . . . " began Mr Darrel.

"Miss Farrow."

"Yes, of course. Miss Farrow. This is Craig. He is new to the school. I wonder if you wouldn't mind settling him into class."

Without waiting for a reply, Mr Darrel turned on his heels and rapidly exited leaving Craig standing looking at the teacher with what appeared to be some contempt.

"Right. You go and sit over there," said Miss Farrow hurriedly pointing in the direction of an empty chair next to mine.

Craig sauntered over and sat down heavily with a sigh. I leaned over towards him.

"She's useless," I whispered. "She hasn't even given you a pencil or a book."

"What's all that fuss?" barked Miss Farrow.

"Sorry Miss," I began. "But Craig doesn't have an exercise book."

This was a cue for the supply teacher to rummage around in various cupboards, it being quite obvious that she didn't know where anything was kept. Eventually, Joanne Swift, the class swot (who I secretly fancied - but that's another story) got out of her seat, walked to the correct cupboard and got one out then handed it to Craig.

As soon as she had sat down, I continued my game. "Please miss, he doesn't have a pencil either." My comment had the desired effect as a ripple of sniggering ran round the classroom.

Miss Farrow found a pencil and slammed it down on Craig's desk. "Anything else?" she asked impatiently.

As she turned away, I whispered to Craig; "Watch this. She walks like a duck?" Another bout of sniggering broke out from those close enough to hear.

I should explain at this point that our desks in those days where arranged in pairs, all facing the front of the class. So you usually developed a good relationship with the person sitting at your neighbouring desk. And Craig and I hit it off immediately.

What was it that made him seem such a hard case, even at the age of ten? It wasn't something I questioned but his arrival certainly seemed a pivotal moment in my life. For Craig was indeed tough. I realise now that much of that came from his home life. I was later to learn that he had moved school seven times in just three years. He told us fanciful stories of his mum's battles with various figures of authority although looking back it was clear that many of Craig's bruises didn't just come from the rough and tumble of boyhood. I can also surmise that his 'nomadic' education was in no small part due to his mum trying to keep one step ahead of the authorities. And to keep them away from the succession of men in her life - who Craig would refer briefly to as 'Uncle Tom' or 'Uncle Bob' or 'Uncle Garth' or whatever. It was funny though how he never talked about them other than by referring to each of them in turn as 'Mum's latest.'

Anyway, I made him laugh and he soon established himself as someone not to be messed with around school. Not that I think I ever saw him threaten or hurt anybody. He just had that aura about him. And for the first time in my life I had protection.

It was playtime a few days later that I first saw Craig in action, so to speak. We were wandering aimlessly round the playground when he suddenly stopped in his tracks.

"Look over there," he said pointing in the direction of a particularly chubby ten year old whose name I neither knew nor cared to know. "Come on."

Craig walked straight up to the boy then eyed him up and down carefully. "I'm hungry. Give us that," he demanded, pointing to a huge paper bag the boy held tightly in his fist.

"No," he replied, his mouth full of sweets.

"Don't you think you've had enough already, doughnut boy?" I mocked. Craig laughed.

8

The boy eyed Craig nervously. In response, Craig grabbed the bag from his hand and walked away.

"What we got?" I asked peering at the contents of the bag.

"Mojos," replied Craig. "And fruit salad and black jacks."

"Bagsy the blackjacks!" I cried thrusting my hand in.

SHANE

As soon as we'd finished the bag, Craig had already spotted someone else.

"Who's that?" he asked pointing across the playground at the only black boy in the school.

"Oh he's another new kid," I answered. "Joined a couple of weeks before you."

We walked over to the boy who was very obviously on his own. Black children in those days were so unusual where we lived that I don't think anybody knew what to make of him.

As we got closer, I began to appreciate his size. He was huge. He could certainly pass for 12 or 13 years old. But this didn't seem to daunt Craig in the least. Reaching out he grabbed the bag of crisps in the boy's hand.

"Salt and vinegar - my favourite," said Craig.

Immediately the boys other hand shot across and grabbed Craig's wrist in a vice like grip.

"Don't you know it's rude to steal," he said in a calm voice.

Craig looked up at him and the boy met him with a steady gaze. Then he wrenched Craig's hand from the packet of crisps.

The expression on Craig's face changed from one of condescension to one of admiration.

The boy, now offered the open packet to Craig. "You only had to ask. Theft is a crime you know. You could go to prison for five years for that. I should know. My dad's a solicitor."

"Oh doesn't he talk all hoity toity," I laughed.

"What's your name, muscle man?" asked Craig, ignoring my comment and taking a huge handful of crisps.

"Shane," replied the boy.

"I'm Craig and this here is Snide? You wanna join my gang Shane?"

Shane examined us both carefully for some time before finally answering. "Yeah. OK."

And so our unholy partnership became a trio. Craig immediately saw Shane's potential I guess because, although regarded as hard, he was in physical appearance quite a small, scrawny specimen. And I suspect he knew that if he ever did get into a confrontation, he wouldn't necessarily come out of it too well. Particularly as we were on the verge of joining secondary school where we would be minnows in a much bigger pond.

So Shane gave Craig protection and Craig gave me protection. But Craig was always the leader of our gang. And Shane and I never questioned that.

If truth be known I always preferred Shane to Craig. I think in hindsight we probably had more in common. Shane's dad was indeed a solicitor - although I only ever met him on a couple of occasions. In fact in all the years I knew him I never ever visited Shane's house. Well not until we'd both finished school (but that's another story). I knew where he lived, one of the big detached houses up Spring Hill, but I was never invited round. Shane always came calling for us.

We got on well, me and Shane. On the rare occasions that it wasn't all three of us together, we would talk endlessly about anything. Shane saw himself as an authority on everything from politics to science and, although I wasn't always taken in by it, I nevertheless respected him as a fountain of knowledge.

It was never quite the same with Craig. When you were in Craig's presence it was almost as if you were in awe. You waited patiently to be called to the table rather than offering up anything yourself. Unless it was a sharp throw away one liner about someone. Then I was at liberty to wax lyrical. That was my role in the group. Shane didn't even have that. When we were together he was always the quietest of the three.

10

I think Shane's greatest strength, in my eyes at least, was that he was Mr Dependable. He was as straight as a die. The acronym WYSIWYG could have been written for him.

Craig on the other hand had a personality that was far more impenetrable. He could be quite secretive at times, particularly about his home life. I guess looking back that hanging around with us was his escape from all that.

THE DEN

I can't remember when we discovered the den. It feels somehow as if we always knew it was there but there must have been a time before. It was so well hidden that I can't quite recall if we ever discovered it or if one of us knew about it beforehand and simply introduced it to the others. Funny thing was it was always ours. On the rare occasions other kids came across it, they already knew not to enter without permission. The den was the property of 'Craig and his mates'.

It was a simple concrete structure hidden by overgrowing brambles and bracken at the top of a disused railway embankment. Far below, along the course of the now lifted railway track, a footpath had been constructed although it was never well maintained and the depth of the cut meant it regularly flooded in winter leaving it virtually impassable to all but the most persevering of walkers. Even in summer it remained a cool damp haven, the sort of place you might escape to on the hottest of days if it wasn't for the clouds of midges angrily circling the few stagnant pools of water that survived all but the most severe of droughts.

Shane had assured us that it was an old air raid shelter although who it actually served, at the top of a railway embankment at least 200 yards from the nearest house, we were never quite sure.

The roof was made up of a single slab of reinforced concrete that someone had hacked away in one corner to let in a small amount of light and far too much rain. The walls were of similar concrete construction with a simple narrow opening forming the only way in and out. This was the part we needed to maintain as it frequently became overgrown with the ubiquitous brambles and bracken that dominated the upper slopes of the cutting.

To make it even more secret, we had cut a winding path through the undergrowth to join the entrance to the main footpath that ran alongside the fencing at the top of the cutting. In doing so we ensured that the doorway could not be seen from the footpath and passers by could quite literally pass us by without even noticing the shelter was there, particularly in summer when brambles and bracken were both in full leaf.

The floor was simply earth but, having the shelter of the concrete roof (except for the corner with the hole) it was dry for most of the year.

I have a vague recollection of a determined effort we made one summer, I think it was 1975, to furnish it.

It began when I had salvaged an old carpet from my house. We'd had new ones - our first ever fitted carpets, along with our first colour TV, all bought after we won £200 on the premium bonds.

After much struggle rolling it up we carried it the mile or so from my house to the den, Shane shouldering the weight of it throughout, with me and Craig holding up either end.

We felt so pleased with ourselves once we'd unfurled it. Unfortunately, unbeknown to us, the carpet was infested with fleas from our cat. And with nothing else to feed on they all turned on us. That led to a fair bit of ribbing from the other two. I seem to recall that for a short time I was nicknamed 'Fleabag'. It was all taken in good faith though. After all Craig and Shane were my mates. But God help anyone else who tried to call me by that name. Like I said before, I was protected by my friendships with Craig and Shane. Nobody dared tease me.

Shane provided a faux leatherette pouffe which we took turns to sit on. Then, inexplicably Craig turned up at my door one morning with an old armchair. It looked like the sort of high backed sit up and beg chair that a pensioner might inhabit in an old people's home. But Craig simply said he'd 'found it.' He offered no other explanation and, of course, we didn't ask for one.

It was quite a task dragging it down to the den. It had stout wooden legs but no casters, so we had to carry it the whole way on what turned out to be one of the hottest days of the year. Once again Shane's strength was indispensable otherwise we might never have got it there. However, we soon realised that it was a wasted journey when we tried to get it through the narrow doorway. It was far too big. And it certainly wouldn't squeeze through the hole in the roof.

In the end, we broke it up and, despite the heat of the day, set fire to it.

Unfortunately, with it being a dry summer, the grass we had laid it down on also caught fire and we soon had a major incident on our hands.

Craig made the executive decision to do a runner so that, when the fire brigade finally turned up, we were perched on a bank a couple of hundred yards away under the guise of curious witnesses. It gave us a strangely excited feeling of power knowing that all this mayhem had been caused by us yet no one would ever know.

After the fire, which spread to the surrounding foliage, our den became cruelly exposed to the outside world and we lost interest for a while. We certainly gave up on trying to furnish it. It was quite clear now that the narrow opening precluded the entry of anything resembling real furniture. So the pouffe significantly became the centrepiece of the den. And as such it was only right and proper that it became 'Craig's Seat of Office.' We all accepted that without question - even Shane who provided it.

The summer of 1975 was a special one for us as it marked the transition from Junior to Secondary School, in our case Streetside Comprehensive, a monstrous 1960s brick and concrete creation internally decorated in the harshest hues of purple, orange and green. Not that we cared about the colours of the walls. We had far more important things to worry about. Whereas, before the summer holidays we were top dogs in our Junior School, we now suddenly found ourselves as small fry. Not only did we have to contend with sharks in the form of 5th form alpha males, we also had to absorb the output of our rival junior school, The Lindun, a leafy establishment based on the 'right side' of town.

However, despite being naive 11 year olds, quite unaware of the prejudices held towards us by all and sundry, we soon established ourselves on the Secondary School scene, thanks in no small part to Craig's reputation, Shem's muscle and my . . . well . . .wit!

So, whilst we rebuilt our power base, the den went on the back burner for a few months.

Then came 1976.

1976

THE
LONGEST SUMMER

CONTENTS

THE LONGEST SUMMER

For people of a certain age, 1976 means just one thing - the long hot summer. In these days of climate change and global warming the summer of 1976 could quite easily be forgotten, but not by us. To put it into perspective, the summer of 1975 was a dry one. The autumn, winter and following spring were similarly dry. So when the summer of 1976 turned out to be one of the hottest and driest in living memory, things began to get serious. A Minister of Drought was appointed by the government for the first time. In fact, by August the drought had become so severe that some reservoirs began to dry up and trees even began to shed their leaves.

That was when Viktor turned up.

His name, I was later to learn, was Viktor Kapalski. Funny how now, as I write it down for the first time, I realise that, having only seen it written once, I have absolutely no recall of how it is spelt. It somehow looks more authentically Polish when you include Ks in the spelling instead of Cs. Looking at it, I'm not even sure if his surname shouldn't have been Kapowski - with the emphasis, given his personality, on KAPOW!

Anyhow, I never called him by his name and certainly never referred to it when I was with Craig and Shane. We just talked about him as 'The Tramp' - or worse. In fact, now I come to think about it, I never called him anything, even after I learned his name. For his part he simply referred to me as 'Boy.' Nothing more than that. Just 'Boy.'

The story of Viktor begins, as you might have already gathered, on a particularly hot day in August 1976.

Monday 9th August: Scramblathon

"Go on then Snide, off you go."

The voice was slightly mocking, the sort of tone that coming from most people would be offensive. But from the mouth of a friend it stopped just short of the line.

And I knew why Craig was mocking me. Because I was scared of heights and he knew it. Not only that, but since he'd found out about my Acrophobia, all of his new games seemed to revolve around various battles against gravity.

His latest creation he had entitled 'Scramblathon'. Basically it involved free-wheeling on a bike down the side of the cutting at breakneck speed, hitting the footpath at the bottom and then pedalling as hard as possible to see how far up the other side you could get before gravity pulled you to a halt.

There were three routes down. The first, called the 'Wimps Route' was the gentlest of slopes, although even this had one or two tree roots lurking which, if not negotiated, could throw you off your bike and into the brambles. The second was 'The Slalom' and was slightly steeper with two sharp bends that involved skilful use of brakes and transfer of body weight to negotiate. Finally came 'The Death Run'. This was straight down the cutting at the steepest possible angles hitting the path at the bottom with a juddering thump which, if you weren't careful, threw you clean over the handlebars.

And despite my best efforts to avoid it, today was the day I had been elected to take on The Death Run for the first time.

As I sat at the top looking down I considered all of the awful possibilities that awaited me. Even if I used brakes all the way (for which I would no doubt be mocked) there was still the moment where you came to a halt halfway up the other side, staring up at the sky with the unthinkable prospect if your brakes weren't strong enough, of rolling backwards.

I silently cursed the day I'd ever mentioned the fact that I had acquired a second hand bike. Before that, the only bike that ever made it to the cutting was Craig's gleaming red Chopper. With it's plunging narrow handlebars and padded L shaped seat it was to 1970s boys the epitome of cool. And to Craig it was his pride and joy. I sometimes think it was just about the only thing in the world he owned. He had told me that one of his mum's boyfriends had bought it for him although he wasn't sure why because he didn't seem to like him. But he was very keen on Craig making good use of it. I guess he just wanted him out of the way as much as possible, but I never said anything.

Craig certainly didn't possess much else. This was in no small way reflected in his clothes. In all the time I knew him I only ever saw him wear one of three t shirts; a plain white one, a ripped blue one with Slade written across the chest and a khaki green long sleeved affair which looked two sizes too big. His jeans always looked like the same pair and on his feet he wore a battered old pair of brown corduroy pumps.

Shane had a bike but he told us flatly that his mum and dad didn't allow him to take it out on his own and he certainly couldn't bring it down to the cutting.

Then, a few months ago, a neighbour offered me their son's battered old bone shaker, complete with flat tyres. Never having had a bike, I gratefully accepted and spent the next fortnight rolling down the garden over and over again until I finally got my balance.

Naturally, I was over the moon and it wasn't long before Craig and Shane knew about it. That was when Craig suggested I bring it down the cutting. And that was why I now found myself perched precariously on the launch pad at the top of The Death Run staring nervously down into the abyss.

"I think he's scared," grinned Shane.

"Yeah. Well maybe Mummy might let you bring your bike down tomorrow," I replied.

Craig laughed.

Turning back to face the slope I slowly released the brakes. The sudden acceleration took me by surprise and I gasped in shock. "Oh no, oh no, oh noo-oo." My voiced trailed away into the depths of the cutting. It all happened so fast that it was over before I had time to think. One second I was hurtling downhill, the next I was halfway up the other side, brakes jammed on, feet desperately trying to get a grip on the dry crumbling earth.

"You forgot to shout the word," Shane called out.

Dismounting with great care I cupped my hands to my mouth and fuelled by the adrenaline rush of my first Death Run, I shouted at the top of my voice; "Scaramblathon!" Seconds later came the echo, rebounding of the brickwork of the road bridge that crossed the cutting 100 yards or so away.

"Beat that then," I shouted back to Craig.

But he was already on his way. No brakes from Craig though. Then, as he hit the path at the bottom his bike's narrow handlebars took on a mind of their own, turned sharply through ninety degrees and he was thrown horizontally across the path colliding with a sapling growing out from the base of the slope on the far side.

Shane rushed down to his aid but Craig was already on his feet, more concerned about his bike than himself.

"Bollocks!" he cursed, then without further ado he was wheeling the still intact Chopper back to the top.

Shane waited then walked back up with me. "Your turn," I said pushing my bike towards Shane as we reached the top. "And don't forget to shout the word." Shane showed no hesitation, lining the bike up then pushing himself off. He braked a little at first then put his head down and free wheeled. It was timed to perfection and, as he crossed the path at the bottom, a cry of "Scramblathon," resounded around the cutting. Once on the far side his legs pumped hard on the pedals and he finally came to a standstill considerably further up the embankment than my feeble effort.

"Ha. In yer face," called Craig waving his hand at me in a rude gesture. "Now watch the master at work."

Throwing his leg over the saddle like a cowboy mounting his horse he hurled himself off the launch pad screaming "Scramblathon," as he went. This time, as he reached the bottom, he braked sharply. Momentarily, his back wheel slewed sideways then, raising himself out of the saddle he started to pedal furiously.

However, it was clear he didn't have Shane's strength and he ended up well short of him.

"Ha. In yer face!" I screamed at the top of my voice.

"Ha in both yer faces - losers," called Shane from his lofty position.

And this time it was Shane's turn to laugh.

Monday 9th August: The Spy

Having exhausted ourselves on the Death Run and with the heat of the day beginning to smother us like an oppressive blanket, the decision was made to retire to the cool sanctuary of the den.

I led the way along the winding path, relieved to be free of the ordeal. As I reached the entrance I paused. Looking back now, I can't quite recall which of my senses it was that alerted me to the fact that something or someone was in there. Was it a sight, a sound or even a smell? Whatever, it was enough to stop me in my tracks.

I sensed Shane at my shoulder. "What is it?" he asked.

I peered inside, my eyes gradually becoming accustomed to the gloom.

"Look!" I hissed, pointing into the far corner.

On first inspection it appeared to be a pile of old rags, an assortment of tattered clothes, tied up by a piece of rope which had been secured rather ornately with a bow. Looking more closely, I could make out a pair of army type boots sticking out of the bottom. And lying on top, at an angle lay a flamboyant fedora hat which had obviously seen better days. The bundle was surrounded by an assortment of plastic carrier bags. One was stuffed with more rags and at least two others appeared to be full of scrunched up tin cans.

Craig joined us and, leaving our bikes leaning against the outside wall, we ventured inside the doorway. As we entered, the smell hit us - a rank stench that caught the back of the throat. It most closely resembled a cross between rotting fish and ammonia.

"Is that a person?" whispered Shane.

As if in reply, the bundle suddenly let out a loud, long, rasping snore.

"Jesus Christ!" cried Craig.

It was enough to wake our visitor.

"Whassat. Who's zere?" came a voice from somewhere deep inside the jumble of clothes that now began to stir.

Quickly, we took to our heels, Craig stopping to grab his Chopper, and didn't stop running until we reached the road.

The path that ran along the top of the cutting emerged onto the road through a gap in the hedge. Here the road crossed the cutting by way of a bridge bordered on either side by a low wall built of industrial blue brick. We crossed the road to take advantage of the shade afforded by the trees on the far side.

Here Craig scrambled up on to the wall, hanging his legs over the far side. Shane joined him but, having had enough of heights for one day, I opted to keep my feet firmly on the pavement and merely leaned over.

We were unusually silent for a while although I guess we were all thinking the same thing. If it had been kids in our den we would have turfed them out. But an adult?

It was Craig who finally broke the silence. "Did you hear his accent?"

"Sounded Russian to me," said Shane authoritatively.

"Whooo ees zeer?" I crowed in a grossly exaggerated accent.

"Of course, you know what this means," continued Shane. "He could be a Ruskie spy."

Craig and I turned and stared at him in disbelief. "A spy!" exclaimed Craig incredulously. "What do you mean, a spy?"

"Well you heard his accent," explained Shane. "He's probably working undercover as a tramp."

"Doing what?" I asked.

Shane pondered this for a moment then his eyes widened. "The RAF base!" he said, swinging himself back onto the pavement. "It's just up the road. I bet he's out to steal secret papers and take them back to Moscow."

"And now we've blown his cover," added Craig.

"Just smelt like an old tramp who'd pissed himself to me," I said.

If my intention was to make the others laugh, it failed miserably.

"We could be in big trouble," said Shane. "Let's get out of here before he tracks us down."

"Yeah he's probably got a gun," added Craig. He stopped and looked around. "Hey Snide, where's your bike?"

"I left it at the den," I replied.

"Better go and get it then," said Craig. He paused, examining my face closely. "You're not scared are you?"

"No, "I said, turning to cross the road. I stopped. "Well aren't you coming with me?"

"No chance," answered Craig. "We'll wait here."

Not wishing to lose face, I strode purposefully across the road and pushed my way back through the gap in the hedge. As I approached the den though, I slowed down. I was still pretty convinced it was just a tramp but what if Shane was right? What if he was a secret Soviet spy?

I decided to approach cautiously. As I made my way along the winding path that led to the doorway of the den I stopped every few steps and held my breath, listening for the slightest sound coming from within. Eventually, when I was only a few feet away I heard a familiar snore. That was no spy. What did Shane know anyway?

Nevertheless, I grabbed my bike and made off on it as fast as I could pedal.

It was only as I burst back through the gap in the hedge that I realised that Craig and Shane had gone. Some friends they were. "Chickens!" I cursed under my breath as I turned my bike and headed off in the direction of home.

Tuesday 10th August: Campaign of Action

I was interrupted from devouring a bowl of rice crispies the following morning by a sharp rapping on the door. It had to be Shane, I thought - nobody else knocked our door like that.

Normally I was pleased to see any of my friends standing on the doorstep but, having been deserted yesterday, I was far from inclined to indulge in friendly chat with either Shane or Craig.

Putting my breakfast to one side I made my way through to the hall. I could see from the outline through the frosted glass that it was indeed Shane. I took a deep breath and opened the door.

"Alright Snide," said Shane grinning.

"Alright," I replied in as much an uncommitted a voice as I could muster.

"Me and Craig are going down the swimming baths today. You coming?"

In truth I hated the local swimming baths. Apart from the fact that in the summer holidays it was so overcrowded you couldn't actually do anything in there, the chlorine was so strong it left you with a sore throat for the rest of the day. And besides, unbeknown to Craig and Shane, I couldn't actually swim. "No thanks," I said digging my hands into my pockets awkwardly.

"OK then," said Shane obviously totally unaware that I was annoyed with him. "See you. Oh and if you're not coming with us, you could go down the den and see if that tramp's still there."

"I thought you said he was I spy," I replied.

"Nah!" exclaimed Shane. "Me and Craig talked it out on the way home yesterday. Well it wouldn't make sense would it? I mean, did you smell him? PU!" Shane held his nose with his right hand and pulled his left arm down as if flushing an imaginary toilet.

I couldn't help laughing. "Yeah. I might go down and see what's happening."

Having finished off my breakfast and thought about it though, I felt a little bit apprehensive.

The thing was that, in a way this man was a challenge to our authority as a gang. And in all our time together, we had never been challenged. And I for one didn't quite know how to react.

In the end, with nothing else to do, I decided to approach with caution. And so with the relentless sun beating down on me from a clear blue sky I mounted my bone shaker and rode down to the railway cutting.

I don't know whether he heard me coming but any idea of a stealthy approach was quickly extinguished when a head appeared in the doorway of the den and I found myself staring into two fiery eyes.

"Aach - you again. Why you here?"

"I . . my . . "

Unable to think of anything to say I turned, jumped on my bike and for the second time in two days, pedalled away as fast as I could.

"Well he's got to go," announced Craig firmly.

It was late afternoon and Craig and Shane, both stinking of chlorine, had met up with me in the park.

"But how?" I asked.

"We could start a campaign of action," suggested Shane.

"Yeah, I like that. A campaign of action," said Craig, repeating the words thoughtfully. "We need to do something to drive him out."

All three of us stood a while in silent contemplation.

"Stones," cried Shane, suddenly.

"And water bombs," added Craig with a crafty grin. "All over those smelly bags."

"How?" I asked.

"Guerrilla raids," proclaimed Shane with some authority. "Like with a grenade strike. Run up to the entrance, throw the stone in and run."

"And we can drop the water bombs through the hole in the roof," added Craig. "So who's going first?"

Then, as if reading each others' minds, Craig and Shane both turned to face me.

"Me?" I shouted.

"Yeah," said Craig. "And give him some lip while you're at it."

My heart quickened but looking into the eyes of my two friends, I knew the decision had already been made.

"When?" I asked, a certain squeakiness in my voice giving away a nervous tension that had begun to build somewhere deep inside my gut.

"No time like the present," said Craig. "I tell you what Snide, you can use my Chopper to get away quicker. Well come on then."

We made our way out of the park which bordered the cutting, Shane and Craig stopping from time to time to pick up, then discard potential stones.

We scrambled down the bank of the cutting and started along the footpath. Suddenly, lying at the edge of the path, I caught sight of something large and angular sticking out of a pile of clinker. It was a broken half brick. I picked it up. "What about this?" I asked.

"Snide! Are you mental or what!" cried Craig.

I felt a warm glow of pride inside. This would show them I was no coward. Suddenly the feeling of fear and apprehension gave way to one of excitement as a burst of adrenalin took hold.

"Come on," I said. "Let's do this."

We clambered up the other side of the cutting, Craig and Me trailing behind as we pushed our bikes up the steep bank. Soon we were stood at the end of the path leading up to the den.

"What if he's not there?" I whispered.

Craig didn't reply. Instead he pushed his bike towards me.

I slowly made my way up to the entrance, turning the bike around so I could make a quick exit. As quietly as possible I pulled out the stand and leant the bike on it.

I peered through the doorway, my heart beating in my throat.

There he was, slumped in the corner with his head down, an empty bottle lying next to him.

It had to be now.

As I fished the brick out of my pocket I noticed my breath coming in short sharp bursts. Surely he could hear me.

Summoning all of my strength, I hurled the brick in his direction.

"Commie bastard," I shouted. Then I turned and mounted the bike.

What happened next all seemed a bit of a blur. There was a roar of rage from inside the den followed by the sound of footsteps. Panicking, I put my foot on the pedal and pushed, but nothing happened. The bike wouldn't move. Looking, I realised that the stand was still down. But it was on the opposite side to the pedal my foot was still perched upon. Then, as I tried to simultaneously balance and kick the stand away I tilted to one side and crashed into the brambles.

I looked up to see the tramp was now standing over me. He began shouting something in a foreign language.

I disentangled myself from the bike, scrambled to my feet and hastily remounted.

As I turned to go, our eyes met, briefly.

It is a moment I will never forget.

For, although his words were angry, his eyes showed fear, even a certain sadness. For the first time, I found myself looking, not at a stupid, smelly tramp whose only purpose in life was to be despised and mocked. I saw another human being.

And I suddenly felt ashamed.

Finally, I got the stand up and pedalled away with the tramp's curses still ringing in my ears.

Shane and Craig were stood where I had left them. They were both laughing - Craig so much that tears were streaming down his face.

I laughed with them but, it felt forced and contrived. In my mind something had changed.

"Did you hit him?" asked Shane eventually.

"Course I did," I replied. "Well you heard him didn't you?"

"Could be dangerous," said Shane. "If you hit him on the head, you could have given him a brain haemorrhage. He could die. Then you'd be done for murder."

"No I couldn't," I replied. "I'm too young."

"No you're not," said Shane. "Criminal age of responsibility. It's ten. I should know."

"Well it was a bit mental throwing a brick at someone," added Craig who was still laughing.

We started back towards the park.

"Water bombs next," said Craig at length.

"Well I've done my bit," I added. "Your turn next Shane."

"Yeah. I got some balloons at home. We can use those." continued Craig.

Shane, as unflappable as ever, said nothing.

Saturday 14ᵗʰ August: Water Bombs

We didn't meet up again for a few days. I had no idea why but sometimes Craig simply vanished off the face of the Earth. And without our leader, Shane and I rarely got together. To be honest, I didn't feel like doing much anyway. Just as you thought the summer was as hot as it could get, it suddenly became even hotter.

I had resorted to fishing the old inflatable paddling pool from the garden shed and filling it with water. It wasn't a very good idea though. At first it leaked water, then I realised it was leaking air as well. By mid afternoon, the parched, yellow grass had swallowed up more than half of the pool's contents and what was left had warmed in the midday sun to the point where it no longer served its purpose as a coolant.

I spent much of my time the following day trying to patch up various leaks and punctures using a bicycle repair kit but in the end, it all became too much of an effort . Sitting under a tree with an ice cold drink was far less strenuous. It also gave me an opportunity to think.

Something had touched me when the tramp and I made eye contact. This was a real live human being, just like me. Yet he was living like that. Alone, no money, unwashed, in a foreign land. How on earth did he ever end up in such a situation? And how must he have felt when I, for no reason at all, hurled a brick at him?

The trouble was Craig and Shane.

As far as they were concerned he was fair game. And if I wanted to be part of the gang, I would have to go along with them. It left an uncomfortable feeling in the pit of my stomach.

I didn't in fact see Craig or Shane for another four days. In the end, I decided to go and visit Craig myself.

Craig's house was on a large estate on the edge of town. Like many of the houses on the estate it was a shabby red brick, red tiled affair with small windows and an untidy garden. Parked at the side of the house was a rusting car whose engine had long since been removed and parked at the side of the car was Craig's bike.

Suddenly, the gate at the side of the house swung open and Craig appeared dragging a large bin bag behind him.

"Here they are," he said without even looking up at me. "Trouble is I think they're too heavy to carry on my bike."

I smiled at how we hadn't seen each other for days yet Craig was picking up the conversation where we'd left off as if all of the intervening time was an irrelevance.

He dragged the bag round to the front of the house then sat down, exhaling noisily. "Phew. It's hot!" He wiped his hand across his forehead.

That was when I noticed his black eye.

"Who did that?" I asked.

Craig looked up at me sheepishly, then back at the house, then at me again. He appeared to be about to speak but changed his mind - and the subject.

"It's the water isn't it? It's too heavy."

I opened up the bag and looked inside. There were about ten balloons in all, already filled with water each tied in a knot at the neck.

"Wouldn't it be easier filling them at the den," I suggested.

"No," answered Craig. "You need a tap to get the pressure."

He paused for thought. "Hang on, I've got an idea. Come on."

31

"What about Shane?" I asked.

"Let's ring him," replied Craig. Leaving the bag behind, he climbed on to his bike and started off down the path, turning right into the road.

To be honest I'd forgotten that Craig's house didn't actually have a telephone. All his calls were made from the local phone box on the corner.

Craig pulled up and leaned his bike on its stand. He fished around in his pockets examining their contents carefully, then turned to me.

"You got 10p?"

Lucky for him I had. And lucky he phoned Shane when he did because he was just about to go out to town with his mum.

Trying to get Shane out was never easy, we both knew that his mum didn't approve of Craig. In fact I'm not even sure if she approved of me. Shane had once said she'd lectured him about mixing more with the children of the professional classes and not the local riff-raff. I didn't understand it at the time but I guess she was just a snob - pure and simple as that.

Anyway, Shane got his own way (just before Craig's 10p ran out) and soon we were sitting on the bowling green in the park. The bowling green was one of our favourite spots that summer, on account of the fact that it was the only thing still being watered (although even that was under threat with a hosepipe ban imminent). What that meant was that in the hottest part of the day we could go and cool down by lying under the sprinkler.

"So what are we doing here?" asked Shane.

"Watch," said Craig.

Walking across the green, he fished a balloon out of his pocket, pulled the end of the hose off the sprinkler and shoved it into the neck of the balloon. Immediately it began to inflate. When it was full enough, Craig gripped the neck between his thumb and forefinger, cupped its weight with his other hand and threw it hard in our direction. As it flew through the air, water fountained out of the neck soaking me and Shane.

"Now do you get it?" he laughed.

"Oh yes," shouted Shane. "Genius!"

I laughed with them but inside I again had that uncomfortable feeling - something like guilt, disapproval and the feeling of being coerced all rolled into one.

We filled one balloon each before heading off in the direction of the den.

All three of us lay flat on the concrete roof of the shelter, the hot surface scorching our skin. Looking through the hole we could just make out in the gloom the tramp's collection of bags.

"There's your target," Craig whispered to Shane. "It looks like it all needs a good wash anyway." He stifled a giggle. Craig tapped me on the shoulder and we backed away to the safety of the undergrowth. Shane took one last look then threw the water bomb through the hole. There was a sloshing sound followed by silence. Shane crawled forward and pushed his head through the hole. Then he pulled himself up and shouted, "Direct hit. And he's not in there."

"Are you sure?" said Craig.

"Deffo."

"Come on then." He grabbed me by the shoulder and I followed as he made his way down the path and through the doorway. "We can do a better job if we attack from within."

"What you gonna do?" asked Shane, his face reappearing at the hole in the ceiling.

"This," said Craig, upending each bag in turn and emptying the contents all over the floor. He then released the neck of his water bomb aiming the water all over the bags' contents.

He held the balloon close to his groin. "Look at me having a wee," he laughed. "Your turn Snide."

I walked over and reluctantly emptied my balloon.

"Actually I can do better than that," giggled Craig. And with that, he undid his trousers and urinated all over the small pile of clothes that had been contained in one of the bags.

"Ha ha ha," shrieked Shane. "Makes no difference cos he stinks of piss anyway."

But Craig hadn't finished. He was in full flow now. Seeing the tramps half full bottle, he picked it up and smashed it against the wall. "Dirty bastard!" he shouted. He then started to kick the clothes all over the floor and grind them into the earth with his foot.

At the time, I'd never seen aggression like it from anybody. But looking back it seems clear that all that pent up anger in Craig wasn't really aimed at the tramp. It was aimed at whoever had given him that black eye.

After what seemed an age, Craig calmed down and marched out, with me trailing behind in stunned silence. Shane had lost interest and was sitting on the fence when we emerged.

"I've got to go," I said and made off in the direction of home. And to be honest, I don't think I'd ever felt so relieved to get away.

Saturday 14ᵗʰ August: From Safety to Where?

There comes a point in your life as you grow up when you have to make a big decision. Do you stay safe, go with the flow and hold court with the masses? Or do you go out on a limb, exposed, naked, and stand up for what you believe in, for what you know is right - regardless of the condescension and cynicism of those around you?

Some would describe it as a moment of truth, although it's often never that simple.

The question was; did I go along with my friends, my gang, and continue to bully and persecute a man who, for whatever reason, I had inexplicably developed an unspoken affinity with? Or did I go with my instincts and offer friendship to someone who, despite coming from a different world to mine, was undoubtedly alone, frightened and in desperate need of a helping hand.

When explicated in such terms, the choice became black and white.

The night following the water bombing however, was a particularly difficult one. My conscience had already decreed that I should make amends with the old man (for that was how

I now referred to him in my own mind). It was the least I could do.

If I befriended him however, what would Craig and Shane say? And if I spoke to him behind their backs, how would they react if they found out? After all, I had a standing amongst my peers. I wasn't nicknamed Snide for nothing.

The oppressive heat of the night didn't help my thinking. Sleep was difficult. Eventually, after endless tossing and turning beneath my nylon sheets, I slipped out of bed, crept downstairs and tiptoed into the kitchen. Opening the fridge I took out a carton of milk and poured some into a glass.

I closed my eyes savouring the cool white liquid as it blissfully slipped down my throat.

As I put the glass down and opened my eyes, my attention was immediately caught by an advert printed on the side of the milk carton. It was an appeal for a missing boy printed on behalf of his family. The tone of the message was restrained but it was enough to set me thinking again about the old man in the den.

Where was *his* family?

Who cared enough about *him* to help him in his plight?

Did he really have nobody? And if he did . . .

Maybe, just maybe, I could be somebody. I didn't have much to offer - I was just a 12 year old boy. But loneliness and social isolation are harsh companions. Even at my tender age, I had already learnt that.

I thought again about Craig and Shane. They would certainly turn on me if they found out. But then again they didn't have to know.

It would just have to be done in secret . . . if that was at all possible.

Exhausted now, I crawled back upstairs and into bed, determined to sleep on it.

In reality however, my mind had already been made up.

Sunday 15th August: Contact

If I had any doubts about when I would make contact with the old man, my decision was made for me the next day when Shane rang to say that he and Craig were going swimming again and did I want to come?

As soon as I had said no, I knew that this had to be the day.

I arrived at the den later that morning and was surprised to find a makeshift washing line, made out of string, hung up between two trees just outside the den's entrance. Draped across it, rather haphazardly lay all of the old man's clothes, drying in the sun.

I paused on the footpath, nervously - not quite sure what to do next. I didn't have time to think though as a noise behind me made me turn round.

And there he was, standing right in front of me angry and defiant.

"You!" he barked. He looked around suspiciously. "Where your friends?" he asked.

"I'm . . I came on my own," I stammered.

"Why?" he snapped. "Huh? - Why you always round here?" He looked over my shoulder at his washing line. "You did this?" he threw his left hand out gesticulating angrily towards his drying clothes.

"My friends did it," I began. "But . . . but I felt bad. I wanted to say sorry." I looked at the ground waiting to be chastised but the old man said nothing. At length I looked up again and was surprised to see his face had softened and that he was studying me carefully.

"This is no trick?" he asked, looking around him again.

"No," I replied.

"Hmmph. Maybe they need a wash anyway," he said with the faintest glimmer in his eyes. He obviously didn't know that it wasn't only water his clothes had been doused with.

"Your friends say sorry too?" he continued.

"No," I said. "They don't know I'm here."

The old man walked past me and into the den. I followed him to the doorway.

"I need drink," he said pulling a small bottle of what looked like vodka from his pocket. "This summer. Is so hot." He unscrewed the cap and took a large swig. "Your friends, they broke my last bottle!" he exclaimed bitterly, sitting down. "You come in."

I moved inside the doorway, baulking at the smell, then sat down opposite the old man.

For a while neither of us spoke. Something about him intrigued me though and I wasn't about to leave. I watched as he took another slug of vodka, grimaced, then turned to me.

"I know why you always hanging around," he said after studying my face again. "This is your place?"

"It's our den," I confirmed.

"It's our den," he repeated to himself, quietly. "And now, it is mine. Soon I move on, but for now I stay here."

He spoke with such conviction that I felt it would be pointless to argue. I looked at him blankly.

"Don't worry. This is not the end of the world," he continued. "You think it is but there are more important things than this. Yes?"

"Yes," I replied, not really sure of what he meant.

"You young. You think you got it hard because you not got enough things. But you know you got plenty. What you want? New bike - huh? Yes, I hear you talk with your friends. Let me tell you something boy." He stopped to take a little more from his bottle. "New bike? Won't make you happy. Your friend. He has new bike. He is not happy."

I looked at the old man, puzzled.

He continued. "I tell you, I hear you talk. Child doesn't need toy or bike. Child needs love. You have love. Your friend, he has nothing. He has bike, but this does not matter. He has nothing. You understand this."

"What do I understand?" I asked.

"Why else you here?" replied the old man. "Look at me. I stink yeah. Stink of piss. Stink of this." He shook his bottle angrily in my face. "I just a stinky old man. But you come back to see me. Why - huh?"

I shrugged my shoulders.

"Because you know what is to care. Because you have someone cares for you. Someone who loves you."

I looked down at the ground and felt my face reddening. That was the second time he'd mentioned love. And to boys of my age, it wasn't the sort of word we ever used.

"Hah!" the old man laughed. "So you telling me your mum not love you? Your dad? Huh?"

"Well yes but."

"But?" He fixed me with a steely stare, his pale blue eyes unwavering beneath their overgrown eyebrows. "You young. You always try to be, what is the word . . cool. When I was boy, there was no time for cool. When I was same age as you, my country was taken by Germans. My father was . . " He paused for a moment, his eyes clouding. Then he drank some more from his bottle.

"You lost him?" I asked at length, my curiosity overcoming me.

"Lost him?" shouted the old man. "They shoot him in front of me. I watch him bleed to death. Then they take me from my mother. Take me to camp." He dropped his voice. When he spoke again, his voice was almost childlike. "I never get to see my mother again."

I looked at him horrified. He returned my gaze with sad but challenging eyes.

"What sort of camp was it?" I eventually asked, fearing the worst.

"Death camp," he muttered, staring now at the ground. "We given no food. We all starving. Then, British soldiers come. They rescue us. Some dead though. Many dead. The smell of death. It everywhere."

He turned to face me again. "You think I stink huh? Nothing like smell of that camp. Smell of death. Hmmm." He closed his eyes for a moment and started to breathe heavily.

"But they saved you," I persisted.

"Huh?" He opened his eyes with a start. "You young, you think you got it hard. You know nothing." He closed his eyes again, then pulling his hat down, drew himself up into a ball.

Sensing the conversation was over I took my leave, determined to return tomorrow.

Monday 16th August: Eric

Any thoughts of a quick return to the den were quashed early the next morning when Craig and Shane turned up on my doorstep.

"We're going to the park," said Craig excitedly. "Eric's having a fire!"

For many years our local park had been managed by a keeper called 'Ernie', a dour man in his 60s. He walked with a pronounced limp and, on his right foot, wore a special shoe with a huge, almost circular, platform sole. This earned him the nickname 'Ernie Round Foot.' I had been led to believe that this was due to the fact that he had been born with one leg shorter than the other but that garnered little sympathy from any of the local children.

The simple fact was that Ernie hated all children, seeing us as a nuisance spoiling his otherwise pristine park. And so we hated him - and did anything we could to wind him up. Our favourite was to walk on his precious bowling green. Set one foot on the green and you could guarantee he would be straight out of his hut shouting, "Clear off. I can get the police round here in minutes!"

Of course we knew he never would, mainly because the police wouldn't be in the slightest bit interested. So we just wound him up even more, then ran away laughing. As far as we were concerned, he was fair game.

Then, one day he was gone. Nobody knew whether he had been sacked, retired or even died. But suddenly, there was a replacement - Eric.

Eric was tall and thin, in his early 30s with long hair which he usually tied back in a ponytail. He wore a kaftan coat, which reeked of petunia oil, hugely flared jeans and dark glasses. Shane had assured me that the glasses were due to the effects of taking drugs although he never expanded on this.

Eric couldn't have been more different to Ernie in personality, a point emphasised the first time we came across him as we were taking a short cut across the bowling green. He just waved in our general direction then went back to smoking his cigarette.

In fact he showed little interest in the job of park keeper as a whole. He certainly didn't care what we got up to in there. Consequently, we didn't pay much attention to Eric.

That was until the bonfires started.

It all came about as a result of a number of fallen trees in the wood adjacent to the park, brought down the previous winter in a severe gale. Eric had taken it upon himself to cut them up with a chainsaw and burn them one by one. To this end he had dug a fire pit on the edge of the woods and dragged two tree trunks close to the edge to act as makeshift benches. Then with the aid of brushwood collected from round and about and large quantities of paraffin, he lit the lot. We had watched his preparations from a distance on many occasions. Then one day, having spotted us, he invited us over.

That was the start of a wonderful friendship.

Eric was a great raconteur and he certainly had lived an amazing life. He had visited countries in every continent of the world, acted as a roadie to some of the most famous bands around, been stung by scorpions and bitten by snakes . . . the list of stories was endless. At the time I was well impressed with Eric, although looking back now with the wisdom of age I'm not so sure how much of what he told us was true.

As spring turned into summer however, Eric's fires became less frequent and we saw less of him. So it came as a surprise when Craig broke the news to me about this one, especially considering that today was going to be another scorcher - certainly not a day for warming yourself in front of a roaring fire.

As we approached the park, we could already smell the acrid stench of wood smoke, held captive by the heavy summer foliage and the confines of the cutting. Then, as we climbed up the bank we saw him sat on his bench, smoking his cigarette.

Craig was first on the scene, sitting himself down next to Eric.

"Hey dudes," cried Eric. "How you doing?"

"Do you need some help?" asked Shane.

"Sure do bud," replied Eric. "This log ain't gonna take unless we get plenty of brush round it. Can you lot round some up?"

"Go on you two," ordered Craig. "I'll stay here with Eric."

Craig was our leader, and as such it was only right and proper that he should sit at Eric's right hand and pass his orders down to us mere minions. Although, It was obvious with hindsight, that Craig idolised Eric and he probably saw him as the dad he never had.

Shane, eager as ever, marched off into the woods with me in hot pursuit.

We soon found some broken branches, small enough to drag back to the fire but big enough to please Eric.

We didn't speak much as we gathered the wood. Unusual, I thought, as me and Shane normally got on so well.

Then, as we made our way back, Shane broke his silence. "Craig's not happy with you," he said, avoiding eye contact with me.

"Why? What have I done?" I asked.

"When we water bombed the tramp," explained Shane. "Craig reckons your heart wasn't in it. Thinks you've gone soft on us."

"No!" I replied. "But when he weed on his clothes?"

"That was so funny," laughed Shane, totally misunderstanding me. "I bet the dirty sod went mental when he got back."

"Yeah," I said, forcing a smile that felt more like a grimace.

"Anyway," continued Shane. "Craig says you owe the gang a favour."

"What sort of favour?"

"Dunno," replied Shane.

We didn't speak again until we got back to the fire.

"Hey," said Eric as we dragged the last branch to the edge of the pit and hurled it in. "I was just telling Craig here, you gotta be real careful this summer with fires."

Every time he spoke, I wondered why Eric sounded like a cross between The Fonz from Happy Days and Cliff Richard! A strange combination indeed.

"Yeah," continued Craig. "Everything is so dry that if the fire took hold in the undergrowth . . . whoosh!" Here he threw his arms in the air. "The whole wood would go up. Wouldn't it Eric?"

"Too right dude," replied Eric. "It's tinder dry."

"Tinder dry," echoed Craig.

As if to impress upon Eric that I'd taken on board his every word, I proceeded to walk around the edge of the fire pit kicking away any looses debris that might spontaneously ignite and set the whole wood ablaze.

I sat down next to Shane.

"Eric was telling me how he drove across the Sahara desert in a Land Rover," said Craig, casting an admiring gaze in the direction of his hero.

"Really!," cried Shane. "Wow! Didn't you run out of water?"

"Well, it was tough going man," began Eric. Then he went on to describe in detail yet another of his amazing adventures.

Soon, there was enough heat coming from the fire for Eric to prepare his 'World Famous Open Air Lunch.' First he fished out of his rucksack a sliced white loaf and a bottle of milk. Then from his lock up box he produced a kettle, sugar, a tub of margarine and a long, ornate toasting fork. Walking over to the outdoor tap at the side of the pavilion, he filled the kettle and sauntered back to the fire. We knew what would come next.

"Tea and toast chaps!" cried Eric in a mocked up posh voice.

"Rather old chap," replied Craig.

"How super," said Shane.

"Why thank you my good man," I added.

This was a cue for all three of us to burst into peals of laughter whilst Eric set up the kettle on a hook over the fire.

It's true what they say about food cooked over an open fire - it always tastes better. And I think with Eric's pseudo American twang, it almost felt like we were real life cowboys.

On this occasion though, my mind was on other things and, to my surprise, I found my mouth was dry. So much so that the toast stuck in my throat until I managed to force it down with tea.

Shane's warning had obviously begun to trouble me. And even though the tramp wasn't mentioned for the rest of the day, and thankfully we didn't go to the den, I somehow felt I was living on borrowed time as far as Craig was concerned. I knew I would be expected to do something for his 'Campaign of Action' and now that I had met the old man face to face, that could become very complicated indeed.

Tuesday 17th August: A Second Meeting

I left for the den early the next morning, mainly to avoid Craig and Shane and determined to find out more about the old man.

To my surprise, on my arrival I found him nowhere to be seen. His belongings were still there, the bin bags in which they were stored neatly stacked in the corner with his ubiquitous bottle of vodka (emptied) beside it.

My curiosity was aroused however by a smaller bag which had been stuffed away underneath the rest but whose corner was clearly jutting out for all to see. Unlike the others, it appeared to be made of leather (or PVC). It definitely hadn't been there the other day. I could only assume the old man had taken it with him on that occasion. I surmised that it must therefore be of great importance to him.

Why hadn't he taken it with him this time? I wondered. It was clearly worth investigating.

Looking over my shoulder to make sure the coast was clear, I entered the den and pulled the bag out by its handle. It was a strange looking thing, almost like a ladies handbag but considerably battered. Checking the doorway again, I carefully unzipped it. The sound of the zip seemed to echo around the den and I felt sure that someone, somewhere would hear it, immediately assume that I was up to no good and enter the den to catch me in the act.

But of course, nobody did.

The bag fell open under the weight of its contents. Inside I could see what could only be described as the old man's most personal possessions. Most interesting of all was an old passport with a large spread eagle on the front. In gold letters above the eagle was written the word POLSKA. So he was Polish!

I opened the passport and flicked through it. It had been stamped on his entry into the UK. The date was 5th June 1946 - 30 years ago. I turned to the photo ID. It was long since out of date. It showed a young man who, without the hat, scruffy hair and beard I barely recognised. Only the eyes stood out, staring into the camera just as he had stared into mine a few days earlier.

I looked at the name; Viktor Kapalski. Date and place of birth; 14th July 1918 - Gdansk, Polska.

How did he end up here? I wondered.

I carefully put the passport back in the bag and noticed an old sepia photo. I took it out and looked more closely. It showed Viktor again, about the same age, hand in hand with a woman. They both looked very happy.

I was so engrossed in the photo that I didn't hear the approaching footsteps until it was too late. Suddenly Viktor was standing in the doorway holding a large bin bag stuffed with what appeared to be tin cans.

I quickly stuffed the photo back into the bag and tried to zip it up.

"Ah boy," he said. "You come back."

He put down his bin bag by the entrance to the den. "I get 1p for each can. I collect enough, then I eat."

I breathed a sigh of relief. At least he wasn't angry.

"You look in my bag," he said pointing at me.

I didn't reply.

He stared at me for some time then joined me on the floor.

"Here," he grunted pointing to the bag. I handed it over.

Viktor unzipped it, took out the photo and looked at it. As he did so, I felt an overwhelming sadness sweep over him.

"Her name is Dorothy," he began. "We meet when I first come to England. We love each other with a true love. I miss her." He said no more but as he continued to stare, tears welled up in his eyes.

Still I said nothing.

"We married six months - then she die." He muttered something softly in Polish at the photo then carefully put it back into the bag.

"Why," I began nervously. "Why did you leave Poland?"

"Hah!" he exclaimed, cheering up a little. "When British soldiers come to liberate us, they say plenty of jobs in England. Polska, it destroyed. I young man then. I go to England to find work, make money to take back home. But then I meet Dorothy. We marry." Here he dropped his voice again. "She get ill and then she die. Then I alone."

"Why didn't you go back to Poland?" I asked.

"I have job in England. I make good money. But I have great sadness. No wife, no friends. Only this." And in saying so he fished a fresh bottle of vodka from his pocket, unscrewed the lid and took a large swig from it.

Grimacing and coughing, he placed the bottle on the floor, replacing its top carefully. "She my only friend now," he said, sadly.

I didn't know what to say.

Viktor picked up the bottle again and waved it angrily in my face. "You see boy!" he said. "She take all my money. Soon I broke. Lose my job, lose my home. Now I live here alone with her." He looked me in the eyes again. "But I leave soon. I have second home." He started to laugh to himself. "Viktor has two homes you see boy. My other home is in middle of road."

He threw back his head and laughed. I didn't quite get the joke but guessed the vodka was starting to take effect. He certainly seemed to be talking nonsense. How can you live in the middle of a road for goodness sake?

"I know what you think," he laughed. "I read your mind. Crazy man living in middle of road. In England you call it cent-eral reser-r-rvation."

Suddenly it hit me like a thunderbolt. There WAS a well known tramp in our town who had built himself a makeshift home in the central reservation on the ring road.

"You don't mean opposite St Paul's Church?" I asked.

"Yeesss!" exclaimed Viktor clapping his hands together in joy. "But council men come and turn me out. Pull down my home. So I come here. But soon I leave. I go back to road. Rebuild my home there. Hmm, yes - soon I leave you and horrible friends alone." He closed his eyes and pulled his hat down. I guessed the meeting was over.

I blinked in the bright sunshine as I emerged from the den. Speaking with Viktor again had been interesting. But it didn't help matters with Craig. In fact it made them worse. There was no way I felt, that I could continue with the Campaign of Action - especially if Viktor said he was leaving soon anyway. I would have to tell Craig and Shane that I'd talked to him and he'd promised to leave in the next few days. That would at least buy me some time. And if he did leave, all would be well. If he didn't . . . well, I would have to cross that bridge when I came to it.

Wednesday 18th August: The Deal

"You did what?" gasped Craig, his mouth half open in surprise.

"I talked to him," I replied.

"Talked to him." repeated Craig with more than a little irritation. "But that wasn't the deal. The deal was to carry out the Campaign of Action and drive him out." He paused. "Wasn't it?"

"Well, yes. But listen," I persisted. "I told him he had to go. And he promised he would in a few days."

"A few days!" repeated Craig again. "How many days?"

"Well err . . three I think," I lied.

"Three days from yesterday?" asked Craig.

"Yes."

We were sitting on the edge of the woods trying to get some shade from the harsh midday sun. Fortunately for me, both Craig and Shane seemed to have lost some interest in the den but I knew I had to broach the subject of the tramp before Craig did.

"Right then." said Craig at length. "That means he'll be gone by Friday." He stopped and looked at me coolly. "If what you say is correct."

I looked across at Shane who shrugged his shoulders at me.

"I found out more stuff about him," I continued, hoping that I might begin to persuade them that he was actually an OK sort of person. "He comes from Poland and his wife died and . . ." I paused as I caught sight of the expression on Craig's face then continued, valiantly. "And, he's the same tramp that lives in the central reservation on the ring road."

"Oh I know," said Shane, coming to my rescue. "Opposite St Paul's church."

"Yeah, that's right" I confirmed.

"Well he can sodding well go back there," said Craig. "Dirty bastard."

We sat in silence for a while but I could sense Craig was seething. I think Shane showing some genuine interest in Viktor had wound him up even more.

"I tell you what Snide," he said eventually, his voice trembling with rage. "If he's not gone by Friday, then you're gonna have to show your loyalty to MY gang."

I didn't quite like the way Craig emphasised the word 'MY'. If I didn't feel like I was on borrowed time before, I certainly did now.

Craig continued. "The deal was the Campaign of Action and if he's not gone by Friday, then we continue it." He stopped and turned, his cold eyes challenging me. "You will continue it."

"What do you want me to do?" I asked apprehensively.

"You'll see," replied Craig calmly. "I got to go."

Shane and I watched him lumber off across the park on his Chopper.

When I felt he was far enough away to be out of earshot, I spoke.

"Shane. He's just an old bloke who's fallen on hard times. I don't want to do this campaign any more."

Instead of replying though, Shane surprised me with an entirely new take on the matter. "How long has he been living in this country?" he asked.

"Thirty years," I answered. "I found his passport. It was stamped on entry in 1946."

"And how long has he been living like a tramp?" continued Shane.

"Not sure," I said. "Most of that time. His wife died soon after he married her. Then he went off the rails. Why?"

Shane looked deep in thought. "You know that means he's probably an illegal alien," he said with his usual air of authority.

"What do you mean?" I asked, genuinely puzzles at never having heard the phrase before. "He comes from Poland, not outer space."

"No you dimwit!" cried Shane. "Illegal alien is a legal term. They use it a lot in America. It means illegal immigrant. If the authorities catch up with him, he'll be sent back to Poland."

I tried to take all of this in. "But he had a job," I protested.

Shem shook his head wisely. "He would have been on a VISA which would have expired."

"But he married a British woman," I persisted. "That makes him legal."

Shane frowned at me. He always did that when he knew he was wrong.

"Well whatever," he said. "He needs to be out by Friday. And you owe the gang one."

I tilted my head back to allow my face to catch the sun which had moved around enough to be once again clear of the trees.

"Yeah, and I'm not happy about it. Bloody gang!" As soon as I'd said it, I regretted it. The last thing I needed right now was for Shane to tell Craig that I wanted out.

I just hoped against all the odds that by Friday, Viktor and his belongings would be gone. Then we could get back to normal. But somehow, I doubted it.

Friday 20th August: Deadline Day

I kept a low profile all day Thursday but was hardly surprised when Craig and Shane called for me quite early on Friday.

"Give him a chance!" I blurted out as I opened the door. "He said he would go some time today." I looked at my watch. "It's only half nine."

"Yeah, and he's still there," said Shane. "We've already checked."

"And you need to know," continued Craig. "Exactly what you're gonna have to do if he's not gone by noon."

"Noon?" I echoed. "Why noon?"

"Because we decided, at a gang meeting this morning."

"What gang meeting? I didn't know anything about a gang meeting."

"Makes no difference," said Craig. "You're outvoted two to one anyway, so no point you being there."

"So what have I got to do then?" I asked nervously.

In reply, Craig reached into the plastic carrier bag he was holding and pulled out a clear, unlabelled plastic bottle.

"Guess what this is?" he leered, unscrewing the cap and pushing it towards my nose. "I got it from our Shed. Jim uses it to light the barbecue."

Cautiously, I took a sniff. The powerful smell of paraffin immediately caught the back of my nose.

"And guess what you got to do with it?" continued Craig, producing a box of matches from the pocket of his jeans and shoving both paraffin and matches towards my unwilling hands.

My heart missed a beat as I realised what they had in mind.

"Me and Shane will lure him out. You do the rest," said Craig.

"Everything?" I asked.

"Everything."

"Even his passport, his photos?"

"Everything!" repeated Craig, his voice hardening a little.

I looked stupidly at the bottle and matches and said nothing.

49

"Well if you're not up to it," replied Craig, exchanging glances with Shane.

I looked at Shane. Shane quickly looked down, intensely scrutinising the pattern on our doormat.

If there was ever a moment to stand up for myself, this was it.

But now that that moment had come, I froze.

Like a coward I took the paraffin and matches.

"OK. I'll do it."

Why, you may ask, did I agree to it? Because it was easier to go with the flow than risk losing my friends. Well that was my reasoning at the time. Looking back now, it was probably the most cowardly and stupid decision I have ever made in my life.

But standing there on my own doorstep, at the age of 12, I bowed to peer pressure. And by verbally agreeing to do it, I had dug myself in deeper still.

There was no going back now. The deed had to be done.

"We'll be back at twelve," said Craig.

I looked again to Shane for some support, but received none. "Twelve," he repeated, finally looking up. Then patting me on the shoulder he said; "You know you've got to do it Snide."

As I watched them walk off up the garden path, my mind immediately set to work. I needed to warn Viktor but not lose face with my friends - but how?

As soon as they were out of sight, I set off for the den.

I found Viktor awake and sorting through his baggage.

"Ah boy!" he cried. "You come to see Viktor one last time huh?"

"You're leaving?" I asked.

"I go to my other home now," he replied.

A rush of relief swept over me.

"Your horrible friends. They pay me visit this morning. You very stupid boy to make friends like that. They no good."

"What did they say?" I asked.

"Hmm. Call me names," muttered Viktor. "Tell me to get out. I say nothing back. But I going now. Enough - huh? You understand?"

"Yes," I replied.

I looked at him one final time but he had lost interest in me and had returned to sorting through his belongings.

It was just before noon when Craig and Shane called for me.

Considerably more relaxed, I picked up my small rucksack that contained the paraffin and matches.

"Let's do this!" I said confidently as I shut the front door behind me.

Craig, now on his Chopper, led the way with me and Shane in pursuit.

When we reached the cutting, I marched on towards the door of the den. Soon this would be all over. I could announce to Craig and Shane that he had gone and everything would go back to normally.

As I reached the doorway of the den, I stopped and looked inside.

At first I couldn't quite believe my eyes. There was no sign of Viktor, but his bags were still there!

I ran in and started rifling through them. At least his leather handbag wasn't there. He must have taken it with him.

What was I to do?

Craig was now standing in the doorway. "Looks like we're not needed," he said turning to Shane who was stood somewhere outside.

"Hang on," I said, desperately trying to buy time. "We can't do it in here. This is our den. Let's take them outside."

Craig immediately beckoned to Shane and the two of them proceeded to drag the bags out into the bracken.

I followed them out, my sense of guilt and betrayal almost too much to bear.

"Do it," ordered Craig.

Slowly I unscrewed the top from the bottle and poured its contents over the bags. Then, with trembling hands, I struck a match and dropped it onto the pile. Immediately, the whole lot ignited.

I felt numb.

"Yeeeah!" screamed Craig, running back into the den.

As the fire took hold, Shane and I also retreated into the safety of the shelter.

"Well done Snide," said Craig.

Ceremoniously he picked up his seat of office and sat himself down upon it. "I officially declare that the den is once again in our hands!" he cried throwing his arms in the air.

Any celebration, on his part at least, was short lived though as the den slowly began to fill with smoke.

"I think we need to get out of here," said Shane, nervously.

We didn't need telling.

However, as we reached the doorway, we were hit by a wall of heat and smoke. The tinder dry bracken and undergrowth that the bags had been thrown into had now also caught light, making escape through the doorway impossible.

All three of us backed away and were driven further inside as wave upon wave of thick, choking smoke started to pour into the confines of the den.

"We gotta get out of here!" cried Craig.

"Through the hole in the roof!" shouted Shane. As he was the tallest he tried first but, even standing on tiptoe, only his finger tips reached the edge of the hole - not enough to get a grip.

"Stand on the pouffe!" I shouted, dragging it over.

By now the smoke was so thick that all three of us had begun to cough and visibility was rapidly deteriorating. What made things worse was that the hole in the roof was acting as a kind of chimney drawing even more smoke in through the doorway.

Shane tried to climb on to the pouffe but lost his balance as he lost sight of his feet and crashed to the floor.

"Get down low!" I cried, remembering a fire safety film we had watched at school. "Smoke rises. The cleanest air is at ground level."

In response, we all lay on the floor. Here the air was a little clearer - enough for us to see each other, but still choking.

"We're going to die!" gasped Shane.

Suddenly, we became aware of a commotion outside.

"Nooo!" cried a voice that was familiar to me but which, in the confusion of smoke, heat and panic, I could not identify. "What ees happening here?"

It was Viktor.

"HELP!" I screamed.

For a moment there was silence. Then, above our heads, there came the sound of footsteps on the roof. Instinctively, I looked up at the hole and was relieved to make out through the smoke the dim outline of a face, a bearded heavily lined face. It peered into the gloom then disappeared again, coughing convulsively.

After what seemed an eternity, Viktor's face reappeared. "Here boy. You come. Grab my arms."

Quickly, I got to my feet, clambered on to the pouffe and stretched my arms upwards. Strong hands gripped my wrists and I felt myself being lifted. As my head emerged, I breathed deeply then coughed. My eyes were streaming from the smoke as I blindly pulled my hands through the hole and gripped its rough sides. With the help of Viktor's hands under my arms, I hauled myself up and threw myself flat on my stomach on the roof of the shelter.

"My friends!" I gasped.

Taking a deep breath, Viktor rolled back onto his front and dangled his arms again through the hole. Within seconds he was pulling upwards and Shane's head emerged.

"Craig! Come on!" he shouted, looking down as he scrambled out.

Viktor reached in again but this time, there was no hand for him to grab.

"He can't reach. He's too short!" shouted Shane.

Suddenly, an idea came to me. Jumping off the roof, I ran around the edge of the blaze and was relieved to see Viktor's makeshift washing line lying on the ground. I quickly coiled it up and threw it onto the roof.

Viktor needed no explanation and immediately began to feed the end through the hole.

At first there was no reaction.

"Grab the rope you stupid boy!" shouted Viktor in frustration.

"Craig. Craig. Where are you?" screamed Shane.

Finally, after what seemed an eternity, there was a weak tug on the rope. Immediately all three of us began to pull and, very soon Craig was lying face down on the concrete, coughing and spluttering.

I looked at Viktor, who was sat a little way away, his handbag slung over his shoulder, getting his breath back.

"You saved our lives," I gasped.

Craig and Shane looked on but said nothing.

Somewhere in the distance, we could just about make out the siren of what we guessed was a fire engine.

"I'm out of here," spluttered Craig and, staggering to his feet, he made off in the direction of the park.

"Me too," added Shane, following him.

I watched them disappear down the side of the cutting then turned back to Viktor.

But he was gone.

I walked as far forward as the smoke and heat would allow and looked over the edge of the roof. The bags were still burning but the bracken, around it had nearly burned itself out. The fire however, was now steadily advancing and spreading out along the top of the embankment.

It was also clear, from the approaching sound of its siren, that the fire engine was now very close. And here I was, standing over the seat of a deliberately started fire with my hands reeking of paraffin.

I decided that it was time that I too made my exit.

Friday 27th August: News

The fire made the front page of the local newspaper.

'ARSON VANDALS BLIGHT LOCAL PICNIC SITE' screamed the headline. *How, in their wildest dreams they could ever describe a dilapidated World War Two air raid shelter as a picnic site I will never know. But that was newspapers for you. I was at an age where I was starting to appreciate things like that.*

In fact, I learned a lot of things that summer:

That it IS right to stand up for what you believe in, even if you have to suffer the consequences in terms of how your peers view you.

That you should never take people at face value. First impressions are always important, BUT sometimes they can be completely wrong.

That you should never assume that those people who you surround yourself with, necessarily think in the same way you do. And sometimes, the reasons for their ways of thinking are far more shocking than their own words and actions.

We never saw Viktor again. He didn't return to the den.

In the days following the fire, I was never quite sure whether he knew that we'd set fire to his things. I hope he didn't. I hope he returned to the den that day, saw the fire, heard my scream for help and set about rescuing us - without ever discovering his burning belongings. That is something I will never know. We never got the chance to speak again.

And I mean NEVER.

It was the following week that I heard the news.

We were due back at school a week on Monday and, somehow fittingly, the great drought of 1976 was about to break.

I had spent the afternoon down the park with Craig and Shane. But it had been a subdued day. The heat and, more importantly, the humidity had become almost unbearable. And as morning turned to afternoon, the ubiquitous blue sky of the summer of 1976 had begun to fade into a milky white. By early evening it had turned to an angry, threatening hue of copper.

Then the thunder came. And how it came! I can never recall seeing lightning like it!

Dusk came early that night.

Then the power was cut.

All that we were left with for entertainment was the radio. Why we ended up tuned into our local radio station, I cannot remember. Probably my parents were listening out for why we'd lost our electricity. It was of little interest to me - until the news bulletin came on.

"A man died today after being hit by a car on the town's ring road opposite St Paul's church. Police said that, despite the accident happening around lunch time, his blood alcohol level was way over the drink drive limit. The identity of the victim is, as yet, unknown. Anybody with any information on the man is urged to contact police immediately so relatives can be informed."

A thousand thoughts raced through my head. Was it Viktor? The accident was certainly in the vicinity of his makeshift home. But, if it was Viktor, why did they not know his identity? Surely he would have been carrying his handbag, complete with passport.

But then again, what if he hadn't been carrying it?

The next day I decided to dedicate to tracking down Viktor.

Firstly, I went to visit the site of his temporary home, or at least where its last incantation had been cleared from the central reservation. But that gave no clues. There was no sign of the shelter Viktor claimed to have been rebuilding. In desperation for answers I spent the entire day walking the full length of the ring road, but to no avail. I even visited the den, but again, there was no sign.

More thunderstorms set in during the afternoon so I made my way reluctantly home. I had already decided against contacting the police. After all, what information did I really hold. Viktor could be anywhere.

So that was it. The summer of 1976. The longest summer.

And Viktor - if you're still alive somewhere and reading this right now - I'm sorry. I wish I'd got to know you better. You were a good man.

As for the gang, we continued to hang out and went on to spend many more summers together as we progressed through our secondary school years, starting with the summer of 1977 - the year that we embraced punk rock!

1977

PUNKS

CONTENTS

PUNKS

A steady drizzle fell from a steel grey sky, a fitting setting for the scene that it looked down upon. A typical council house on a typical council estate on the edge of town. A place where the tangled overgrowth of opportunistic mother nature lay in chaotic juxtaposition with the left behind cast offs and clutter of man.

Two boys in their early teens stood at the bottom of the path that dissected what was once a garden, now overgrown with nettles, butterfly bushes, brambles and anything else that wasn't too choosy where it grew. Near the front door, a rough circle of barely visible soil, choked with weeds, supported a handful of straggly, out of control rose bushes which, despite their neglect had begun to bloom in defiance of the drab summer they were so unlucky to have been thrown into.

To the side of the house lay a rusting wreck of a car, it's engine long since removed. Looking at it, one drew the impression of a project that, for whatever reason, never quite got off the ground.

Securely chained and padlocked to the drivers door handle was a bicycle, a Raleigh Chopper. This too looked like it had seen better days, adding to the general air of despondency about the place.

The two boys, nervously shuffling their feet as they decided on their next move, made for a strange pair. One, thin, gawky and awkward in his stance, took in his environment with a certain nervousness - so obviously out of his comfort zone. The other, smartly dressed, broadly built and with an inner calm and confidence that could never go unnoticed, stood motionless, waiting.

At length, the first spoke. "Well there's no sign of his motor bike. He must be out."

The other nodded in assent. "Come on then. Don't want to keep Craig waiting do we?"

Taking one final, furtive look around, the thin boy started to stride, purposefully up the path, his comrade in pursuit.

They stopped at the front door for a brief moment and listened. From an open upstairs window came the sound of music. Not the bland, sanitised music that radio stations had been churning out for years now. No. This was different. High energy. Fast. Furious. With vocals to match. And as far as these boys were concerned, this music represented a bright new future.

The thin boy? That was me. The other of course, was Shane.

I knocked loudly on the door. The music stopped suddenly. Then there was silence. I knocked again.

"Come on then. Open up. We're getting soaked out here!" I shouted.

The sound of footsteps was followed by what appeared to be some sort of a struggle as the front door finally lurched open with a shudder.

And there in the doorway stood Craig. And what a sight he was, wearing a fluorescent green and black hooped mohair sweater, ripped combat trousers covered with zips and huge safety pins and a battered old pair of black Dr Martens boots. His hair had been dyed blond and rather erratically spiked using what appeared to be wallpaper paste.

"Alright boys," said Craig in a slightly forced cockney accent. "You took your time."

"Yeah. Well you know how it is," I replied. "Shane had to get changed at mine. You know what his mum and dad are like. If they ever found out he was walking around the streets dressed like this, they'd kill him."

Craig laughed then examined both of us more closely. "Where d'you get the drainpipes Snide?"

"Market. Sad old loser there thought I was into rock and roll or something. Only cost two quid. They stink a bit though."

"They don't half," added Shane, turning his nose up.

Craig turned to Shane. He was wearing an old leather jacket over a plain white t shirt. His jeans were black but were still far too flared for his liking.

"Need to do something about those," said Craig pointing at them. "Hippy trousers! They look like sails. Put on a pair of roller skates and the wind would carry you down the street in them."

We all laughed though I could sense Shane's discomfort.

Craig opened the door wider and ushered us in. "It's alright. He's out."

"Yes. We saw his bike was gone. Is he out all day?" I asked.

"Down the pub," replied Craig. "Won't be back until chucking out time. Unless the pigs do him again for drink driving."

I breathed a sigh of relief. Although Craig was never explicit about his mum's boyfriend, Jim, we got the impression that he wasn't the most pleasant of people. Especially when he'd had a skinful.

Craig booted the base of the front door to shut it then started to make his way upstairs. Shane followed closely on his heels and I trailed behind taking in the interior of Craig's home as I did so.

It wasn't my first visit but nevertheless, the shabbiness of it all left me breathless. At first sight it appeared as though someone had begun stripping the wallpaper in the hall at some distant point in the past but had then given up. In places where the bare plaster showed through, a layer of grime and filth had deposited itself leading one to the conclusion that any thoughts of redecorating had long since been abandoned. There was no carpet, only a grimy rug in the middle of the floor stained with what appeared to be lumps of congealed mashed potato.

And the smell! It could only be described as a cross between unwashed socks and stale cabbage.

But, at the end of the day we had embraced the punk rock scene and Craig's house was definitely what we would describe as punk.

Shane loved it more than me. I think it was his way of secretly rebelling against his mum's relentless cleanliness.

Despite the passage of twelve months, we still weren't allowed into Shane's house and Craig and I were of the firm belief that, given the choice, his mum wouldn't have us in his life either!

Craig's room was like the rest of his house, a confused mass of distempered rubbish. Pride of place though was given to his ghetto blaster. This gleaming, monstrous piece of audio machinery stood on top of a battered chest of drawers, none of which seemed to shut properly, mainly due to the fact that either their runners were broken or their fronts were hanging off.

"I got the Pistols on," said Craig enthusiastically, pressing the play button. Immediately the room was filled with the strains of God Save the Queen.

"She needs saving," I shouted smugly over the din of the music. "She's so old. She'll be dead soon."

Craig laughed and started pogoing, a dangerous activity in a room where you were hard pushed to see the floor for clutter.

Shane sat on the bed, crossed his legs and started tapping his feet to the beat in a rather stilted manner.

"Good innit Shane!" cried Craig as one particularly high pogo nearly took out the single bare light bulb that hung grimly from the ceiling.

"Yeah cool," replied Shane unconvincingly.

I sat down next to Shane and picked up an old copy of the New Musical Express, or NME as it was known.

"Mickey down the market told me about this new band," shouted Craig as the song playing on the cassette reached its climax. "They're from round here. Listen." He ejected the tape and put in another. Without any introduction, another high energy song thundered through the speakers.

"Who are they?" I asked.

"Enemies of Promise. They're playing at JBs at the end of the month."

"What's the song?" asked Shane.

"Working down to Zero."

I leaned back against the wall listening to the new sound and flicking through the NME.

At length, Craig exhausted himself and leaned out of the open window. "It's stopped raining," he said.

"We going to visit Eric then?" asked Shane getting up and stretching.

"Yeah," I added. "He was going to tell us more about his days as a roadie."

The tape ended abruptly. Nothing to do with the song. It had just run out of tape. Craig lifted his donkey jacket off the hook on the back of his bedroom door and threw it around his shoulders like a cloak. "Come on then."

As he made his way through the door, you could see that on the back of the jacket he had written, in white gloss paint, the word HATE in huge letters.

I smiled. Nobody was quite sure what cool was at that time but Craig certainly had it in buckets.

We found Eric, sitting on his log stoking up yet another bonfire. His fire pit had originally been set up to burn a number of trees that had blown down in a severe gale in the winter of 1975. But, having run out of wood, he had started making excuses about certain other trees needing coppicing and the fires had continued, unabated.

"Hey dudes," he called, waving in our general direction with one hand before drawing heavily on a suspiciously fat roll up that he held in the other.

"What's with the hair, man?" he asked, pointing at Craig's blond spikes.

"Told you. We're all punks now," said Craig, his artificial cockney accent surfacing again.

"That's not music," retorted Eric. "It's just a row. They can't even play their instruments. Or sing. Now if you want to hear some real music, you should listen to Purple Kaleidoscope. They're a prog rock band from the late 60s. I was a roadie with them for a while. Have I never told you about that?"

"No," we all chorused in reply, although in truth we had heard all of his stories many times before. But, like any good story (and I was never quite sure how much was truth and how much fantasy), they were always good for a retelling.

That was the cue for an awesome hour of sex, drugs and rock 'n' roll. And as Eric, the master story teller weaved his way through his tales of debauchery, I imagined myself living life on the road as part of a hard working, hard playing rock band. And by the faraway look in Craig's eyes, he was doing the same.

"And what about you Shane?" asked Eric as he finished. "You don't look the sort to be into punk."

"Why not?" asked Shane, spitting into the fire as if in an effort to underline his punk credentials.

"Well boys like you," began Eric.

"Just cos he's black, doesn't mean he has to be into Soul and all that crap!" I interrupted.

"Yeah!" cried Craig in support. "What's the matter? You a racialist or something?"

There was an awkward silence.

Shane eventually broke the impasse. "Actually, I quite like soul . . . . well some of it is OK . . . isn't it?" There was another awkward silence broken eventually by a roar of laughter from Eric.

"You kids!" he said. "You make me laugh."

"We're serious!" cried Craig, angrily. "We're the future and the future starts now."

"Yeah," Shane and I chorused together, although I don't think either of us quite knew what he was talking about.

The next morning however, we were about to find out.

Tuesday 2nd August - The Band

It wasn't even nine in the morning when Craig phoned. I always knew when it was Craig because you heard the beeps of the public callbox as he struggled to put his coins in.

"Hey Snide. Come round our house and bring Shane with you. I've got something to show you."

"Is *he* in?" I asked cautiously.

"He'll have gone by eleven. He's always first in at opening time."

"OK. We'll be round about eleven then."

I met Shane, as always, at the bottom of his road. Although his mum and dad were both at work, Shane reckoned that his neighbours had formed a network of spies who could recall with

68

absolute clarity the times and descriptions of any visitors to any house in the street. And if he was spotted at their front door, it would inevitably get back to Shane's parents and that would mean big trouble.

"So what's this all about?" asked Shane, who today, not having had the opportunity to change his clothes at mine, was dressed as if he was about to spend several hours swotting at the local library.

"I don't know," I replied. "But he sounded pretty excited."

I looked at my watch. It was still quarter to eleven so we decided to approach Craig's house with caution. We needn't have worried. The motor bike was gone.

Craig beat us to the front door and beckoned us in.

"Come on. Upstairs!" he shouted, running up to his room.

It was obviously our turn to try and shut the front door today and, yesterday's rain having soaked into the exposed wooden frame, it was more difficult than ever. Shane used his muscles to try a few shoulder barges but it was to no avail. I tried reopening then slamming it as hard as possible but this just rattled the glass, which was already loose and cracked, to the point where I thought it might fall out.

Eventually Craig's head appeared at the top of the stairs.

"Just boot it at the bottom," he called out.

Shane indicated to me to stand aside then, taking a few steps back, took a run up and leaped two footed at the bottom of the door. It shut with a loud bang.

"Of course, you realise we've got to open it again at some point," I said.

"No we haven't," grinned Shane. "We'll just go out the back."

We made our way upstairs and found Craig standing, hands on hips, over what appeared to be an upturned tin bath, which was balanced precariously on top of an old wooden crate. Much of the rubbish on his bedroom floor had been piled up under the window as if to emphasise that the bath now had pride of place in Craig's affections.

"Well?" he began. "What do you think?"

69

Shane and I stared at it dumbly.

Craig then proceeded to pull from the back pocket of his combat trousers two long, stiff wire brushes.

"They're drum brushes," he announced. "Listen."

He pulled up a stool that appeared to have been confiscated from the kitchen and started hammering the brushes against the bottom of the bath.

I was surprised, firstly because it actually sounded quite good and secondly because Craig seemed a natural at drumming.

Eventually, after Craig had burned himself out, he stood up and tucked the brushes back in his pocket. "Boys," he announced. "*We* are forming a punk rock band."

Again Shane and I stared at him.

"But we've got no instruments," I said at length.

"No - you haven't Snide. But Shane has."

A worried look started to spread over Shane's face. "Oh no!" he cried. "No way. My mum wouldn't allow it. Besides it's a classical acoustic. You can't play punk on a classical acoustic."

"It's still a guitar," grinned Craig. "And besides, once we get good, we can save up for a real one."

He turned to me. "And you Snide," he continued. "Will be our singer."

"Me?" I echoed. "But I can't sing."

"You don't need to be able to sing. It's punk. Just shout the lyrics," said Craig.

"What lyrics?" I asked.

"Well. I'm gonna write some tonight," explained Craig. "About smashing the government and the state." He punched one fist in the air. "ANARCHY!" he shouted.

We all laughed.

However, in truth, now that the idea was beginning to sink in, it did seem to me that it might be good fun. Shane still looked worried though.

"The only time I'm allowed to take that guitar out of the house is when I go to my Spanish Guitar lessons," he said.

"We can practice in the days when both your mum and dad are at work," said Craig.

"And what about my nosey neighbours?" asked Shane. "Especially that old bag at number 23. She's got it in for me."

"Stuff them. They should mind their own business."

"And where are we going to practice?" I asked.

"Down the den," replied Craig. "We can make as much noise as we like down there. Nobody will hear us."

And so it was decided. With Shane's mum being home the next two days, first rehearsal was arranged for Friday.

Friday 5th August - Rehearsals

We must have looked a strange sight as we made our way down the road in the direction of the den. Craig led the way, his hair spikier than ever, his donkey jacket with HATE written on the back drawing the attention of passing motorists, some of whom felt the need to blow their horns and pass comment through their drivers windows. We of course, replied in kind.

I had been given the job of carrying the tin bath which I had opted, for ease, to place over my head. This limited my view somewhat, allowing me to see no more than a couple of yards in front so I tucked in close behind Shane . As it turned out, I ended up walking too close and trod on his heels several times. Shane for his part was sandwiched between the two of us carrying his precious guitar on his back.

Eventually we reached the den and, as I tried to make my way through the doorway, the tin bath hit the frame with a loud clang which reverberated around my still enclosed head.

"Right," said Craig, placing the wooden crate that was to support his makeshift drum in the middle of the floor. "First thing we need is a name."

Funnily enough it hadn't occurred to either me or Shane that we didn't have a name.

"We need something really punk," I said. "How about The Stinking Jacks?"

"What does that mean?" asked Craig, screwing his face up. "No. We need something political. How about Smash The State?"

"Autonomy for the People," suggested Shane.

"What's autonomy?" asked Craig.

"I know," I chipped in. "It's control of the people by the people."

"Cool," said Craig. "But I prefer Smash The State."

We knew there and then that any further conversation would be going through the motions. Craig had already made his mind up and it didn't matter what Shane or I said or did, Craig would have his way.

"OK," I said after a long silence. "I'll go with Smash The State."

Shane nodded in agreement although he seemed more preoccupied with putting his guitar somewhere where it wouldn't get dirty.

"Come on then Shane. Play us a tune," said Craig.

"Well . . . I don't know that much. I've only had a few lessons. I can play this . . ." Shane proceeded to sit on the upturned tin bath, arranged his guitar on his lap and very slowly started to play some basic chords. At length, he broke into song:

"Oh give me a home where the buffaloes roam
Where the deer and the antelope play
Where seldom is heard a discouraging word
And the skies are not cloudy all day
Home, home on the . . "

"Stop!" shouted Craig.

"What's the matter?" asked Shane in surprise.

"Well firstly," began Craig. "That's a bloody cowboy song. And secondly, you're sitting on my drum kit. How am I supposed to play?"

"But I can only play sitting on something," said Shane.

"Well try sitting on the floor," suggested Craig. "But you're gonna have to learn to play standing up. You can't play punk sitting on your arse."

We all burst into peals of laughter.

"What was them chords you was playing?" he asked.

"C, F and G," answered Shane. "They're the only chords I know."

"Not a problem," I chipped in. "You only need to know three chords to play punk." I turned to Craig. "So where do I come in then?"

In response, Craig fished a folded piece of paper from his pocket and handed it to me. Opening it up I could see several lines of what I guessed were lyrics, scrawled in spider like writing across it.

"Smash The State," said Craig, with a hint of nervousness in his voice.

I looked at Craig then back at the paper. This obviously meant a lot to him but my first problem was that his handwriting was so poor, I could barely decipher it.

"What would be really good would be if I could read it," I smirked.

Craig shot me a withering glance and snatched the paper from me. "I'll read it to you then," he said.

He peered closely then, slowly began to read:

"Smash the state
Just do it mate
No one is gonna tell me
What to do or say
Cos I'm living for today

Anarchy rules
So smash the state
Just do it my mate
No clever trousers
In the government
Gonna tell me
How to behave

Nor the army, nor the RAF
Cos anarchy rules
OK."

He stopped and looked up at me. "Well?"

"They're great!" I said trying to sound enthusiastic but wondering why each verse had a different number of lines and why, most of it didn't even rhyme. However, I could sense a little vulnerability on Craig's part so decided to run with it as best I could.

"Can you play a C Shane?" I said.

After spending a few seconds arranging his fingers on the fretboard, Shane duly obliged and started to strum. Craig leapt up, pulling his brushes from his pocket and started to hammer the tin bath.

Now it was my turn. I really had no idea of what sort of tune to sing so I just screamed Craig's lyrics with as much venom as I could muster but sang them all on the same note, that note of course being C.

As I screamed "OK," to conclude my contribution, Shane stopped but Craig carried on, going ballistic with the brushes as we stood and looked on in amazement.

"That was brilliant!" screamed Craig when he had finally finished.

And to be honest, it really did feel brilliant. It was indeed a very special moment that I shall never forget. I don't think I had ever felt so exhilarated or alive in my entire life. I looked at Shane who smiled back at me. We had been well and truly bitten by the performance bug.

"I'm a guitar hero!" cried Shane, thrashing his C chord with renewed vigour.

Suddenly there was a loud twang and Shane stopped and looked down at his strings in horror. "Oh no! Mum's going to kill me. I've snapped my top E. And I've got Spanish Guitar class tonight."

We both tried to look concerned but, as I exchanged glances with Craig, I noticed his shoulders were beginning to tremble in silent mirth. Then we both roared with laughter until tears ran down our faces.

"Looks like you'd better get down the music shop and buy some new strings before mummy gets home," I joked.

Luckily, Shane saw the funny side of it too. "Well," he began. "You have to expect these set backs when you're a rock star."

"Yeah!" shouted Craig, in excitement. "SMASH THE STATE!"

"Yeah!" we echoed. "SMASH THE STATE!"

Saturday 6th August - Punks Versus Rockers

Punk meant many things to many people (as it still does). To the press, it represented violent yobs vandalising our streets, spitting at people, even mugging old ladies. And there may have been some for who some of this might have been true.

But for us, it was never anything like that. Nothing threatening or sinister. It was just a bit of a laugh. An outlet for our teenage aggression. For Craig it was a means of exorcising his rage at his home life. And with no meaningful parental guiding hand to steady his ship, it meant that he took it to the extreme. Not that Craig or any of us ever talked about our emotions. After all, we were teenage boys growing up in 1970's Britain.

As far as I was concerned, punk was a godsend. To me it was all about being as snide as possible to as many people as possible and that was something I excelled at, even prided myself on. Well - how else would I have gained my nickname.

Shane on the other hand was a different case altogether. Although we never spoke about it, we knew that punk was never really Shane's thing. Before punk came along I remember him telling me how his dad used to take him to a record shop in Walsall called 'Reggae Got Soul.' This, apparently was an Aladdin's cave of rare American and Jamaican imports from artists I'd never heard of and Shane would talk with great enthusiasm and expertise about the sounds his dad brought home with them.

So when punk came along and Craig and I embraced it, Shane obviously found himself with a dilemma, caught between following the music he really loved or keeping in with his mates.

And of course, at the age we were, there was no competition - loyalty to the gang prevailed. To be fair Shane began to feel more included when the whole punk bandwagon progressed and high profile bands such as The Clash and The Ruts started to play their own reggae songs. I think it was something to do with solidarity between punks and black boys, both feeling that they were part of an oppressed minority picked on by the media and the police.

And it was Shane who was now locked in my bathroom changing into his punk gear. He had got away with the broken string incident the previous day, having persuaded his mum that he had broken it at home whilst prepping for his Spanish Guitar lesson. Keen to encourage her boy in his quest to learn a musical instrument she drove him straight down to the music shop in town and bought a whole new set of strings.

Shane had endured a hairy moment when the shop keeper recognised him, having seen all three of us lurking outside the shop a few days earlier. However, his barbed comment of; "Not got your friends with you today then?" drew no comment from Shane's mum and he had escaped unscathed.

After what seemed an age Shane finally emerged from the bathroom, a plastic bag containing his neatly folded home clothes in his hand, which he placed carefully on top of my chest of drawers.

We had managed the previous afternoon to turn his flared jeans inside out and, using my mum's sewing machine, had hemmed in the flares so they now looked a little more respectable. Also we had found some green paint in my dad's shed and painted SMASH THE STATE on to both of our t shirts.

"What time did Craig say?" asked Shane.

"Half ten, outside Cyclops Records," I replied. "There's a few others coming down who Craig knows."

Shane looked at me uneasily. I read his mind instantly. Being the only black boy on our estate, Shane had learned the hard way about irrational prejudice and hatred and this was always more likely to manifest itself when meeting new people. His sheer size meant that usually it was low key and behind his back but there had been occasions when older kids, even adults had given him unnecessary grief simply because of his looks.

If Craig and I were with him of course, we would have nothing of it. And our reputation as a gang, especially among our own age group, was such that most people steered well clear of us.

In town though, dressed as punks you were never quite sure who you'd meet, how they would react and how things might pan out. So in that respect I guess we were all on our guard. It was just that in Shane's case, I guess it felt more personal.

Craig was waiting alone outside Cyclops when we arrived.

"Alright boys!" he shouted. "I just been telling a couple of Rockers how crap their music is. Ha ha. Bloody headbangers."

"Yeah," I added. "I can still smell their patchouli oil. Phew!" I held my nose in exaggerated gesture.

Craig laughed but Shane's attention had been caught by something over both of our shoulders.

"You know those rockers," he said. "Were they wearing denim jackets?"

"Yeah. Losers," replied Craig. "Why? What's up?"

In reply Shane pointed behind us. We both turned round.

"Hello. Looks like we've got us some trouble," said Craig as a group of four lads slightly older than us and all dressed in denim approached.

"They don't look too happy," I remarked.

This wasn't the first time I had been involved in confrontations with other groups based on my choice in music. At the time, your identity was intrinsically linked to the type of music you followed. You were either a punk or a mod or a rocker or whatever. But you couldn't be into more than one of these. To do so would be sacrilege. The unwritten rule was that you followed your chosen genre and everything else was rubbish.

It was strange though, when meeting rival groups, how much more empowered I felt whenever I had my mates around me. If I had been alone, I would have run. No doubt about it. But with Craig by my side and Shane's muscle behind me, I almost enjoyed moments like this.

The biggest of the four boys stepped up pressing his face close to Craig's. I didn't recognise them as being from our school so they obviously weren't aware of his reputation.

"My mate says you've been taking the piss," he hissed through gritted teeth. "Stupid little punk. You think you're so . . "

"Jesus Christ!" I interrupted. "What's that smell? Did someone die?"

The boy turned his attention to me. "You looking for trouble?," he virtually spat in my face.

"Your mum too poor to afford toothpaste is she?" I quipped. "Or did you just forget to brush your teeth today?"

The boy looked temporarily at a loss and took a step back. "You what?"

"Your breath stinks like manure mate!" I added. "What did you have for breakfast? A horse shit sandwich?"

"Right that's it!" shouted the boy. "No dirty little punk's gonna talk to me like that!"

He raised his fist and was ready to strike when a hand flashed out from beside me and grabbed his wrist in a vice like grip. It was Shane.

"I think you need to calm down," he said in a low voice.

"You better do as he says," added Craig. "Otherwise I'm gonna have to let him off his leash."

Here he turned to the other three, unclipped a huge safety pin from his trousers and bent it open, pointing the sharp end at them.

"And you three, you want some of this then?" he said, scowling.

"Now piss off!" I sneered.

The boy looked at Shane and at Craig then pulled his hand away.

"Just watch it next time," he muttered, turning to go.

"And oi!" I called.

The boy, who with his friends had started to amble away, stopped and turned to face me.

"You're going the wrong way. Chemist is that way," I continued pointing up the street. "I believe they do a very nice line in dental hygiene."

The boy scowled at me one final time then turned and walked off.

I continued, nevertheless. "Unless it's the barbers you're after. Looks like you need a good haircut as well. You could get a discount if all four if you go. They might even wash it for you if you're lucky."

Craig and Shane both sniggered.

I turned to Shane who looked a little shaky like he was still feeling the after effects of the adrenaline burst.

"Nice one Big Man," I said patting him on the shoulder.

Craig looked at him with pride. "Come on," he said to both of us. "I want you to meet some new friends of mine."

The rest of the day passed relatively uneventfully. Craig did indeed introduce us to some older boys with similar taste in music and, after they had been told the story of our face off and how Shane had scared off all six of them (well sometimes it's good to exaggerate), we hung around the Oasis market with them listening to music and looking for cool additions to our wardrobes.

It was never easy looking for clothes though, because Craig was always the one wanting to buy stuff and Shane was usually the only one of us who had any money. Consequently, on more than one occasion Shane would lend Craig a couple of quid. Craig would always reply with; "I'll pay you back next week." But, of course, he never did.

Tuesday 9th August - Groupies

It was a few days later and we were back down the den rehearsing. We'd tried doing a couple of cover versions but being confined to one acoustic guitar and an upturned tin bath severely limited us. So we usually reverted to playing our one and only song 'Smash The State.' And that wasn't going too well either.

Craig, having felt that he'd made his contribution to the song, was now applying pressure to me and Shane to improve it.

"It needs a second chord," he said. "Try F."

Shane and I exchanged glances. Then Shane spent some time forming the chord shape with his fingers before strumming a rather muted F.

The problem was though, as anyone who has tried to learn guitar will know, that changing from one chord to another quickly and smoothly takes a lot of practice. As a result, the song ground to an undignified halt every time a chord change was attempted. With practice this was reduced to more of a hiccup but it was still enough to make the song sound disjointed.

Craig then turned his attention to me. "You're only singing one note Snide. Can't you do something more interesting."

The truth was I knew this already but was at a loss as to what to do. After all I'd never written a tune before. And even when I did eventually come up with something that closely resembled a melody, Craig thought it sounded too happy.

"Sounds like a bloody pop song!" he grumbled.

It was at this point that all three of us noticed the sound of giggling outside. Craig was first outside to investigate.

"Alright girls," we heard him say in his fake cockney accent.

Shane and I looked at each other in surprise.

I should point out at this point exactly where we stood as far as girls were concerned. All three of us were thirteen years old. And in that respect we were in the early stages of awakening to our sexuality. Twelve months ago our reaction to girls would have been overwhelmingly negative. Girls might as well have been aliens as far as we were concerned. They held no interest to us since they were irrelevant to the lives we led.

Now however, although we'd never really talked about it, we found ourselves behaving differently in the company of the opposite sex. For me personally, it was a feeling of excited nervousness and a need to impress . And from what I'd seen from Craig and Shane, they felt the same. Our sexual awakening was in its earliest, most formative stage. But it was undoubtedly there.

Shane and I sauntered out, hands in pockets, trying to look nonchalant.

Three girls were standing around Craig. They were about our age though I didn't recognise them.

"Was that you playing just then?" asked the smallest of the three, a slim black haired girl dressed in a tight t shirt and flared jeans. My eyes immediately became riveted to her chest as I noticed that she was wearing a bra.

"Yeah. We're a band," said Craig, continuing as best he could in cockney mode.

The girl exchanged glances with her friend and they both giggled. The third, standing slightly behind the other two stood awkwardly staring at the ground.

"Do you know any David Cassidy?" asked the black haired girl.

"Or David Essex?" added her friend.

"No!" replied Craig emphatically. "We don't do any of that crap. It's so lame."

The third girl muttered something to the ground about Donny Osmond but nobody took any notice.

"So what do you do then?" asked the black haired girl.

"We're punk ain't we," answered Craig. "You wanna hear us play?"

My heart missed a beat. Surely he wasn't being serious.

"Yeah. OK," replied the girl. "Who's the singer?"

"Me," I said, blushing.

The girls followed us into the den and stood in the doorway looking like they were fully prepared for a quick exit if it became absolutely necessary.

"What is this place?" asked the second girl.

"It's our den," answered Shane. "Cool isn't it?" he smiled hopefully at all three but his friendliness wasn't reciprocated.

"Come on then Shane!" exclaimed Craig confidently. "Let's do Smash the State. You ready Snide?"

"Snide?" interrupted the second girl looking me up and down with genuine interest. "That's not your real name is it?"

"Err no," I answered awkwardly.

"What is it then?" she persisted.

"He's just Snide. Alright?" snapped Craig.

The two girls giggled again. The third girl shuffled her feet on the floor and edged towards the door.

"Okay. 1,2,3,4!" cried Craig and, slightly out of time with each other, we launched into Smash the State.

If anything, the presence of an audience made us perform even worse than usual. Shane got his fingers into a tangle when trying to change chords, producing something that had neither melody nor rhythm. And for my part, I had completely forgotten the tune I had come up with earlier and ended up trying to cover up my ineptitude by shouting the lyrics even more aggressively than usual. Then, as we came to the final verse, my mind went completely blank and, rather than stand doing nothing I actually started to dance.

The song ended in chaos with Craig trying to make the best of a bad job by beating the hell out of his tin bath. But rather than sounding like cool drumming, it now suddenly sounded like . . well like someone beating the hell out of a tin bath.

All three girls faced us smirking. Eventually the dark haired girl gave her verdict. "I think you need a bit more practice boys." And with that they left.

Craig put his hands on his hips and looked at us both in disgust.

"What d'you call that!" he exclaimed, angrily.

He pointed a trembling finger at Shane. "You need to learn how to play that bloody guitar. And you Snide need to learn how to sing."

He stormed out leaving Shane and I looking bemused.

Having given Craig a few minutes to calm down we emerged to find him sitting on the fence at the side of the footpath that ran along the top of the railway cutting where our den was located.

"The trouble with you two is you don't know how to play punk properly," said Craig without looking up. We said nothing but joined Craig on the fence and sat in silence for some time.

"Right," said Craig at length. "This is what we need to do. The end of this month, Saturday the 27th, Enemies of Promise are playing at JBs in Dudley. We're gonna get tickets and we're gonna go and learn how to do this thing properly."

"We'd never get in," I said. "We're too young."

"And my mum and dad would never let me out," added Shane.

"You two are always so negative," complained Craig. "Look Snide. We could get in. It's easy. You know Tony and Chris we met down Oasis on Saturday? They're going and they're fifteen. Nobody's gonna stop them getting in. So we dress up in our punk gear, spike our hair, wait outside the venue until they turn up and get in with them. What do you say?"

I didn't want to speak out of turn again but it all sounded a bit dodgy. Punk gigs were renowned for getting out of hand (well that's what it said in the papers).

"Well . . " I began.

"Did you say Saturday the 27th?" interrupted Shane.

"Yeah."

"In that case I just might be able to do it," said Shane. "We've all been invited to a wedding. Some friend of my mum. But if I cried off sick, I'd be free to go to the gig. They wouldn't be home until after midnight. I could get back before them and they'd never know!"

My heart sank. I'd hoped that with Shane's support we could talk Craig out of it. Now I was in the minority, I had no chance.

"Snide?" asked Craig again. "Come on. It'll be a laugh."

"Okay," I said, trying to summon some enthusiasm. "I'll do it."

Wednesday 10th August - Shane
The Entrepreneur

By the next day I had manage to convince myself that going to see Enemies of Promise was a good idea after all and had even cleared it with my mum to stop out late that night to go to a family wedding that Shane's parents had invited me to. Not strictly true, but enough truth embedded in the story for me to cover my tracks if I got found out.

We had arranged to meet down the den again to discuss our plan of action and when I arrived I was relieved to find that, although Shane and Craig were both already there, there was no sign of Shane's guitar. At least we weren't going to be rehearsing today.

"Alright Snide," called Craig. He was sitting on his upturned tin bath with Shane. Like myself, both had opted for casual dress. It felt quite a relief not to be a punk just for one day.

"Tickets are £1.50 from Cyclops Records."

"That's a bit much isn't it!" I exclaimed.

"Yeah, but worth it I reckon," replied Craig.

"Plus we need to get some proper gear to wear," added Shane.

"And I know where I can get hold of some alcohol," grinned Craig.

I felt my heart begin to sink again. I couldn't help feeling we were getting out of our depth here.

"So we need to make some money pretty damn quick," concluded Craig. "Any ideas?"

I sat down on the floor and exhaled noisily. "My mum won't give me any money without knowing exactly what I'm spending it on. What about your mum Craig?" I didn't bother asking about her boyfriend, Jim. He never did anything for Craig. At least her previous bloke had occasionally bought him stuff. This one spent his entire dole on booze and fags leaving Craig's mum to stretch what little money she had on paying all the bills.

"Nah," replied Craig, without explanation.

"Well I see it like this," began Shane. "Nobody is going to give us the money so we will have to earn it."

"Yes but how?" I asked.

A certain sparkle in Shane's eye told us that he had come up with one of his 'Great Ideas.'

"I've got a great idea," he said.

"What is it?" I asked, dubiously.

"Car wash!" exclaimed Shane. "It's easy money. All we need is a bucket and a sponge and we're up and running."

"A car wash," repeated Craig, thoughtfully. "Not a bad idea. How much do we charge?"

"Dunno," replied Shane.

"50p?" I suggested.

"Yes, that's good," said Shane. "Do sixty cars and that's £10 each. Easily enough to get tickets and anything else we need."

I did a quick mental calculation. "Sixty cars and we got fifteen days. So that's four cars a day. I think we could manage that."

"Right then," said Craig. "Shane, you buy the bucket and sponge. We can pay you back out of our takings."

"Don't we need a company name?" asked Shane.

Oh no, don't start all that again I thought.

Ignoring Shane, Craig continued. "Snide, you can do all the talking with customers. You're good at all that stuff, being brainy and everything."

I nodded in consent.

"Right then," concluded Craig. "We start tomorrow."

Friday 12th August - A Fair Day's Pay

As it turned out, it rained all day Thursday so it was Friday when we finally congregated at the park ready to embark on our new venture. I was first to arrive, followed by Craig wearing his full punk gear including his donkey jacket with HATE written across the back and his hair freshly spiked that morning. I didn't say anything.

Finally Shane appeared carrying a bright red bucket. As he got nearer we could seen that he was wearing brand new Adidas t shirt, track suit bottoms and trainers.

"My dad said that if I was starting a new business, he was prepared to invest in me," he said by way of explanation, although I'm not sure at the time if Craig or I knew exactly what he meant.

We had opted to meet at the park with the intention of going on to the new estate bordering it. This area of town had many detached houses so we reasoned that potential customers there would be more likely to pay for someone to wash their cars for them.

After wandering around aimlessly, trying to pluck up the courage to approach a house, Craig finally stopped outside a smart semi detached with a lime green Mini on the driveway. "We'll start here," he announced and marched up the garden path.

As we reached the front door, Craig positioned me in front of him. "Go on then Snide," he said.

Up to this point, a car washing business had seemed a great idea. But now, as I faced the front door, it suddenly seemed a lot more complicated. Shane had supplied the bucket and sponge but we had no washing up liquid, no water and, most importantly, no idea what we were doing!

I took a deep breath and knocked timidly on the door. It was immediately opened by a portly middle aged woman wearing a bright pink house coat. She looked down her nose at all three of us.

"Yes?" she enquired in a voice that seemed rather too posh for the house she lived in.

"We err . . Car wash," I stammered, nervously. Then, feeling Craig's elbow digging me in the ribs, I tried to be a little more assertive. "We noticed you car is dead filthy," I began.

"I beg your pardon?" interrupted the lady, indignantly.

Shane stepped forward. "What my friend means is we are offering a car wash service in this area and were wondering if you . ."

He didn't need to carry on. Having taken one look at Shane, the lady slammed the door in our faces.

Immediately, Craig pushed past us both, opened the letter box and shouted; "Get stuffed then you fat cow!" through it.

"I'll call the police if you don't go away!" came a rather panicked reply from within.

This was a cue for us to run for it. And we didn't stop running until we got back to the safety of the park where we collapsed on the grass.

"Hey dudes, what's going down? You in trouble again?" said an all too familiar voice.

"No Eric," said Shane, having been the first of us to get his breath back. "We've been doing our car wash business. But Craig shouted some pretty rude stuff at a woman and she threatened to call the police."

Eric laughed. "Hey listen Craig, man. You've really got to learn you can't go abusing your customers."

"She deserved it," replied Craig. "She was such a square."

"Looked pretty round to me," I quipped. Craig and Shane laughed.

"Seriously man," continued Eric. "Look at you. You can't wear that jacket. It'll scare the customers off. And that hair. You got to do something about that hair. Come on."

Eric marched off in the direction of the pavilion with the three of us in pursuit. He stopped at the outdoor tap that stood to the side of it. "Right. Kneel down," he said to Craig. Surprisingly, Craig did as he was told. Suddenly Eric grabbed Craig by the shoulder and thrust his head under the tap, turning it on as he did so.

"Jesus Christ!" screeched Craig as the freezing cold water flushed through his hair and down his back .

"Wash it out man," ordered Eric. Again Craig obliged.

Ablutions completed, Eric hung Craig's jacket up to dry and we all crashed out on the bowling green.

"Now then. If you wanna make money out of this business, you got to treat customers with respect," said Eric. "Make yourselves sound professional. Tell them you're offering a car wash service in the area."

"That's what I did," replied Shane. "But that woman took one look at me and slammed the door in our faces."

"Yeah, well . . ." began Eric.

"Is that 'Yeah well' as in 'Yeah well' cos she's a racialist like you?" said Craig.

"I'm no racist man!" cried Eric, putting his arm round Shane's shoulder. "Me and Shane are cool right?"

Shane smiled at Eric by way of reply.

"Come on," I said. "Let's give it another go."

"Yeah, but maybe not on that street," added Shane.

It actually took half a dozen attempts before we finally got our first customer. Of the five refusals, two had said no politely, one shut the door on us without speaking, one told us to get lost and one initially agreed but then refused to give us any hot water! At last though, we finally had someone who said yes and had agreed to pay the full fifty pence.

The car in question was a Land Rover and looked easy enough at first sight. However, it soon became apparent that washing a car took far longer than we'd imagined. For a start, we realised the limitations of three people trying to wash a car with one bucket and one sponge. Inevitably, at any one time, two of us were standing by watching the other one work. Shane was the only one who was tall enough to reach all the way across the roof so he did the top. I did the windows and sides and Craig did the wheels and front, but not until after we'd had to request a refill of our bucket.

Finally we knocked on the owners door to collect our fee.

"Fifty pence please," I said holding out my hand. The man looked rather surprised, then stepped out onto the driveway to inspect our handiwork.

"But you haven't rinsed it yet," he said. "You need to rinse it to wash the all of the dirt off. Where's your hose?"

We all looked at each other stupidly. "We haven't got one," I mumbled.

"Haven't got a hose," the man repeated. "So not only have you used my hot water, now you want to borrow my hose!" None of us replied.

"Very well," said the man at length. "But I think, if I'm going to let you use my hose, the least you can do is clean the inside of my car as well. I'll even let you use my vacuum cleaner. Hang on."

He went back into the house then reappeared through the side gate unwinding a long green garden hose. After connecting it and showing us how to use it he disappeared into the house.

"Come on. Let's finish this quick otherwise we'll be stuck here all day," said Craig.

"Yeah. I'll ask him for the vacuum cleaner," added Shane. "One of us can rinse while another does the inside."

"You really value your life Shane, don't you!" I exclaimed, sarcastically. "Don't you know that would mean mixing electricity and water. That's lethal that is!"

And so it was that after rinsing, *then* drying, *then* polishing (the owner insisted on it), *then* vacuuming, we finally got our first payment.

"This is going to take for ever," I moaned as we trudged back to the park. "Four customers in a day? We've only just managed one!"

"We'll do better tomorrow," said Shane reassuringly. "There'll be more customers at home at the weekend. And I know where we can get our hands on a hose."

"Where?" I asked.

"Eric," replied Shane. "We can borrow the one he uses on the bowling green. He's cool. He'll lend us it."

"And tomorrow, we'll tell them interiors is an extra 20p," added Craig. "You never know. We might make even more money. And we need two more buckets and two more sponges. You can sort that out Snide."

"Ok," I replied dejectedly.

And with that last thought we split for the day, determined that tomorrow would be the day our business really got off the ground.

Saturday 13th August - Competition

"Oh yes," continued the third customer of the day. "She's a GTi you know. 2.8 litres. 0 to 60 in 10.7 seconds. That's the turbo you see."

After making a brisk start, this man was making serious inroads into our time. And even though it was quite obvious that we didn't have the slightest interest in his car, he continued to roll out its technical specs to us ad nauseum.

"And you see in there," he added pointing through the side window. "Walnut dash. None of your plastic rubbish."

"Yeah." I butted in. "But it's not a real sports car, like a Ferrari or a Lamborghini, is it? It's just a Ford Granada."

The expression on the customer's face hardened. "Yes, well you be careful while you're washing her. That's all. Don't want any damage to the paintwork." At this point he turned to address Shane directly. "You got that son?" Shane nodded. Craig and I exchanged glances and Craig mouthed; "Racialist. Another one!"

Having finally got rid of the persistent petrol head, we made good time. Working now with three buckets and Eric's hose (Shane had been absolutely correct - Eric had handed it over without fuss), Craig and Shane were soon tidying up whilst I knocked on the door for payment.

Obviously still smarting from my comments, the customer examined his car's bodywork closely, looking for the slightest smudge, smear or scratch to complain about. In the end, without further comment, he emptied the contents of his pocket into his hand and sorted through a collection of copper coins.

"You got any change?" he said at length. "I've only got 37p here. I've got a pound note though."

"No problem sir," said Shane fishing from his pocket the fifty pence piece from our previous job. "We've got change."

"Oh," replied the man, looking a little deflated as he begrudgingly removed a note from his wallet and handed it to Shane.

"Thank you," said Shane, giving the man his change. "Glad to be of service."

"And drive carefully," I added as we turned to go. "Don't go picking up too many speeding tickets." Craig and Shane both held it in until they heard the front door shut then roared with laughter.

"You're so bad Snide," laughed Craig.

We decided to take a break and made our way back to the park, Shane with the hose coiled round his neck and me carrying the three buckets neatly stacked inside each other.

Just as we turned the final corner and saw the green expanse of the park in front of us, Shane stopped dead and pointed.

"Hey, look."

We followed his gaze and were surprised to see, a few doors down on the opposite side of the road, two boys vigorously at work washing a car!

"Are you thinking what I'm thinking?" said Craig slowly.

"Competition?" I asked.

"Yeah. Come on. Let's find out what they're up to."

It was only as we got closer that it became obvious to us that they were twins. They were also quite large.

"Hey Tweedledum and Tweedledee!," I shouted.

The two boys, who were so busy at their job that they hadn't seen us standing at the bottom of the drive, stopped and looked up.

"Who are you calling Tweedledum and Tweedledee?" shouted one of them in reply.

"He's only joking," said Craig, making his way up the drive. "Is this your dad's car?"

"No," replied the other.

"So why you washing it then?"

"For money," replied Tweedledum, bluntly.

"We wash people's cars. Then they pay us. Seventy pence each," continued Tweedledee.

"Oh no. That can't be right," said Craig, menacingly. "Cos that's what we do. And this is our patch. And you Tweedledum!" He stabbed a finger into his chest. "And your brother here, are trespassing on it."

"Says who?"

"Says me. And you see him over there," continued Craig, pointing at Shane. "If you mess us around, I'm gonna let him loose on you."

Tweedledum stepped forward and used his full body weight to push Craig backwards. "I'd like to see him try," he snarled.

On cue, Shane stepped forward. We all knew Shane as a gentle giant but he had his role in the gang. And when Craig was threatened, his role was to step in and play the heavy.

Suddenly the front door flew open and a man in his sixties marched down the drive.

"What the blazes is going on here?" he demanded.

"These boys are trying to intimidate us," shouted Tweedledum.

"Oh? And why is that?"

"They say we're working on their patch."

"What rubbish!" shouted the man. "Why you two boys have been washing my cars for years."

He turned his attention to us. "And as for you three. I don't know who you are but you're certainly not from round here. Now clear off or I'll call the police."

"That's twice in two days," I muttered under my breath.

Reluctantly, Craig and Shane retreated with the twins watching them triumphantly.

"We'll get even with those bastards," muttered Craig as he passed me. "Come on."

"Council of War?" asked Shane.

Craig nodded in assent. "Yeah. Council of War."

Sunday 14th August - Industrial Espionage

The next day we were back down the park and were surprised to see, emerging from the bowls pavilion, Eric.

"Oh hi dudes," he waved as he caught sight of us sprawled out on the green.

"What are you doing here on a Sunday?" I asked.

"Just come to pick something up," answered Eric tapping his nose in what I guessed was a gesture that meant 'But don't tell anyone else you've seen me here.' As he did so, he hastily stuffed a small paper bag into his jacket pocket. "So how's your car wash business going then?"

"We've got rivals," replied Shane.

"Yeah. And they need putting in their place," added Craig.

"It wasn't the Clarkson twins was it?" asked Eric.

"Probably," I replied. "They were definitely twins. Looked like they enjoy their food."

"Yeah. That'll definitely be the Clarksons. Nice lads, Rick and Rob, but they know how to handle themselves you know."

"Do they have plenty of customers then?" asked Shane, ignoring Eric's comment.

"Regulars," answered Eric. "And lots of them."

"If we could get the addresses of their customers," said Shane, thoughtfully. "We could move in on them next Saturday."

"Why Saturday?" asked Craig.

"Because if their customers are regular, then chances are they do the same cars every Sunday. So we go round the day before and offer to undercut them."

"By undercut, do you mean offer to do it cheaper?" I asked.

"Yes," continued Shane. "They told us they charge seventy pence. We only charge fifty. Some might say no to us out of loyalty but I bet we could win enough over to make a decent bit of money."

"So how do we get the addresses then?" asked Craig, rolling over onto his stomach.

"Only one way," I said. "We've got to go undercover. Spy on them."

"Spy on them?" cried Craig. "How?"

"We'd have to be careful," I said. "If they saw us hanging around, they'd guess what we were up to straight away."

"So what! What if they did!" shouted Craig getting to his feet and brushing grass off himself. "We'd show them, wouldn't we Shane?"

Shane gave Craig a knowing look. "It'd be better if they didn't see us."

"Shane's right," I added. "Besides, it would be a laugh spying on them and them not knowing what we were up to."

It was early afternoon when the three of us reconvened at the edge of the park. Shane had gone home and returned with an old note pad and pencil and Craig had picked up his Chopper bike for the purpose of 'Drive Pasts.'

For my part, I'd been round the estate doing some early reconnaissance and had come across the twins working in a nearby street.

"Address?" demanded Shane, his pencil poised in preparation.

"32 Richmond Gardens," I replied.

"Okay," added Craig. "We'll give it 15 minutes, then I'll do a drive past."

And so, settling ourselves down under the shade of a tree, we idled away the first half of the afternoon. Every so often Craig would leap up onto his bike and disappear, returning a few minutes later with another address.

It was on his eighth return however, that he broke some disappointing news. "14 Bamber Gardens," he panted as he slithered to a halt on the grass. "But we got a problem boys. They've spotted me!"

"What did they do?" I asked.

"Just a load of shouting and flicking the Vs."

"Do you think they know what we're up to?"

"No. They just wanted to shout a load of abuse at me. Bastards!"

"Right. We need to ditch the bike then," said Shane. "Have you got your lock?"

"Yeah," answered Craig, fishing the padlock and chain from his pocket. "I'll go and chain it to the pavilion."

As he cycled off, I turned to Shane. "So what do we do now? Continue on foot?"

"It's the only way," replied Shane, standing up and stretching. "We're gonna have to keep our distance though."

As soon as Craig returned, we set off in the direction of Bamber Gardens. Reaching the corner, we were relieved to see we hadn't lost them. They were working on the car next door. "That's number 16," said Craig to Shane who duly wrote the address down in his note book.

"We best wait here," whispered Shane. "If we hang around behind these conifers, they won't see us."

Nonchalantly we slunk behind the trees so that we were now stood on the edge of the driveway of the corner house.

"We need to be careful," I said, lowering my voice. "This road is a cul-de-sac so, at some point they'll be coming back this way."

"No problem," answered Craig. "They carry all their equipment round on a big trolley. We'll hear them coming a long time before they reach us."

We were interrupted by the sound of a front door opening.

"Oi you three!" came an irate voice. We turned round to see a wiry bespectacled man glaring at us from his doorstep. "What do you think you're doing on my driveway? Clear off!"

"Well at least this one hasn't threatened to call the police," I muttered under my breath.

"Go on!" continued the man. "Get back to your own estate you yobs!"

Slowly, we began to walk away.

"And I won't forget your face in a hurry sonny," the man shouted after us. We didn't turn round to see which one of us he meant but I had my suspicions.

We returned later but there was no sign of the Clarksons. So, deciding that nine addresses was a reasonably good haul, we called it a day.

"We'll give these a go next Saturday then," I concluded. Shane and Craig both nodded.

"We'll take a couple days off," said Craig. "Most of these will be back at work tomorrow anyway."

"I reckon we should just concentrate on making enough money to buy the tickets," I added. "That's £4.50."

"And the booze," said Craig. "I can get my hands on a Watney's Party Four for 85p."

"So with bus fares, that adds up to about £6," I concluded. "How much have we made so far Shane?"

"Two pounds. So that's eight cars to do and we've got nine addresses here," replied Shane, holding up his notebook.

"Yeah, but they won't all take us on," said Craig.

"We'll do it," replied Shane, confidently. "We can do a few Thursday and Friday."

"So what are we gonna do tomorrow then?" I asked.

Craig stopped and turned to face us with a glint in his eye. "Band practice!" he said.

Monday 15th August - A Near Miss

It was the first time we had practiced in nearly a week, the last time being when we had humiliated ourselves in front of that group of giggling girls.

Craig had good reason for reassembling us though. Having sulked and refused to talk about the band for a couple of days, he had now written a second song and was eager to share it with us.

"It's called DESTROY THE SYSTEM!" he declared triumphantly, waving another tatty piece of handwritten paper under my nose.

To my relief Craig had appeared to take more care with his handwriting this time. Under the heading DESTROY THE SYSTEM by KHAISER CRAIG (I didn't ask why he'd decided to call himself that!) he had written:

Destroy, destroy, destroy
Destroy the system. The people in power
It's coming slowly. Their final hour.
Anarchy for us. Rise up and fight.
Stand up and shout out. For your rights.

A decent start I thought - at least it rhymed. Then it went downhill somewhat into a general rant.

Destroy the police state cos the kids are OK
We gonna take no more crap from the men in authority
Fight, fight, fight
For what is right
Destroy, destroy, destroy - the system

"Good innit," said Craig proudly. "And I've got the drumming to go with it." And with that he produced his brushes from his jacket pocket and started to hammer his tin bath whilst screaming the lyrics.

Shane had already started to strum along with a new, slightly melancholy chord. "I learned it last week at my guitar lesson," he said by way of explanation. "It's called E minor. And I can do A." Here he changed his fingers surprisingly smoothly to play his other new chord.

"I love it!" cried Craig. "Come on Snide. Let's do this. 1-2-3-4!"

Immediately he launched into his drumming with Shane reverting to E minor. The juxtaposition of manic percussion and melancholy chord sounded a bit odd at first but after finally finding my rhythm, I started to sing.

"Destroy! Destroy! Destroy!"

"Woohoo!" cried Craig over the din. "Go Snide go!"

And so it went on for the next couple of hours as we alternated between 'Smash the State' and 'Destroy the System'. Each time we played the songs they seemed to fit together a little better. My singing became more rhythmic, Shane's chord changes became smoother and Craig . . . . well he was just Craig!

Looking back on it now, I realise that it was just a load of rubbish but then, we felt like trailblazers - trailblazers at the forefront of a new era in music. Setting new standards. Setting the world on fire.

Eventually, Shane broke the spell. "I can't play any more. My fingers are sore," he complained, carefully leaning his guitar up against the wall of the den.

"That's alright Shane," said Craig. "I'm knackered as well."

Shane stood up and looked at his watch. "Oh my God. Its ten to twelve. My mum will be home in ten minutes. I've got to go!"

"Hold on Big Man," said Craig, reassuringly. "Don't panic. I'll give you a lift on the back of my chopper."

"Hurry up then!" cried Shane, his voice rising in panic.

Craig made his way out of the den and picked his bike up. Shane grabbed his guitar, zipped it into its canvas bag, slung it over his shoulder and climbed onto the back of Craig's saddle.

"Hold on tight," called Craig, raising himself up to a standing position and beginning to pedal as fast as he could.

I watched as they swerved onto the main path and headed in the direction of the main road. Then there was silence . . . . . followed by a loud crash!

Quickly I ran in the direction of the sound and found Craig and Shane both lying on the pavement, Craig's chopper on its side with the front wheel still spinning furiously in the air.

"What the hell happened?" I exclaimed as I reached them.

"Bloody car!" cursed Craig, sitting up and examining a badly grazed hand. "I was just getting onto the road and he came out of nowhere. Forced me to swerve. You OK Shane?"

Looking a little shaken, Shane got slowly to his feet and brushed himself down. "I think so," he said eventually.

"What about your guitar?" I asked.

In response, Shane unzipped the bag, pulled out the guitar and looked at it carefully. "Holy crap!" he gasped as he turned it over. It was easy to see why. For there, extending the full length of the body of the guitar, was a giant crack.

"My mum's going to kill me."

Carefully, he slid his guitar back into its bag and, standing Craig's bike back up, remounted the saddle.

"See you later Snide," said Craig, as he got back on himself.

"Yeah, see you," muttered Shane.

And with that, they teetered off up the road.

Tuesday 16th August - Insight

Shane had phoned me on Monday evening with the bad news.

"Hi Snide. I'm not coming out again until Saturday."

"Why not?"

"Because of what happened to my guitar. It's got to go to the shop today to be repaired. Not only that but mum saw Craig giving me a lift on the back of his bike. She went mental!"

"Oh Christ," I replied.

"I've only been allowed out Saturday because Dad wants to support me in our car washing business."

"Even with Craig being part of it?"

"He doesn't know about Craig. He thinks it's just me and you."

"Oh. That's probably best."

"I've got to go anyway Snide. Mum's given me a list of jobs to do round the house today to go towards paying for the repair. See you." And with that he'd put down the receiver without waiting for a reply.

All of which left a bit of a hole in my week but I decided to go and visit Craig the next morning anyway.

So, having approached with caution and checked Jim's motor bike had gone, I found myself knocking on the front door of Craig's dilapidated house on my own for once.

After much struggling, Craig wrenched it open. "Where's Shane?" he asked.

I explained.

It was at this point that I noticed the huge bruise on Craig's arm. Craig often had bruises and both Shane and I were pretty sure they were something to do with Jim. But Craig was always dismissive of any discussion about what went on in his home life and we had learned to avoid that particular topic of conversation.

On this occasion though, the bruise was so large and obvious, I felt I had to say something.

"What happened to you?" I asked pointing.

Craig looked down at his arm then, without replying walked upstairs to his room.

I followed him up to find him perched on the edge of his bed. He sat quietly looking pensive - most unlike his usual ebullient self.

"I know what you and Shane think," he said, avoiding eye contact with me. "He's alright most of the time, Jim. He usually leaves me alone."

I nodded awkwardly, not really sure what might come next or how I should react.

"It's just when he's had a skinful," Craig continued, staring at the carpet. "He goes a bit mad sometimes."

There was a long silence. Eventually I said; "Oh. God." I didn't know what to say really. I felt well out of my depth.

I decided to try to change the subject. "Do you fancy going down the park?"

But Craig was on a roll now. "He hits Mum sometimes." He bit his lip and the expression on his face turned to one of anger. "The bastard! When I get older, he's gonna pay."

I laughed, more in embarrassment than anything, then realised how inappropriate a reaction it sounded.

There was another long pause then, suddenly, Craig appeared to snap out of his gloom. "Come on Snide," he said, grabbing his donkey jacket. "Let's go down the park then."

Thursday 18th August - Good Grafters

It was now only nine days to the Enemies of Promise gig and we were still four pounds short of the money needed to buy our tickets (and Craig's booze). So, despite Shane's absence, Craig and I decided to resume the car washing business on our own.

Fortunately we still had two buckets and two sponges and Eric was once again more than happy to lend us his hose pipe. I had even got my hands on a genuine chamois leather cloth, which I found amongst some clutter under our kitchen sink. What we were not in possession of however was the list of the Clarkson twins' customers, which was written in Shane's note book.

It was Craig who had the idea of revisiting our own customers from the previous Saturday.

"Well it's worth a try," I said. "But it was only five days ago. We might not have much luck."

I was right. The first customer on our round wasn't at home and the second politely declined.

And so it was that we found ourselves knocking hopefully once again on the door of Petrolhead Man, the owner of the Ford Granada.

"Oh, it's you two," he said looking slightly disapprovingly at us. "Where's your friend?"

"He couldn't make it today," I answered.

"Pity," continued Petrolhead. "I liked him. He was a good grafter."

"We can do just as good," said Craig.

"Well," began Petrolhead. "She is a little dirty. I took her out for a spin on Sunday you know. To the countryside. Got quite a bit of mud on her sills. It was well worth it of course. Great fun negotiating those winding country lanes. Special sports suspension you see. Grips the road on the most uneven of surfaces. And the dual disc braking system is a godsend when you meet someone coming round a blind bend at sixty miles per hour."

He stopped and looked at us as if waiting for a reaction. Awkwardly, I looked over at Craig whose eyes had appeared to glaze over.

"We can vacuum and polish the interior for an extra 25p," I offered, desperate to change the subject.

The man scratched his chin in an exaggerated thoughtful gesture.

"OK boys. You've got yourself a deal," he said at length.

Immediately, we set to work, filling buckets with hot water and attaching the hose pipe. In some perverse way, hearing Shane's praises being sung seemed to spur us both on to prove that we were 'good grafters' too.

We decided to start at the top and soon realised how much we missed Shane's height. Being slightly taller than Craig, I opted to work on the roof whilst Craig did the windows.

Everything was going well until I inadvertently got the chamois caught around the car aerial. It was a trendy aerial that, as on most modern cars, emerged from the front of the roof at a very oblique angle. The problem was that, being quite old, the chamois had a hole in it and somehow the hole had hooked itself over the end of the aerial, sliding down its length until it was well and truly snared.

I stood back from the car with my hands on my hips. "Damn!" I cursed.

"What's up?" asked Craig.

"My chammy's stuck," I groaned.

Craig examined it closely. "You just need to unhook it," he said.

"I can't reach it enough," I explained.

"Then give it a flick," suggested Craig.

I tried once or twice but it was stuck fast around the base of the aerial.

"You're not trying hard enough," said Craig. "Let me have a go."

He leant forward and grabbed the end of the chamois but, being shorter than me, he had even less purchase on it.

"Well it's flexible this aerial isn't it," said Craig. "So if I just give this thing a tug." He pulled and the aerial bent towards him a little but the chamois remained firmly lodged.

Craig was now starting to get irritated. "Stupid bloody thing!" he exclaimed. Then grabbing hold of the end of the chamois, he gave it one enormous yank.

There was a loud crack.

Then the chamois, complete with broken aerial shot over Craig's head and into the hedge behind us.

"Holy crap!" gasped Craig.

I looked over to the house and saw the horrified face of Petrolhead standing at the window. Seconds later the front door was thrown open.

"What have you done?" he shouted as he ran towards his beloved car.

"My aerial! My streamlined, lightweight alloy aerial!"

He turned to Craig his face gradually turning from red to purple. "Bloody hooligan! You've defaced my beautiful car!"

Craig walked over to the hedge and carefully disentangled the broken aerial from the chamois. Then slowly, almost reverentially, he offered it in his open palm to Petrolhead.

Petrolhead's hand lashed out to take the aerial and, as it did so, Craig flinched and raised both his hands to his face in protection.

"You'll pay for this," said Petrolhead lowering his voice.

"Well actually - they won't," came a familiar voice from behind us. "They're under age so they can't be sued for damage to property."

All three of us turned round to see Shane standing there.

"And even if you did try to sue, they have no legal assets with which to pay you compensation."

"Hi guys," he said to us . "I remembered we'd arranged to wash cars today so I rang dad at work and he's let me out."

"Oh, your dad who's a solicitor?" I said breathing a sigh of relief.

"The very same," replied Shane. "A solicitor who specialises in liability and compensation law."

Petrolhead stared at us open mouthed, then at the broken piece of aerial in his hand.

"We're really sorry mate," said Craig, looking genuinely apologetic. "If you want we can finish the job off for free."

Petrolhead looked dumbfoundedly at us then appeared to swell up, his face darkening again as he did so.

"I think he's going to blow," I muttered to Shane. "LEG IT!!!"

Grabbing our buckets and sponges we took to our heels and ran. As we did so we could hear the demented rantings of our most loyal customer (well we had completed one and a half jobs for him) echoing down the road.

Eventually we reached the sanctity of the park and seeing Eric making his way into the pavilion, followed him through the open door.

"Hey dudes! Cool it!" he cried. "What's going down?"

"We've just upset another customer," I explained.

Eric started to laugh, then looking us up and down, the smile suddenly vanished from his face.

"Hey. Where's my hose?" he demanded.

All three of us looked at each other.

"Holy crap - again!" said Craig.

Eric opted to return to the address alone to retrieve his hose, telling us to look after the pavilion in his absence.

It was a longer absence than any of us anticipated. Having waited for the best part of an hour, Eric finally appeared, his hose pipe coiled over his shoulder. And for the first time in the year and a half we'd known him he looked genuinely flustered.

"Jesus, you've really pissed him off," said Eric. "He thought I was one of your dads at first. Wanted me to pay for some aerial you broke? Refused to give me the hose back. In the end, I said he had illegal possession of council property. As soon as I mentioned the law, he went all funny. Dunno why. Handed it back to me muttering something about bloody lawyers!"

We all laughed.

"I don't get it. What've you guys said to him?"

"Shane's been quoting the law at him," I explained.

"Well I tell you what. You need to steer well clear, for now at least," concluded Eric.

We stayed a while before, remembering that we still needed to earn four pounds, we went back out on the streets. Eric even let us take his hose back out again.

This time we got lucky with a couple of addresses from the Clarkson's list, both of whom took up our offer of an internal vacuum for an additional 25p.

"So that's three pounds fifty we've got now," said Shane as we ambled back to the park. "That's just one more pound needed for tickets."

"And I think I can actually get the booze for free," said Craig.

"How?" I asked.

"I know where Jim keeps his secret stash. He thinks nobody knows about it but I do. It's not beer. It's whisky. He's got a whole box of miniatures. He'll never miss if a few of those go missing."

My heart sank again.

"I had whisky at Christmas," said Shane. "It burns your throat man. Gives you a warm glow though."

"It'll give you more than a warm glow, the amount we're gonna have," said Craig, with a grin.

My heart sank even further.

Saturday 20th August - Dodgy Dealings

We had continued to work our way through the Clarkson Twins' list on Friday and made the final pound we needed to buy our tickets. We decided nevertheless, to try the last three names on the list on Saturday morning, if only to provide us with a bit of spending money.

It was a hot, sunny morning so we started early. As it turned out, the first two opted to remain loyal to the Clarksons, but the third, a scruffy man with a ruddy face, gladly accepted.

"It needs a good scrub," he said.

"We can do the inside for an extra twenty five pence if you like," I said, hopefully.

"Oh no. Absolutely not," he replied firmly.

Shane went to fix up the hose allowing Craig and I to fill the buckets. I gestured to Craig as I turned the hose on. "Hey, that was a bit strange," I said quietly for fear of being overheard.

"What was?" asked Craig.

"He was pretty adamant he didn't want us going inside his car. I wonder why."

"What's the matter?" asked Shane joining us.

"I was just saying, it's funny he didn't want us going into his car," I said.

"Maybe he doesn't trust us," suggested Shane.

"Why?" asked Craig. "What's he got in there that's so valuable." He dropped his sponge into a bucket and sauntered over to the driver's window. "Can't see anything," he said, pressing his nose up to the glass.

I joined him, peering hopefully into the back. "Hang on," I said. "What's that on the back seat?"

Shane was by my side now, also looking into the back.

"Looks like a cardboard box with some white powder in," I said. "Doesn't look like it's worth much."

"No?" said Shane standing up straight and staring at me with excited eyes. "You know what that is don't you?"

"What?"

"Drugs!" said Shane, dropping his voice to a whisper.

Craig immediately filled the void left by Shane at the window and gazed in. "Wow! There must be a couple of pounds of the stuff there."

"Quick!" shouted Shane suddenly. "He's watching us. Buckets!"

Immediately we each grabbed a bucket and began scrubbing the car vigorously.

"It's OK," hissed Shane at length. "He's gone." He dropped his sponge back into a bucket. "Now then. First of all we need to ascertain what drug it is. I know a bit about these things. My dad has defended several people charged with possession of drugs over the years and I would say, in my expert opinion, that that is cocaine."

"I thought you said your dad was a compensation lawyer," said Craig.

"Well he is mainly," replied Shane. "But my dad does all sorts of legal stuff. And I'm telling you that's cocaine. There's only one way to really find out though."

"How?" I asked.

"You rub it on your gums and if they go numb it's cocaine."

The owner appeared at the window again and in response, we began furiously to work our way over the bodywork with our sponges.

"So who's going to test it?" asked Shane eventually. "Cos if it is cocaine, the relevant authorities will need to be informed."

"I'll do it," volunteered Craig.

Suddenly the front door opened and the car's owner walked out. "How are you boys getting on? I bet it's thirsty work on a day like today. Can I get you all a drink of squash?"

"Thank you. That would be nice," I answered.

"NO! Thank you," said Shane giving me a knowing look.

The man looked slightly taken aback. "Oh well. If you get thirsty, just give me a knock." He went back into the house.

I turned to Shane. "What was all that about?" I asked. "I could do with a drink. It's really hot today."

"He saw us looking in," replied Shane. "He could spike the drinks with knockout drops then take us prisoner in his house."

"Well I'm gonna find out what we're dealing with here," said Craig, taking one last look at the house then trying the back door.

It opened.

Craig leaned in, licked his finger and stuck it into the box. Then withdrawing his hand, he shut the car door and held his finger up to us. It was coated with a thin layer of the fine powder.

"Yeah," said Shane. "No doubt about it. That's snow alright."

"Snow?" I repeated.

"Street name for cocaine," explained Shane.

"Why snow?" I asked.

"Cos it's purest white of course," said Shane, raising his eyebrows.

"Doesn't look very white to me."

"Nor me," added Craig.

"That's cos its dirty. Probably been mixed with other stuff. Flour, chalk, scouring powder. They use all sorts."

This didn't seem to daunt Craig in the slightest. "Well I'm going to try it anyway. Here goes."

Slowly he raised his finger to his mouth, then puling his lips back into a grimace he carefully rubbed some of the powder over his gums.

"What can you feel?" I asked.

"Nothing," replied Craig, in disappointment. He wiped the rest of the powder onto his jeans and ran his tongue over his gums hopefully.

Immediately a look of horror and disgust came across his face.

"Eugh. Ah no. That's vile that is. Tastes disgusting!"

"Spit it out. Spit it out!" shouted Shane. "It might be poisonous. They do that sometimes."

"Now he tells us," I said, under my breath.

Obviously troubled by the taste more than any threat of poisoning, Craig tried to spit out the last remnants of the powder.

"The actions of a true punk," I said to Shane, jokingly. He didn't reply.

The front door opened again and the owner came out. "If you don't mind boys. I just need to get my fertiliser out of the car." He opened the back door. "Ah. There it is," he said, carefully picking up the box.

"Fertiliser?" I repeated.

"Yes," replied the man. "I need to give my plants a feed."

"What's in it?" asked Craig, his face starting to turn a pale shade of green.

"Oh it's a traditional mix," answered the man. "Dried fish for nitrogen, blood for iron and bone for phosphorous."

Craig let out a loud groan and gripped hold of his abdomen.

"Oh dear. Is he alright?" asked the man. "I think maybe the heat has got to you sonny. Maybe I'll get you that drink of squash after all."

"Yes," I confirmed. "I think that would be a very good idea."

How Craig managed to finish the job after that I don't know but we did indeed finish it and got paid one pound for our troubles.

"Right, that's it," said Craig as we packed up. "I'm finished with car washing. Let's leave it to the Clarksons."

And on that point, both Shane and I were in total agreement with him.

Monday 22nd August - Tickets

We'd all made an extra special effort to look the part when we went into town to finally buy our tickets. Craig had found some green food dye in the back of a kitchen cupboard and dyed the tips of his spikes with it. He also appeared to be wearing some sort of make-up on his cheeks but neither Shane nor I pursued that. I wasn't quite sure whether he was emulating someone famous or just trying to disguise yet another bruise. He certainly seemed extra hyper that morning.

Shane had come to my house, as usual, to change into his modified jeans and t shirt. He had also acquired a rather expensive looking leather jacket which his mum apparently approved of.

For my part, I had also got me a leather jacket. Mine however had been bought second hand from the rag market and I wore it with the collar turned up, trying to look like Jean Jacques Burnell on the cover of Rattus Norvegicus - my favourite album at that time.

As we got on the bus, we turned heads (which was exactly what we wanted) and Craig did his bit by rounding on one lady who was looking at us in a particularly disapproving way and saying; "What you staring at?"

Craig had decided that he was going to buy the tickets and most of the bus ride was taken up by Shane carefully counting out all of the loose change we'd amassed from our car wash business to check that we definitely had the required amount.

The bus stopped right outside the arcade where Cyclops Records was situated. It was our favourite record shop because they stocked all the latest punk records and often had our favourite music playing in there as well. We also loved their carrier bags which had been personalised with the shop logo - a one eyed demonic monster wearing a huge set of headphones.

As we entered the shop, Craig walked up to the counter, dug his hands into his pocket and emptied its contents onto the counter.

"Three tickets for Enemies of Promise at JBs," he said.

The assistant, a young, smartly dressed man with neatly styled spiky hair (you could at best describe him as 'a sanitised punk') looked at the crumpled pound note smothered by a huge pile of coins. Then he looked at Craig.

"How old are you son?"

"I'm not your son mate," replied Craig. "And what's it to you? Pretty boy!"

I smiled. Craig was always entertaining when he had one of his hyper moods on him.

"Well you ain't sixteen," continued the assistant, ignoring Craig's rudeness. "Minimum age for that gig is sixteen."

Craig looked at a bit of a loss. "Well," he said at length. "They're not for me are they. They're for my brother and his mates."

"Oh yeah," said the assistant. "That them over there is it?" He pointed at me and Shane.

"No," replied Craig, sulkily.

The assistant took a deep breath and looked at the money again. "Ok. If that's what you want," he said, beginning to count out the coins.

Having ensured Craig had given him exactly the right amount of money, he rummaged under the counter and produced three tickets on fluorescent green paper. "There you go. But don't go bringing them back next Monday saying they wouldn't let you in."

"Cheers mate," said Craig, snatching the tickets and holding them up triumphantly to show us. Shane gave him a big thumbs up.

I, on the other hand, had that sinking feeling in my stomach again, like a condemned man taking another step towards the gallows. It wasn't that I didn't want to see the band live. It was

110

just I'd heard so much about fights and people being injured at punk rock gigs. And we were only thirteen. What would we do if it really kicked off?

I tried to convince myself that the stories I'd heard were just hype and propaganda put about by a middle aged, middle class, right wing press who wanted to suppress the kids' freedom of expression. But somehow, now I knew we were definitely going, those particular sound bites seemed to ring hollow.

Craig noticed the look on my face. "Brilliant innit Snide," he said. "Tell you what as well. Look what I got." He opened his jacket and patted the inside pocket which was bulging. A faint clinking sound arose from its interior.

"Jim's secret stash," he said, lowering his voice, as if I hadn't already worked that one out.

I managed a weak grin.

We walked outside and bumped into Tony and Chris.

"Hey, it's the preschool punks!" cried Tony, whacking Craig on the back. "Love the jacket Snide."

I looked at the ground awkwardly. "Cheers," I said grinning, stupidly.

"So what are you three up to then?" asked Chris.

"Just bought these," said Craig producing the tickets from his pocket.

"You're kidding," said Tony. "You can't go there. They won't let you in. You gotta be sixteen."

"So?" replied Craig. "We look sixteen."

"No you don't!" said Tony. "They've got bouncers on the door. You've got no chance."

"I thought you said you were going," said Shane.

"We are," replied Tony. "But one of the bouncers is Chris's uncle. He's already guaranteed he'll get us in."

"I tell you what," suggested Chris, looking across at Tony. "You come with us. I can get you in. But I'm warning you now. It can get pretty rough at these gigs. Don't come crying to us if you get hurt. Cos we won't want to know."

"No problem," laughed Craig. "We can take care of ourselves, can't we Shane?"

"Sure thing," replied Shane, confidently.

My stomach tightened even more. But I knew I had to go through with it now. Craig had already picked up on my trepidation and would be sure to be testing me out in the coming days. As far as he was concerned, If I didn't go with them, I'd be letting the gang down. One thing was for certain though. Craig and Shane were going to be looking forward to Saturday a hell of a lot more than me.

Saturday 27th August - The Gig

It had been a quiet week. With our car wash business effectively closed down and with persistent rain preventing us from venturing outside, it was a case of sitting around indoors wasting time.

Craig and Shane spent much of the week round my house. Apparently Jim had been on the warpath after discovering several of his whisky miniatures missing. Fortunately for Craig, Jim hadn't suspected him. Unfortunately for Craig, Jim had blamed his mum resulting in a huge row and fight.

As far as Saturday went, little was mentioned of it, apart from a few barbed comments to me from Craig, who suspected I wasn't fully up for it. To be honest, he needn't have worried since I had already resigned myself to my fate.

Apart from that, everything went to plan. I got clearance from my parents to go to Shane's family wedding and, on Saturday morning, Shane had developed a mysterious belly ache, resulting in him being left at home alone by his parents.

And so, that evening, we found ourselves standing in a shady recess between the main entrance to Dudley Zoo and the front of JBs. Craig had already started on the whisky miniatures when he met us. Wasting no time, Shane immediately downed one leaving me the as only one still sober.

"Come on Snide," urged Craig. "Get it down you."

I unscrewed the top and put the bottle to my lips. In truth, I had tasted beer occasionally (and thought it tasted disgusting) but had never tried spirits.

I tipped the bottle up and swallowed hard. Immediately my mouth went numb. Then I felt the burn in my throat and, seconds later, a curiously pleasant warm feeling in my stomach. The taste though was revolting.

"Eugh!" I coughed and spluttered. "Jesus!"

"Good huh," laughed Craig.

I looked down at the bottle in dismay. I'd only drunk half of it. Thinking it would be best to get it over with as soon as possible, I raised the bottle again and drained it. Again I coughed as the fire spread down my throat.

Craig was just rummaging in his pocket for another when we spotted Tony and Chris walking over.

"I thought it was you three," began Chris. "What you doing skulking round here? The zoo doesn't open for another ten hours."

Tony laughed.

In response, Craig reached into his jacket and pulled out two miniatures, offering them to Chris.

"Oh nice one man," said Chris taking them and passing one to Tony.

Looking back, I guess it was my first real experience of being intoxicated and I was pleasantly surprised at how, within a matter of minutes, the knot in my stomach relaxed and for the first time I began looking forward to getting in to the gig and pogoing.

With Tony and Chris having quickly dispatched their miniatures, we sauntered over to the queue.

"Oh yeah!" cried Craig, rather too loudly as he admired the various items of clothing and hairstyles in front of him. "Smash the State!"

"Yeah, smash the state!" I echoed, neither knowing nor caring why I was shouting it.

The queue moved pretty quickly and we soon found ourselves at the front.

"Alright Chris," said one of the two bouncers on the door, a large man with an even larger belly.

"Alright Unc," replied Chris, turning round to the rest of the queue to see if they were impressed that he should be on friendly terms with one of the doormen.

They weren't.

"Are these the three you told me about?" asked the bouncer, looking us up and down.

"Yeah."

The bouncer drew in his breath sharply then whistled.

"Well he'll pass for sixteen," he said pointing at Shane. "But the other two?"

He turned to Craig. "You sure you know what you're letting yourself in for son?" he asked.

"I can handle meeself," replied Craig with the slightest hint of a slur.

"Have they been drinking?" he asked Chris.

"No. It's just his natural ebullient character," I quipped, immediately wondering why I'd said that.

"Comedian eh!" said the bouncer, looking at me now.

"Take no notice," said Chris. "His nickname is Snide. Snide by name, snide by nature. Don't worry. I'll keep them under control."

The bouncer took one final look at me then turned his attention to the ever growing queue. "Go on then. In you go."

Once we'd shown our tickets to the other bouncer and got inside, the alcohol really began to kick in. It was a strange feeling. Time seemed to become compressed - although an hour had passed between our entry and the support band coming on, I can remember very little of either the hour or the support band.

And within what seemed a very short space of time, we had laid down our marker in the middle of the dance floor and were waiting with eager anticipation for the main act, Enemies of Promise, to take the stage.

Right on cue, at nine o'clock, the lights dimmed and the band appeared. With a simple "Good evening," they launched into their first song. Predictably it was 'Working Down to Zero'.

As soon as the drumming started Craig, who by now had consumed far more alcohol than I could ever imagine, beckoned to me and Shane to follow and started to push his way through to the front.

I looked across at Shane, who seemed more in control than either of us. He shook his head and, happy for somebody to make a decision on my behalf, I nodded and stayed put.

It was as they began their fourth song that things started to go wrong.

The first I knew of it was a crowd surge from behind, knocking me off my balance (which at this point wasn't too good anyway) and forcing me and Shane towards the stage.

Turning round, I could see some sort of disturbance taking place at the back of the hall.

I tapped Shane on the shoulder.

As we accustomed our eyes to the gloom, I could make out some sort of fight. In the thick of it appeared to be a group of individuals who looked very out of place. Dressed in denims, with long, greasy hair, they were unmistakeably Rockers.

"I don't like the look of this!" I shouted, having dramatically sobered up.

Suddenly, a surge forced several of the intruders right into our path.

"Hey Snide," shouted Shane. "Look!"

As I followed his gaze, I picked out a small group who I immediately recognised as the Rockers I'd given personal grief to two weeks ago. As if on cue, one of them spotted us and pointed in our general direction.

As in any situation of war, you firstly need to assess your ability to defend yourselves. Shane and I constituted two, yet with their mates around them, they outnumbered us to a point where we only had one option. I looked wildly around me. The entrance was blocked by fighting, but to our left, lay a possible exit - the toilets.

"Leg it!" I shouted, pointing to the Gents door.

Grasping the situation, Shane pushed me forward then ran on in front. He may have had the confidence to handle himself in a one to one situation, but this was entirely different.

We kicked open the door to find a couple of punks, busy emptying their bladders at the urinals.

They watched in confusion as we spotted the frosted glass window to the side, threw it open and scrambled out.

Surprisingly, we found ourselves at the side of the zoo - in the exact same spot we'd stood and drank whisky earlier.

"You OK?" I said.

"Yeah," replied Shane. "Let's get out of here."

Still slightly disorientated and concerned about Craig, we hung about for some time at the bus station. Eventually he appeared, his t shirt looking even more ripped than ever, his lip swollen and split and his eye turning a worrying shade of purple.

"Where the hell were you?" he shouted, spotting us huddled in the bus shelter. "Man, what a fight!"

"We couldn't find you," replied Shane.

Craig shakily walked around us for a while, obviously still intoxicated. "They were there. Those Rockers. The ones we met outside Cyclops. Shane, you should have been there. You'd have annihilated them."

"Bastards!" I exclaimed, although in reality, at that point I couldn't have cared less about who was there, what they stood for or what we stood for.

All I could think about was questioning why we were sitting in a bus shelter in the centre of Dudley at eleven o'clock at night, pissed and having spent £4.50 on tickets to watch a band who we'd seen no more than ten minutes of.

Sunday 28th August - Grounded

The next morning the phone rang early. My dad answered. "6807," he shouted into the receiver. It always made me laugh how he treated the telephone system as though it was some temporary military instillation constituted of paper cups on the end of pieces of string.

"It's for you," he said, handing me the receiver.

"Snide? It's Shane. Bad news I'm afraid. Mum and Dad came back early from the wedding cos Mum had a belly ache." (Oh, the irony, I thought). "Anyway, they found me out. Well, what I mean is they found out and they found me out, if you know what I mean . . . found me out of the house that is."

"Oh no!" I answered, slightly confused.

"Yeah. I confessed everything. I had to. And the bottom line is I'm not allowed out for the rest of the holidays." He paused whilst I said nothing. "So I'll see you in school next week Snide. OK?"

"Yeah OK." I replied. "It was a good night though wasn't it Shane?"

"Wouldn't have missed it for the world!"

No sooner had I sat down than the phone rang again. My dad answered. "6807 . . Yes it is . . Yes? . . Yes? . . No! . . Did he? . . Did he? . . No, I didn't know . . He said he was going to a wedding with you . . What was that? . . Drinking? . . Surely not . . He's confessed everything! . . OK well thanks for ringing, I can assure you that I will deal with the matter. . No, no, I don't allow him out willy nilly . . Craig? . . Well if you want to point the finger at someone, point it at him . . Yes OK . . Thank you, goodbye."

He put the receiver down grimly. The look of guilt on my face said it all.

"Don't count on going out again this holiday," Dad said firmly.

I didn't reply. Now the heavies (in the form of our parents) had taken control of the situation, it all seemed a bit ridiculous. What had we been thinking of, trying to go to a punk rock gig at our age.

That afternoon, the phone rang again. This time I answered. The sound of the pips told me it was Craig.

"Alright Snide?" He sounded surprisingly cheerful.

"Not really," I began. "Shane's not allowed out for the rest of the holiday and neither am I."

"They found out, huh?"

"Yeah. What about you? Don't suppose it really matters with you does it?"

"Well that's where you're wrong," answered Craig.

"Why?"

"Well when I got home last night, Jim still had one on him about his missing miniatures. And he'd been drinking. I could smell it on his breath. Anyway he turned on me and grabbed me. Felt something in my jacket pocket, didn't he. Cos I still had a couple of bottles left in there. Well, he went berserk. I thought he was going to kill me. But mum had had a skinful too. So she stepped in. Never seen her like that before. She was screaming at him, lashing out with her fists, booting him, everything. Anyway, to cut a long story short, she's kicked him out."

"What, for real?" I gasped.

"Not half. He was banging on the door whilst she was throwing all his gear out the bedroom window." He paused. "Then the police came. Carted him away. Haven't seen him since."

"Good riddance to bad rubbish," I said, although in reality this wasn't the first time Craig's mum had thrown Jim out. And on every previous occasion, she had had him back a few days later.

"Anyway," continued Craig. "Mum said that she was really sorry cos she hadn't spent enough time with we lately and that we should do more together. So she's starting by taking me to the zoo today."

I was amazed at the transformation in Craig. Overnight he had transitioned from hard man to mummy's boy. But I wasn't about to say anything. Apart from the fact that he was leader of our gang, I felt fairly sure that within a few days Jim would be ensconced back in Craig's home and the abuse, and all that it entailed, would start all over again.

"OK Craig, see you back in school then. Smash the State!"

"Oh yeah," replied Craig. "That's another thing. Mum wanted her tin bath back so I've been to the den this morning and picked it up. Might have to put the band on hold for a while."

"Okay," I replied, a little disappointed.

"We'll put it down to artistic differences."

Artistic differences? I thought to myself. In other words it's all over.

"OK. See you Snide."

And that was that. We never played as Smash the State again.

I was right about Jim, though. True, it was a few months before he wormed his way back in but, once he had his feet under the table again, things soon got back to normal.

As for punk rock, the energy and excitement of the music and the sheer snideness of it all stayed with me to such an extent that I still listen to music from that era forty five years later.

In the meantime, as 1977 merged into 1978 and our respective puberties went into overdrive, girls began to work their way to the top of our personal agendas, whilst music . . . well that had to take a back seat, for the moment at least.

1978

LET'S TALK
ABOUT GIRLS

CONTENTS

LET'S TALK ABOUT GIRLS

Susan Palin. Now there's a name that would arouse my hormones. With long, blonde hair and an hourglass figure, she had a touch of Joanna Lumley about her. Poshly spoken, she walked like a model on a catwalk, her slightly upturned nose and aloof expression sending out a clear message that she was well out of our league. There was nothing to stop any of us fantasising though, especially when, stripped of her finery, she ran around the school gymnasium, in her bottle green gym knickers!

Not that any of us boys were treated to that very often. By the time we'd reached third year of Streetside Secondary School, boys and girls did PE separately, with the notable exception of the last week of each term.

On these rare occasions, the PE teacher, Mr Price would get out all of the apparatus; climbing bars, box, horse etc. and scatter the mats on the floor in order for us to take part in a game of 'Pirates.' I can't remember the exact rules now, but I seem to recall that it was something to do with moving around a circuit without putting your feet on the floor. 'Apparatus or mats only' was the rule.

Of course, this held no interest to the majority of us boys. As far as we were concerned, pirates was a once a term opportunity to chase the girls around and manhandle them. And with the likes of Susan Palin, that was about as close as any of us would ever get.

Susan, of course, was not the only object of my emerging adolescent fantasies. There was Claire Beatrix, more stocky and socky (the fashion for schoolgirls at that time was to wear thigh length thick woollen socks) and her entire entourage, none of whose names I can recall.

In short, my hormones were well and truly out of control. Even now, I find it hard to explain the convulsive effect that the first waves of testosterone have on a young teenage boy. Everything changes.

One minute you are busying yourself with Meccano and Hornby train sets and your family and friends are your entire world. The next, the demon of sexuality grabs you by the hand and takes you on a journey from which you will never return.

Everything is seen through a distorted lens. Fulfilment of desire becomes your most important goal. And, however difficult, even impossible it seems to reach that goal, you will pursue it relentlessly in the hope that maybe, eventually, your quest will reach its fruition.

Musically, things had moved on a lot since the summer of 1977. We were, all three of us, still into music. But as far as punk rock was concerned, the honeymoon period was over.

For Craig, the moment of realisation came that Autumn when, after discovering that his mum had run out of the peroxide that he used to dye his hair blond, he attempted to use bleach as a cheap alternative. Well, Domestos to be precise.

The consequences were disastrous, even by the standards of Craig's dysfunctional life. Within hours, his stepdad Jim had to rush him into A & E with blistering to his scalp. Over the next few weeks clumps of his hair fell out, with the result that he ended up getting himself the shortest hair cut any of us had ever seen.

At school this earned him the nickname of 'Skinner' amongst the older boys and he became a source of much amusement amongst our peers. But Craig was always an opportunist and, realising his position as the hard man of our year group was under threat, he decided to reassert himself as top dog. The unfortunate boy he picked upon in order to do this, had merely smirked at him one dinner time. As a result, he received the full force of Craig's aggression and rage.

The consequent battering resulted in Craig being suspended from school for a fortnight. But when he returned, his standing as the school's 'Rocky Balboa' had been reinstated. If anything, it was stronger than ever. He may have been a scrawny specimen, but everyone knew now without a shadow of doubt that Craig was a boy not to be messed with.

As for Shane, it had always been obvious that he'd never been into punk rock. So when Craig toned down his image, he took the decision to return to the latest fashion trends, which his parents invariably bankrolled.

He also began to rediscover his own taste in music. He would describe to me the latest Reggae 'Dub' sounds he'd been listening to after visiting the iconic record shop 'Reggae got Soul' in Walsall. And, having heard some for myself on a cassette Shane had compiled for me, I bought into it - big time. Even today, I still enjoy listening to the likes of Augustus Pablo, Prince Far I and Mikey Dread.

My main preference in music though was still punk, or 'New Wave' as it had been renamed, because in short I loved the attitude and energy of it.

For me personally though, a far bigger issue was beginning to impose itself on my personal life. Just when I was beginning to feel comfortable in my own body, I developed the worst problem any teenager could ever imagine - ACNE!

And it wasn't just a few spots. Most teenagers at that time had to tolerate that. No - my face became so pitted and pockmarked that it began to look like something resembling The Somme.

And I was just starting to get into girls!

Disaster!

Monday 31st July - The Professionals

"What? All summer?" gasped Craig in mock horror.

"Well, five days a week for the next four weeks," replied Shane. "They're using me to cover for colleagues whilst they're on their annual paid leave."

"Their what?" frowned Craig.

"Holidays," I said, saving Shane the need for explanation.

"But it's *our* holidays as well!" cried Craig, more in desperation than anything.

Of course, I knew what this was all about with Craig. It wasn't that he was upset at being denied the company of Shane for much of the summer. This was about loss of control. Control of us - the gang.

Ever since Shane had taken up a Saturday job at a shoe shop in town earlier in the year, Craig was no longer calling the shots in terms of where we went, when we went there and what we did. And as leader of our tightly knit gang, he didn't like it.

Not that Shane was in the slightest bit bothered by Craig's outbursts. Shane was a cool customer. Besides, not only did he have a job with a title (assistant salesman and fitter) which he was very proud of, he was also earning serious money.

It was his mother who initially pushed him into Saturday employment. In her words; the work experience he was gaining would be an invaluable addition to his CV. Personally, I think it was more about keeping him away from me and Craig.

She had a point too considering that last summer holidays we'd converted him into a punk rocker, broke his guitar and got him drunk in the middle of Dudley!

"So when d'you start?" I asked.

"In an hour. I'm on my way to get the bus now. Just thought I ought to drop by and let you both know."

"What days are you off?" I asked.

"I've got Wednesday and Thursday this week, then Thursday, Friday next week."

"That's alright anyway," sniffed Craig, casually. "Me and Snide was going down the park to play The Professionals."

Shane gave Craig a slightly supercilious look. "Well I've got to get going," he said awkwardly. "I don't want to be late. The boss doesn't like it."

I noticed Craig flinch slightly at this.

Control, I thought to myself. Definitely control.

Some time later, Craig and I left my house and wandered down to the park. We were a little disappointed not to see Eric.

Still, we always had The Professionals.

If you haven't already guessed, this was a game based on the TV series of the same name and involved Craig and me charging around the woods and park, leaping over obstacles whilst chasing imaginary villains. To be honest, although it was great fun, I'd started to feel a little bit silly playing games like this. After all, we were both fourteen now. I think I was at that point in my life where I felt I should start acting more like an adult. However, the irresistible flame of childishness still burned brightly inside me.

Running into the woods, I spotted Eric's log, leapt over it and lay flat on my stomach clutching my make believe gun tightly. Then, hearing no sound from Craig, I leapt up and, spotting him, screamed; "Get down Bodie! Ruskie sniper at 6 o'clock!"

For some reason Craig ignored me. Instead, he stood, hands stuffed into the front pockets of his jeans, grinning at something or somebody else.

I swung round to see none other than Susan Palin herself, standing with her best mate Terri Donnerly. Terri, who all the boys nicknamed 'Big T,' for reasons I won't go into, was wearing a tight fitting T shirt and jeans. Susan was similarly dressed, although my attention was drawn more to the expression on her face as she regarded me with a look of slightly detached disdain.

"He's a prat ain't he?" quipped Craig.

The nerve of him! He was the one that wanted to play the stupid game. I felt my face flush.

"So what you up to then Craig?" asked Terri, completely ignoring me.

"Just hanging out," replied Craig. "Being bored. That's until you turned up." Again he grinned cheekily at Terri. Then, without warning, he suddenly shouted over to me. "Hey Snide! It's Susan Palin. You fancy her don't you?"

My face turned an even deeper shade of red.

Terri whispered something to Susan who walked over to me, still maintaining her detached air. I wasn't sure whether she was wasting her time on me as a favour to her friend, who obviously fancied Craig, or out of sheer pity for me.

I decided it was probably both.

"Snide? That's not your real name is it?" she said.

"No," I answered awkwardly, feeling like I was being interviewed rather than having a casual conversation.

"So what's your real name?"

I was surprised that, with Susan being in my year group, she didn't know. Mind you, we weren't in the same classes for any subjects and she didn't mix with what few friends I had so maybe, I reasoned, it wasn't beyond the bounds of reasonableness.

"That's for me to know and you to find out," I said, trying my best to sound cool despite the fact that my heart was racing so fast, it felt like it was fit to burst out of my chest at any moment.

Susan continued the interview. "What do you use for that acne then Snide?"

My heart sank. However small a chance I thought I had of making it with her, any hopes had now been well and truly dashed. To her, I was just an ugly spotty nobody.

To make matters worse, I realised not only that I was now staring at her chest, but also that something highly embarrassing was beginning to stir inside my trousers.

No! I thought. Not now - please not now!

I sat down on the log and crossed my legs to conceal my embarrassment. Susan seated herself next to me and continued to look at me quizzically.

Why was she looking at me like that? I thought. Had she noticed?

"I use Clearasil," she continued. "You should give it a try."

I breathed a sigh of relief. She was still talking about my hideous acne. Then the gravity of what she'd said hit me. Clearasil? Susan has a problem with acne? Really? Forgetting my shyness for a moment, I looked across at her freshly scrubbed pink face and studied it for the faintest sign of a spot. She returned my gaze and briefly our eyes met. Immediately, my shyness raced back to the surface.

"Yes. Thank you. I will," I replied, rather shakily.

A prolonged awkward silence ensued during which I stared at the ground desperately trying to conceal with my hands any bulge that might still be visible in my trousers.

After what seemed an eternity, Craig and Terri joined us. "Come on then. Let's go" said Craig.

"Yeah. In a minute," I replied, keeping my hands placed firmly in my lap.

"OK. See you later then, Craig" said Terri, waving.

"See you Snide," added Susan. "And remember - Clearasil."

"Wow. You really made some impression on her!" cried Craig, sarcastically. "Listen. Big T said they might come down the park again later this week. We gotta make sure we hang around here more often. We don't want to miss them. And you never know, Clearasil Kid, you might get lucky with Susan."

Friday 4th August - A 'Chance' Meeting

Craig and I had returned to the park every day that week in the hope of bumping into Susan and Terri again. It wasn't until Friday though that we finally spotted them.

Craig, as enthusiastic as ever, bounded over.

"Hi girls. Fancy a walk in the woods?" he asked.

Terri giggled, then after exchanging knowing glances with Susan, the two of them joined us.

Immediately, Craig paired up with Terri, leaving me in the capable hands of Susan.

As we reached the edge of the woods, we stopped, allowing Craig to usher Terri a suitable distance away.

Spotting Eric's log, I walked over and sat myself down. Susan joined me.

"Are you going to Julian's party?" she asked.

Over the intervening days, I had persuaded myself that maybe there was the smallest smidgeon of a chance that Susan was interested in me after all. Why else would she suggest a way to combat my acne? Maybe because she could see through what was obviously a temporary facial disfigurement.

And now she was asking if a was going to Julian's party? Perhaps, like me, she was thinking long term. Maybe, one day we would be married, with a family. Momentarily, I imagined myself walking arm in arm with her down the aisle, me a handsome young man with an unblemished complexion, her dressed in white to reflect her perfectly scrubbed purity.

Susan broke in on my thoughts. "I'm taking my boyfriend, Peter," she said.

Bump! I was brought heftily back down to earth. So she had a boyfriend. Brilliant! Absolutely brilliant!

"You wouldn't know him," she continued. "He's seventeen. Left school last year. He's training to be a motor mechanic."

I looked at her in horror. A motor mechanic? Surely not. Susan Palin, the classiest girl in our year group and she's going out with a grease monkey.

Suddenly she didn't seem anywhere near as pure and clean as she had a moment ago. In my eyes now, it was more a case of her being slightly shop soiled. I imagined her in his arms, him still wearing his dirty overalls, his oil soaked hands pawing greedily at her body. I felt sick.

"So are you going?" she persisted.

I collected my thoughts. "D'you bean Julian Blandford?" I asked, feeling curiously relaxed now I knew that she was unavailable.

"Yes," she replied. "It's his fifteenth. He's the oldest boy in our year group you know."

I did indeed know who Julian Blandford was. Not only was he the oldest boy in our year group, he was also the richest. His dad was founder and managing director of Blandford Electronics, a major local company and was rumoured to be a millionaire.

And his house - well mansion would be a better word . . .

"Is it at his house?" I asked.

"Yes, of course it is. I guess you've not been invited then."

"Hey Snide!" shouted Craig, having briefly torn himself away from Terri. "What you up to next Saturday?"

"Nothing."

"You are now. We've been invited to a party."

"You mean at Julian Blandford's?"

"Yeah."

"Have we? I don't remember getting an invite."

Craig turned to Terri and rolled his eyes into the top of his head. "I just invited us," he explained laughing. "If we can't get in the front way, we'll climb over the wall at the back. It's easy enough, what with his house being out in the country."

I understood his meaning. The Blandford's mansion was a mile or so out of town and entirely surrounded by fields.

"We could bring Shane along as well," I suggested.

"Oh, yes," cooed Terri. "Shane is so cool. You got to bring him."

Craig looked temporarily annoyed. "Yeah, well I might allow him to come with us," he said. "Hey Snide! It's free booze as well."

My mind went back to the previous summer when, despite our age, Craig, Shane and I had drunk whisky shortly before attending a punk rock concert. And that hadn't ended at all well.

"Great," I replied, unenthusiastically.

The four of us spent much of the morning together, Craig working his cheeky, optimistic charm on Terri with me and Susan playing the part of gooseberries.

However, now I was more relaxed in the knowledge that Susan was already spoken for, we actually began to get on quite well. I guess it was one of those adolescent moments when I realised that it was possible to talk to a girl as a friend, even if it turned out in this case to be a friend who I still had a huge crush on.

Eventually, Craig made our excuses and we left.

"I tell you what Snide," he confided as soon as he felt we were out of earshot. "I reckon I'm in there with Big T. I ain't half looking forward to the party." And with that, he pulled a lewd face and made an exaggerated groping gesture which I took to be a representation of what he intended to do to Terri's breasts. I grinned back at him.

"Whey hey hey!" growled Craig. "Bring it on!"

"Bring it on," I echoed, although in reality I wasn't quite sure what the party had in store for me.

Friday 11th August - Are You Ready to Party?

We had arranged to meet at mine the day before the party in order to go into town to buy some new clothes.

Shane was the first to arrive on my doorstep. We all knew that, with his dad being a lawyer, Shane had plenty of money and it was obvious from his appearance what he liked to spend it on.

Having abandoned his attempt at dressing like a punk last year, Shane now opted for the smart casual look and he pulled it off well. Wearing a crisply laundered and ironed white shirt and smart black trousers, his outfit was completed by a pair of rather expensive looking, highly polished black shoes.

"Hello Shane dear!" gushed my mum as she came downstairs, brushing and smoothing her clothes as if she was about to present herself to royalty.

"Hi, Mrs Percival," replied Shane in his best little boy voice.

"Are you two off to town then?" asked mum, beaming at Shane.

"Yeah. Us two and Craig," I replied.

The smile vanished from Mum's face. "Oh. I see. And will *he* want feeding again?"

"I don't know," I said, slightly irritated by her sudden change in attitude. "Why?"

"Well I don't mind the odd bit of food but he seems to treat this place like a soup kitchen. And as for his appetite. Take yesterday for example. I offered him some toast and he ended up working his way through half a loaf . . . and he finished off the marmalade."

Shane grinned.

"It's not his fault," I retorted. "His mum never feeds him."

"Yes. Well . . ." Mum primped her hair in the mirror. "Come through Shane. Are you hungry?"

"No thanks Mrs Percival. I had a hearty breakfast this morning."

"Of course you did dear," purred Mum.

We sat down.

"How much money are you taking?" I asked Shane.

"Enough," he answered, fishing from his trouser pocket what appeared to be a brand new leather wallet. He opened it and pulled out a substantial bundle of bank notes.

"Phew!" I remarked, feeling quite jealous.

"I'll tell you what as well," said Shane. "None of this comes from my mum or dad. This is all the product of hard graft."

There was a sharp rapping on the door.

Looking through the window I could see Craig standing there, shuffling his feet impatiently. I let him in.

"Alright Snide," he said cheerfully. He pushed past me into the living room. "Hey Shane," he continued. "New nickname for Snide. From now on he's The Clearasil Kid!"

"Leave it out," I said. "And besides, I'm not using it at the moment. I've run out."

"Already?" said Craig, in surprise. "You only bought it a few days ago."

"Yes I know, but I had a bit of an accident the other night."

"What sort of accident?" asked Shane, whose interest had been suddenly aroused by the mention of Susan Palin.

"Well, I woke up in the middle of the night feeling thirsty," I began. "And cos I was half asleep, I just grabbed the first thing to hand and took a big swig of it."

135

At first, Craig and Shane both looked blankly at me. Then slowly, a mischievous smile spread across Shane's face. "No! You didn't . . . did you?"

"Did what?" butted in Craig.

"Drank my Clearasil," I concluded, sheepishly.

"Ha ha ha!" hooted Craig. "Yeah! The Clearasil Kid strikes again."

"You could've poisoned yourself," remarked Shane, also laughing.

I knew it was funny but couldn't help also feeling a little aggrieved. It had always bugged me that whilst my face continued to sprout new spots daily, Craig and Shane's faces had always remained unmarked.

"What's all the noise about?" asked Mum, poking her head around the door.

"Oh. It's you," she said, spotting Craig. "I should've known."

"You got any toast?" asked Craig, hopefully.

"No we haven't," I replied, on Mum's behalf. "I was just telling these two about the Clearasil incident the other night."

"Oh, he's such a fool sometimes," quipped Mum. "It contains alcohol you know."

"Really?" said Craig, his ears pricking up.

"No Craig! Don't even think about it," I said. "Seriously, it tastes disgusting!"

We caught the bus into town and, on arriving were immediately treated to burger and chips at the new McDonalds hamburger restaurant, paid for entirely by Shane.

We then spent some time down the rag market. This was one of the largest indoor markets in the country and included a large number of new and second hand clothes stalls. Both Craig and I favoured the second hand stuff. Firstly it was cheaper and secondly, you could find some real quality items if you looked around.

Inspired by Shane, I had decided to go for the smart casual, sophisticated look and bought myself a really cool shirt and a pair of worn look jeans.

Craig had his own agenda, still opting for the pseudo punk look. It was far more toned down than the donkey jacket with HATE written on the back and ripped combats, that he'd worn all of last summer. But it was nevertheless contemporary.

Shane, already well kitted out, contented himself with purchasing a load of shower stuff, coconut oil for his hair and some posh after shave, being sold at rock bottom price. Having assured us that he didn't need to sample it, it wasn't until we were on the bus home that he discovered that it was undoubtedly fake. In fact it smelt so bad, he left it on the bus.

"Someone's gonna think they got lucky when the find that," said Craig.

"Yeah, until they smell it!" I laughed.

Saturday 12ᵗʰ August - A Bit of A Do

We had no option but to walk to the Blandford's Mansion. It lay halfway down a country lane, nowhere near any bus routes.

As luck would have it, it looked to be a perfect summer evening as we left the houses of Streetside behind and ventured along the network of narrow, winding lanes that led there.

We estimated that it was about thirty minutes walk. This we reckoned would get us there before dark - an important consideration when walking down unlit roads.

However, with our journey less than half complete, the wind picked up and it started to rain. It was only light at first but soon became heavier.

"It's just a summer shower," Shane assured us. "It'll blow over soon."

But it didn't. So, by the time we reached the gates of the house, we were soaked through.

Despite this setback, our spirits had been lifted by a bellyful of spirits, provided of course by Craig.

"Jim gave it me," was always his explanation. Craig's relationship with his stepdad had undoubtedly evolved over the past few months and, although not a healthy one for a fourteen year old boy (as it seemed to be based around the consumption of alcohol), it nevertheless suited Craig in many ways. Most important of these was that Jim seemed to be keeping his temper under control, or to put it another way, Craig was no longer covered in bruises.

Anyway, however he came by it, as we now stood looking down the long driveway that led to an enormous oak front door, we had become oblivious to the weather and filled with an inner warmth.

A car pulled up and two boys I recognised as John Hughes and Anthony Stretch, got out.

"Hey it's Craig's gang," cried John. "How you doing Craig? I didn't know you were coming. You do have invites don't you?"

"No," said Craig, defiantly. "We don't need invites. We invited ourselves."

"Well good luck trying to get in then," added Anthony. "You know they'll have someone on the door. Just saying like."

"Not a problem," I replied. "Cos we're not going through the front door."

"Aren't we?" said Shane, in surprise. "How are we getting in then?"

Anthony and John exchanged glances. "Well, see you in there then boys," said John, as they began making their way down the drive.

Craig turned on Shane and sighed impatiently. "I thought I told you we were going in through the back."

"Through the back?" repeated Shane.

"Yeah. Over the wall."

"But I've got all my best gear on," said Shane, indignantly.

"It'll be OK," replied Craig. "Come on."

And with that he led us along the full length of the front garden wall to a gate.

138

"Right," began Craig. "We go over this gate, follow the wall round to the back of the house, then climb over and let ourselves in through the back door."

We followed Craig over the gate but things began to take a turn for the worse when we realised that, although from a distance it looked green, the field was in fact quite muddy.

"Look at my shoes!" cried Shane, in frustration. "I'll never get these clean. If I'd have known, I would have worn my trainers."

Eventually, having squelched our way halfway around the perimeter wall of the house, we finally had some luck.

"Look here!" said Craig excitedly. We joined him in the gathering gloom of dusk and found ourselves facing a large wooden gate. Craig pushed it and, to our surprise, it opened with a groan.

We crept inside and found our bearings. In front of us was an orchard. Beyond that lay a tall hedge, behind which we guessed was the house itself. In the distance we could hear voices. It had finally stopped raining now so we guessed that some guests were spilling out into the garden.

We passed through the orchard and peering round the end of the hedge saw that this was indeed the case. To our surprise though, amongst them was a significant number of adults. Nobody had said anything about adults being present. We just assumed it was a teenage party, laid on whilst the parents were away.

"This is our chance," said Craig, ignoring this latest setback. "If anybody stops us, we just say we're friends of Julian."

To be honest, if I'd been sober, I don't think I would have had enough confidence to go through with it. But with my *whisky goggles* on, it seemed easy enough.

So, nonchalantly, we walked right through the middle of the crowd in the direction of the kitchen.

I was amazed. Nobody batted an eyelid. Maybe they all had their whisky goggles on too!

Once we were inside, Shane disappeared into the toilet to clean himself up and Craig, having grabbed a can of beer, immediately went off in search of Terri. This left me at a bit of a loss. Eventually, having stood around for some time, being ignored by everybody, I picked up a can of beer myself and went back outside.

The rain had cleared now and my time in the warmth of the kitchen had dried my clothes. It was a strange feeling being in the midst of such a large group of people, none of whom knew me. It was as if I was completely anonymous. And in a strange way it made me feel much more relaxed about the whole party.

I took a swig of beer and, looking for somewhere quieter, ambled in the general direction of the orchard.

It was as I rounded the high hedge and the general hubbub of the crowd died away, that I became aware of another sound. At first, I couldn't quite make it out, but as I moved further into the orchard and the crowd became more distant, it became clearer. It was certainly human. There were two sounds. One was a masculine grunting, the other, a series of soft, feminine sighs. I peered into the gloom, more out of curiosity than anything.

Suddenly an angry voice broke the tranquillity of the moment.

"Oi. Who's that?"

Then, something, or someone leaped out of the darkness and grabbed me forcefully.

"What d'you think you're doing, you little pervert?"

I pulled away in shock and backed myself up to the end of the hedge. Here, there was just enough light from the kitchen for me to see. Stepping forward into the light himself, the owner of the voice grabbed me again and pulled me towards him.

I found myself face to face with a tall, muscular looking lad of about eighteen.

"I'm sorry, I didn't know!" I blurted out.

"Who is it?" came a familiar voice.

"I caught a bloody peeping Tom here, Sue!" he shouted back.

Then, emerging into the half light walked Susan Palin!

Never in my entire life had I wanted the ground to open up and swallow me whole, as much as I did at that moment.

"Snide?" she said, looking confused. "What are you doing here?"

"I don't know. I was just walking in the orchard," I mumbled.

"What! In the dark," barked the lad, aggressively. "You were spying on me and my girlfriend weren't you, you dirty little sod!"

"Leave him Paul," said Susan. "He's alright. I know him." She looked across at me. "We were just kissing. Nothing else."

Now it was my turn to be confused. Why was she feeling the need to explain herself to me?

I realised however, that this was my chance to release myself from the clutches of her Neanderthal boyfriend. So, jerking my upper arm from his grip, I turned and walked very quickly in the direction of the kitchen.

Back inside, Shane had already hooked up with a girl and Craig was involved in a very tight clinch with Terri. All of which left me on my own.

I tried to stick it out as long as possible but there's few things as depressing or as demoralising as being a wallflower at a party.

So finally, I made my decision. Putting down my still half full can of beer, I walked out of the house (through the front door this time) and began the long, treacherous journey home, alone.

Sunday 13th August - The Aftermath

It was late Sunday morning when the phone went. A soon as I heard the pips I knew it was Craig. For once, he sounded subdued.

"Alright Snide?"

"Yeah. Not bad. In truth I was still sore at being left high and dry the previous night at the party. "How about you?"

"Got off with Big T. But then I ended up having too much to drink and threw up on the living room carpet."

I smirked with satisfaction. Serves you right for leaving me on my own, I thought.

"Got a hell of a hangover now. And I can't remember what happened in the end with Big T. I know she got pretty angry with me at one point. Dunno why. She said something about taking liberties. Anyway I copped a good feel of her tits so it was worth it."

"That's probably what she meant by you taking liberties," I said, trying my best to sound concerned.

There was a long silence. Either Craig didn't get what I meant or his hangover was so bad he'd passed out.

Eventually he broke the silence. "Anyway Snide, what happened to you? Me and Shane looked everywhere for you."

I could have vented my anger on Craig at this point but, somehow now it didn't seem worth it. He was obviously suffering enough.

"I got bored," I replied. "So I went home."

"Oh." Craig sounded disappointed. "We thought you might have copped off with Susan Palin. She was there last night you know. Didn't arrive until quite late though."

"No. She was with her boyfriend," I said.

"I didn't see any boyfriend," replied Craig. "Come to think of it, she went off somewhere with Terri in the end." He paused. "Yeah. It's coming back to me now. They went out the front together. Didn't see them again. Anyway I've dumped her. She's so boring. She didn't even have a drink last night."

I took all of this information in, compartmentalising it into important news and trash. Craig groping Terri, Terri kicking off at him and then leaving - that was all trash. Craig apparently dumping Terri (although I'm sure in truth it was the other way round) - that was also trash. But Susan Palin, not with her boyfriend. Now that was interesting. Maybe they'd had a row. She'd certainly stuck up for me when he grabbed me. And she pretty much wanted to make it clear to me that she'd only been kissing, nothing more. Maybe they'd even argued over me and she'd dumped him.

"You still there Snide?" Craig's voice broke me from my dreams.

"Yeah. Still here," I said. "D'you still think I might have a chance with . . . " I was interrupted by the pips. "I'll see you tomorrow Craig. Come round mine at nine. Mum will do you some breakfast." The phone went dead.

I replaced the receiver and sat down on the stairs, deep in thought. So Susan Palin might be available after all. I smiled to myself. Suddenly the world seemed a much happier place.

Monday 14th August - Bored

I wasn't quite sure if Craig had got my final message as the pips went but I needn't have worried. Dead on nine o'clock there came a familiar rapping at the front door.

Mum let him in. "Do you want some breakfast?" she asked in a fairly non committal voice.

"You got any toast?" asked Craig, hopefully.

It was funny how Mum picked up on every single occasion that I failed to say please, but with Craig never said a word.

"He's got no manners, but it's not his fault," she'd once said, so I guess it was something to do with that.

We sat down at the table and between us began to work our way through yet another loaf of bread, pat of butter and jar of marmalade.

"Shane's back at work today ain't he," said Craig, his mouth so full of toast that he sprayed crumbs all over the tablecloth.

"Tell you what though," I suggested. "We could pay him a visit."

Craig needed no second bidding. As soon as I said it, I could see an evil glint in his eye. "Yeah," he said chewing thoughtfully. "Let's pay him a visit."

One bus journey later, we were standing outside Cooper's Shoes in the High Street peering in through the enormous display window.

"I can't see him," said Craig. He stood back from the glass. "Hey, maybe he's lying. Maybe, his mum and dad just give him the money and he pretends to have a job. Maybe he's joined another gang!"

'Here we go again,' I thought.'Control'. There were so many things I liked about Craig; his boundless energy, his eternal optimism, his bravery. But one thing that was beginning to irritate me as we grew older was his immaturity. It had been typified yesterday on the phone by his inability to understand why Terri had dumped him at the party. And this whole gang thing - it was starting to wear a bit thin now. True, I'd sheltered under the protective wing of his hardman reputation when we'd first met and I'd undoubtedly been a more vulnerable person. But we all have to grow up. And whilst Shane and I were slowly altering our outlooks on life, Craig seemed to be stuck in an emotional rut.

My mum's words came back to me: "But it's not his fault." And, of course she was right. Craig had had a rubbish upbringing - a mum who clearly couldn't care less and a succession of stepdads, the most recent, and enduring, of whom clearly had no interest in him either. At least he'd stopped beating Craig and his mum now (as far as I could tell), but he was still a waster who spent all his money on booze and fags. Certainly not the role model that Craig so clearly craved.

"Hold on," I said. "There's Shane, coming out of the stock cupboard. Come on."

We trooped into the shop to discover Shane in mid sales pitch. "Yes, madam, they're all leather uppers." He stopped as he caught sight of us out of the corner of his eye, then continued to tend to his customer.

Eventually, having apparently made a sale, he walked purposefully over to us. "What are you doing here?" he hissed.

"Thought we'd come and see you at work," said Craig.

Shane looked across at a rather superior man standing in the middle of the shop floor who was watching all three of us.

"Look, I'm not supposed to be talking to you when I'm at work," he said. "I'll meet you during my lunch break."

"Actually," announced Craig in a rather loud voice. "I'd like a new pair of shoes. My old ones got ruined on

Saturday night when I was forced by this boy here to walk across a muddy field." He jabbed an accusatory finger in my general direction.

I stifled a giggle. "I'm afraid it's true," I confirmed, in an equally dramatic voice. "It was all my fault."

The man watching us walked over. "Is everything alright here Shane?" he asked.

"Yes thank you Mr Thornton," replied Shane meekly. "These boys were interested in buying some new shoes."

"BUYING!" exclaimed Craig, suddenly raising his voice. "You didn't say anything about having to pay. I've only got fifty pence. Do you have anything for fifty pence?"

"Right. That's it! Get out!" ordered Mr Thornton, whose face had visibly darkened during this outburst. It was quite obvious he'd had enough of Craig.

"Ha ha. In yer face!" cried Craig and he ran out of the shop.

"And you," continued Mr Thornton, turning on me now. "We don't need yobs like you in this store."

I left, feeling a bit sorry for Shane.

My fears were concerned when he emerged for an early lunch hour shortly afterwards.

"I'm really in trouble now," he said, addressing us both, crossly. "Mr Thornton's given me a verbal warning."

"Sorry Shane," I said, digging Craig in the ribs.

"Yeah. Soz," added Craig, looking at the floor.

"Yeah, well OK," said Shane. "Anyway listen. I've heard on the grapevine there's another party. This week!"

"Another party?" Craig and I echoed in unison.

"Yeah. You know Abigail Jones?"

"What the daughter of Mr Jones, the maths teacher? Has a face like a constipated owl?" I joked.

"The very same," replied Shane. "It's her birthday this Thursday and she's having a party round her house. I've got the address here somewhere." He began to rummage in his pockets.

"I don't know about that," I began nervously. "Mr Jones is a bit of a psycho. The school still use him occasionally to give the cane."

"I don't care," said Craig. "He can't touch us out of school. If he does we can do him for assault. My mum told me that. Ain't that right Shane?"

"I believe so Craig," continued Shane, finally unfolding a small piece of paper with an address written on it. "But that doesn't matter anyway because he won't be there. This isn't like Saturday's party. There'll be no adults. They're going away for the night. They're handing the house over entirely to her."

"Wow!" gasped Craig. "Two parties in a week."

We made our plans over a bag of chips, on the pavement outside the Town Hall. Craig decided that, if she was there, he was going to have another crack at Terri and if she wasn't there, he'd go for anything on offer. Shane, had decided to take his brief dalliance on Saturday no further and would be going into the party with an open mind.

For my part, I decided there and then that, rather than being the perennial wallflower, this time I was going to pull.

"Right," I said. "I'm off."

"Where you going Snide?" asked Craig.

"Chemist," I replied, smiling. "To buy the biggest bottle of Clearasil I can find! You coming Craig?"

"Go for it Snide!" shouted Shane.

"Yeah. Snide's gonna pull himself a girlie," added Craig, laughing as he got to his feet.

"Hold on," said Shane. "Before you go. Both of you. Promise me that you will never, ever, EVER visit my shop again."

"We promise," we chorused, much to Shane's relief.

"Thursday then," said Shane. "Let's get ready to party. Again!"

Thursday 17th August - Abigail's Party

Abigail Jones' house was very different to that of Julian Blandford. A drab, semi-detached in the middle of the Hundred Acre Estate, with a small, neatly kept garden and driveway with room for one car.

As Craig, Shane and I approached, it felt strange knowing, not only that we were going to the house of Streetside School's most ferocious teacher, but also that we would be drinking alcohol whilst there. We might even get lucky with a girl.

In Craig and Shane's case, that would be a near certainty. For me, it was more of an optimistic hope.

Shane had kept the piece of paper with the address on but needn't have worried. As we turned into Bankside Crescent, the throb of loud music greeted us and we simply followed our ears.

We were surprised, on arrival, to find the front door had been left on the latch so we could simply let ourselves in. Once inside, we were confronted by a house packed with teenagers of all ages.

"I never knew she had so many friends," I remarked.

"She doesn't," replied Shane. "I'd guess half of these weren't even invited."

"That's a bit rough," I said.

"What do you mean?" retorted Craig. "We weren't invited either!"

"You two might not have been, but I was," added Shane, smugly.

"Yeah, but at least we're in her year group," I added. "Some of these boys look about eighteen."

As if in response to this comment, a huge raucous cheer arose from the kitchen, followed by a loud crash.

Immediately, the living room door flew open and Abigail Jones rushed out, looking flustered. "What's going on in there?" she shouted, barging her way into an even more crowded kitchen.

"Looks like this is going to be one hell of a party!" shouted Craig.

"I'm going to see if she needs any help," said Shane. He followed her into the kitchen and disappeared amongst the throng.

"Come on," shouted Craig. "Let's find us some booze. Her dad will have some stashed away somewhere. Imagine that Snide, drinking Mr Jones's personal supply of liquor."

I laughed, followed him into the living room and watched as he rooted around. It didn't take long. Opening the doors of a sideboard he beckoned me over excitedly.

"Look at this lot Snide!" he exclaimed. "Looks like home made wine. Let's grab a couple of bottles." He reached in and pulled out two large, green bottles with handwritten labels. One, containing a darker liquid was labelled 'beetroot'. The other, lighter one was 'potato'. Craig handed me one bottle and pushed his way back into the hall.

"Let's take it upstairs," said Craig.

Finding the smaller of the two front bedroom unoccupied, we slipped in and sat on the bed. Unlike Craig, I wasn't a drinker but, with Craig egging me on, I tried to match him swig for swig.

"Didn't you say your parents were going away for the weekend soon?" asked Craig.

"Yes Why?"

"Well, you'll have the house to yourself," said Craig, grinning at me.

I immediately read his mind. "Another party?"

"Yeah. Why not?"

I don't know whether it was the booze beginning to work its way into my system, but a party at my house suddenly seemed like a brilliant idea.

"I'll do it!" I cried.

"Woohoo! Nice one Snide. I'll come round Monday and we can plan it."

"Don't say anything to my Mum about it though," I said. "It's gonna have to be top secret."

Craig put his finger to his lips, then burst out laughing.

Having a remarkably high tolerance to alcohol for a fourteen year old, Craig remained steady as he worked his way down the bottle. What happened with me next though was all a bit of a blur.

I remember feeling elated at first. Then numb. Then sick.

The next thing I remember was being shaken awake and finding myself in the bed I'd been sitting on earlier, clutching a teddy bear.

"Snide!" came a female voice. "What are you doing in my bed?"

"Huh?" I grunted. I opened my eyes and found myself face to face with Abigail Jones.

"Do you like my bed?" she asked, pulling back the covers and sitting down next to me.

"Whassat?" I slurred.

"Do you like me?" she added, now sliding under the blanket with me.

Slowly, my head began to clear. I may have been drunk but I knew full well what was happening. Leaning out of the bed, Abigail stretched her arm out and gave the door a hefty shove. It shut plunging the room into darkness.

"Coo! You stink of booze," she said softly, stroking my hair.

I couldn't see her at all but she was close enough for me to feel her breath on my face and smell her perfume.

'My god Snide,' I thought to myself. 'I think you've pulled.' Any other situation and I'm convinced my shyness and lack of confidence would have got the better of me. But here in the dark, we were both invisible. Add to that, the fact that I was mellowed by alcohol, it all made for a perfect set up.

Moving my head forward, I felt my nose bump into Abigail's. Then her lips were upon me, kissing frantically. I tried to reciprocate as best I could but in a strange way, even though I'd often fantasised about my first kiss, it left me cold.

Abigail was oblivious to my indifference though and now I felt her tongue beginning to probe its way into my mouth.

'Oh well,' I thought. 'In for a penny, in for a pound,' and I began to slide my hand clumsily up and down her back. She offered no resistance, so I worked my way round to the front and started to grope at her breasts. She moaned softly and immediately started to wrestle with the zip on my jeans.

149

I could go on but, suffice to say, I had my first ever lesson in finding my way around the female anatomy that night. Not that we did anything other than kiss and fondle. Even if she'd wanted me to go further, the alcohol had rendered me incapable in that department (as she found to her disappointment when she finally did get inside my jeans).

After what seemed an age (and to be honest I was beginning to get a bit bored) we were suddenly distracted by a banging on the bedroom door.

"Abi. It's Amanda. You need to come downstairs. Someone's put vodka in the fish tank!"

"Oh Christ!" cursed Abigail. "My dad's gonna kill me."

Knowing who her father was, I felt genuine sympathy for her. Not that I'd helped matters much. At some point she would find out that someone had been helping themselves to his home made wine as well.

We both climbed out of bed, me wobbling badly as I tried to revert to a vertical posture. I tottered down the stairs after her to be confronted by a scene of utter mayhem. The living room carpet was covered in spilt booze and in one corner it appeared that someone had actually vomited.

"What's that?" she screamed to Amanda, pointing.

"Puke!" replied Amanda bluntly. "That bloody Craig did it! He's as pissed as a newt."

Abigail turned in desperation to the fish tank. It was a lost cause. Not a single fish was left living. All were floating on the surface.

And as if that wasn't bad enough, something seemed to be kicking off in the kitchen as well.

Suddenly Craig appeared at the door.

"There's a fight," he slurred. Then spotting me he shouted; "Snide! It's Shane. Someone's picking on him."

Normally my initial instinct would be to run in the other direction but, numbed by the effects of alcohol and spurred on by feelings of camaraderie with my friends, I lurched through the door, pushing Craig before me.

As we entered the kitchen we were greeted by the sight of Shane and an older boy punching the living daylights out of each other. Eventually the older boy, sensing he wasn't going to win this one, pulled away.

He pointed an accusing finger at Shane who, himself having stepped back, was nursing a split lip.

"You just keep your dirty hands off my sister," he shouted. "Why don't you and your family piss off back to where you come from?"

Shane said nothing but clenched his fists in silent fury.

Craig walked straight up to the boy. "See him," he began, pointing at Shane. "He's my mate! And if you pick on him, you pick on me." And with that he head butted him square on the nose.

His timing couldn't have been worse because, as he did so, the kitchen door burst open and three policeman barged there way in.

"Leg it!" cried Craig.

Luckily for me and Shane, we were stood right by the back door, so we made a hasty exit into the garden.

"Oi!" shouted one of the policemen, spotting us. "Get back here!"

Running onto the lawn, we looked about us desperately.

"My dad will kill me if I get in trouble with the police," gasped Shane. "It's bad enough I got in a fight."

"Quick this way," I shouted, pulling him into a narrow gap between the garden shed and the fence.

We both stood pressed against the shed wall, trying not to let our heavy breathing give us away.

Eventually we noticed the noise dying down in the house and eventually came the sound of the back door shutting.

Shane poked his head out. "All clear," he hissed. Together we crept back across the lawn and peered through the window. The kitchen was empty.

Cautiously, we made our way back into the house and found it deserted except for Abigail and Amanda clearing up.

"Looks like the party's over," said Shane.

"Hi Abi," I said, feeling slightly embarrassed now. "Have you seen Craig?"

"No," said Abigail, firmly. "But when you find him, tell him thanks for puking all over my carpet."

"Do you two want a hand?" offered Shane, apologetically.

"No thanks Shane. Are you OK? That's a nasty cut on your lip."

She got up and examined it more closely. Then, going into the kitchen, she returned with some cotton wool and a small bottle of TCP and tended to his wound.

It may seem ridiculous now, but I actually felt jealous.

We never did find Craig that night. He later told us he'd teamed up with a friend of the boy he'd headbutted and gone back to his house for an all night drinking session.

As for me and Shane, we'd both had enough so, tired and still numbed by the effects of alcohol, we staggered home.

Monday 21st August - Accused

With Abigail Jones' party behind us, I knew that it was my turn next and Craig had come round to help me make plans.

Late that morning though, something happened that forced us to put any thoughts of parties and girls onto the back burner for a while.

Craig and I were sitting in the dining room when there was a knock on the front door. Mum disappeared to answer it.

"Oh hello Shane, dear!"

Craig looked at me with a quizzical frown. I shrugged my shoulders in reply.

Shane entered the kitchen, head down, shoulders hunched forward. It was immediately obvious that something was wrong. Shane was Mr Cool, always in control, level headed. To see him so obviously in an emotional state was something of a shock.

"Alright Shane," said Craig. "I thought you were at work."

"I got sent home," replied Shane, his head still bowed.

"Got sent home," I echoed. "Why? What did you do?"

Mum, also realising something was seriously wrong, pulled out a chair for him. "Come and sit down, love. I'll make you a nice cup of tea."

"Thank you Mrs Percival," said Shane, remembering his manners despite his obviously distressed state.

Craig and I sat in silence, waiting for Shane to tell us more. But he didn't. Instead he remained looking at the floor, lost in his own thoughts. Finally, he raised his eyes to us and I immediately noticed that he'd been crying.

Mum entered the room carrying a tray on which she'd immaculately arranged a teapot, four cups, a jug of milk, a bowl of sugar complete with teaspoon and a packet of chocolate digestive biscuits. Good old Mum - always there in a crisis.

"Now tell us all about it," she said, setting the tray down and busying herself filling the cups.

Shane sighed deeply then began. "It's a bit of a long story really. It all started a couple of weeks ago. Mr Frost, the manager at the shoe shop, called us all together after closing time. He said he'd been doing an inventory and . . "

"A what?" interrupted Craig.

"An inventory," I said. "It's where they check all the stock. To make sure nothing's missing. Right Shane?"

"Yeah that's right," replied Shane. "And that was just the problem. There was some stuff missing. Well, what I mean is, the takings in the till didn't match up to the stock that had gone. Mr Frost said he didn't want to go around accusing his own staff of theft, but he couldn't find any other way of explaining it."

"Bloody hell," said Craig. "Did he know who it was?"

"Well no," said Shane. "There was no way of telling really but he said that he would continue monitoring the stock and till receipts and if any more went missing, he would be forced into taking action."

"And did any more go missing?" I asked. I feared that I knew, not only the answer to my question but also, exactly where this story was going.

"Well yesterday, things got worse. Mr Frost called us all together again and said that the tills were down by over £10. He said that if any of us knew anything, they should come and see him in private.

"Anyway, this morning, I noticed Mr Thornton. Do you remember him? The floor manger who came over to you two when you were in the shop and told you both to leave. Well he was having a conversation with Mr Frost about something.

"Next thing I knew I'd been called into Mr Frost's office. He asked me to turn out my pockets. When he saw my brand new wallets stuffed with notes, he told me that Mr Thornton had seen me stealing from the till. He said he wouldn't involve the police because I was under age but I had to leave his shop immediately. I said I hadn't done anything wrong and that money was my wages, that I'd been saving up. But he wouldn't listen. He told me to go otherwise he *would* call the police."

"He shouldn't have done that Shane. Not without proof," said Mum, putting a comforting arm around him.

"That wasn't the worst bit," continued Shane. "As I was leaving, he said that I should be thankful that he'd given a chance to the likes of me but he wasn't surprised that I ended up stealing from him. He said that we have such a thing as law and order in this country and that me and my kind were expected to abide by it."

"Another bloody racialist," muttered Craig under his breath.

"I'm not having that," said Mum briskly rising from her chair. "Does he know your dad's a lawyer?"

"No," replied Shane. "But I don't want him to find out. He might believe Mr Frost."

"Nonsense!" exclaimed Mum. "What's your dad's work number?"

"021 484 9228," answered Shane.

"Right!" said Mum. "This is a matter for adults to deal with." And with that she disappeared into the hall, where we kept our telephone.

The ensuing phone call was longer than we'd expected. Although Mum kept her voice down to a discrete level, we did hear snippets of her side of the conversation as she raised her voice in anger ". . . talking to a fourteen year old boy like that . . . such a decent lad . . . always polite . . . it's racial discrimination, that's what it is . . . shouldn't be allowed . . . yes I know . . . what with you being a lawyer and all . . . thank you, Mr Small . . . goodbye."

"He's going to have words with him," she said as she returned to the dining room. "Don't worry. He won't get away with this!"

Tuesday 22nd August - Legal Representation

I dearly wish I could have been in that office to see Mr Frost's face when Mr Small introduced himself as Shane's dad and as a lawyer. Not only that, but a lawyer who had a great deal of experience in dealing with claims of unfair dismissal, compensation and most importantly of all, racial discrimination.

We did have the honour of being driven into town with Shane in his dad's Mercedes and walking to the front of the shop with them. But after that it was a case of them leaving me and Craig at the door.

All we saw was Mr Small having a word with Mr Thornton who looked them both up and down with some disdain before accompanying them to Mr Frost's office.

The rest, as I am about to recount, is as Shane told me and Craig later that day.

"Yes? Can I help you?" said Frost, rising from his desk as Shane and his Dad walked through the office door.

"Yes. My name is Gladstone Small. I am Shane Small's father."

"Oh, I see," replied Frost, nervously eyeing Mr Small who, quite contrary to his name, was a large, broadly built man. "Mr Thornton, if you wouldn't mind staying please."

"I'm also giving him legal representation. My card." Here Mr Small pulled a business card from his wallet and handed it to Mr Frost.

Frost's face fell as he read: 'G.W. SMALL - SOLICITOR.'

"I believe you have accused my son of stealing from your shop," continued Mr Small. "Would you mind telling me on what evidence you have based your accusation?"

"Well . . . he was . . seen," stammered Frost. "Tell him please, Mr Thornton. You witnessed the theft. You saw him taking money from the till."

For his part, Mr Thornton seemed to have lost much of his usual composure. "I'm not absolutely certain, sir," he began, unsteadily. "I may have been mistaken."

"So you have dismissed my son without good reason," concluded Mr Small. "Would you say he was a good worker?"

"Well . . . er . . . yes, I suppose so," answered Frost.

"You suppose so. So there is some doubt in your mind."

At this point Shane looked at his dad nervously.

"Has he always been punctual?"

"Yes."

"Reliable?"

"Yes."

"Conscientious?"

"Yes."

"And yet you dismissed him," continued Mr Small. "Tell me Mr Frost. Would you mind explaining to my son what you meant by *his kind*?"

"His kind?" repeated Frost, nervously.

"Yes. You said, and I quote here; 'We have such a thing as law and order in this country and you and your kind are expected to abide by it.'"

"I . . I." Mr Frost's mouth opened and closed like a fish out of water.

"Would I, as his father, for example be included as one of his kind?" asked Mr Small, his voice taking on a slightly harder edge.

Mr Frost gripped the edge of his desk saying nothing.

"Let me put it to you, Mr Frost that such phraseology might be considered by many to be racist."

"I am not a racist," replied Frost, slowly and deliberately.

Mr Small gave him a long, lingering stare then turned to Thornton, who had also gone rather pale.

"As for you Mr Thornton, your initial statement, claiming to have witnessed my son stealing from the till could be construed as malicious. In fact, in collaboration with your superior, your actions could also be viewed as racist."

"Now hang on," began Thornton. "I retracted that statement. I said I wasn't sure."

Mr Small finally turned to Shane.

"Shane my boy, you have many possible courses of action at your disposal, ranging from a simple apology, through having your job back to a full scale compensation claim for unfair dismissal on the grounds of racial discrimination. I don't expect an answer now. I will give you time to think about it. But as my son, I can assure you that you will have access to my full range of legal services entirely for free."

He rose from his chair. "As for you Mr Frost, whatever course of action my son decides to take, I shall be ringing your head office later today to make a complaint about your behaviour. Come on Shane."

Later that day after Shane had told us the whole story, we were sat once again around my dining room table.

"So what are you going to do?" I asked.

"Just going for a written apology from both of them," answered Shane. "I wouldn't want to work there again. And dad said pursuing a case of unfair dismissal on the grounds of racial discrimination would take a lot of time and money and, seeing as how I wasn't paying him, he didn't really want to go down that road."

He sipped from a steaming mug of tea that Mum had made.

157

"He did say one thing though," continued Shane. "He said; 'Beware the power of the law.'"

"Meaning what?" asked Craig.

"Dunno," replied Shane. "But it got me thinking. I might follow in my dad's footsteps and become a lawyer one day."

"You'll have to study hard," advised Mum. "But I'm sure if anybody can do it, you can."

Friday 25th August - Age of Consent

A few days later we were down the den for the first time that summer. Once the centre of our universe, and a symbol of the power of our gang, this dilapidated World War Two air raid shelter now lay largely empty and unused, as it no doubt had done for decades before we ever came along.

I had put together a list of people to come to my party and Shane was writing out the invites (because he had the best handwriting).

I wanted to limit the number of people there to fifteen because I needed to keep it secret from my parents and, having seen what happened at Abigail Jones' house, I was determined to ensure nothing got damaged. After much persuasion though, Craig and Shane had got me to add Susan Palin and Terri Donnerly to the list. Unknown to me, they had also added Abigail Jones.

And it was Abigail who was the hot topic of conversation that morning.

"Well Snide," said Craig, leering lecherously. "You and Abi. Did you?"

"Did we what?" I replied.

"You know," laughed Craig. "Did she let you? You know!"

"I think what he means," added Shane. "Is did you lose your virginity?"

"Eugh no!" I answered, screwing my face up. "She's hideous."

"Well I would," said Craig.

158

"You'd do it with anything!" I retorted. "Even a hole in a fence!"

"Ha ha ha," laughed Craig, jumping up and thrusting his hips backwards and forwards in an exaggerated manner.

"Yeah, but seriously, did you?" persisted Shane.

"No! You must be joking."

"I bet you copped a good feel though," said Craig, grinning evilly.

"I might have."

"Wey hey!" shouted Craig, now pumping his arm in the air.

"You are so crude Craig," remarked Shane, shaking his head. "When are you going to learn that if you want to get a girl you've got to show her a bit of sophistication?"

"Bullshit!" replied Craig. "Just get in there. They love it!"

"Oh yeah? Like Terri," I said. "What was it she called you after Julian's party?"

"I dunno," replied Craig, looking slightly crestfallen. "I can't remember much about that night."

"You never can. Cos you're always pissed. Anyway, I heard she said you were a dirty dog."

"Who told you that?" asked Craig.

"I bumped into Sharon Steel down the shops a couple of days ago,"

"You see," continued Shane. "Sophistication. That's the key to success. Now you just watch the master at work next Saturday."

"Oh? Who have you got in mind?" I asked.

"Susan Palin."

I momentarily felt a pang of jealousy. Then remembering my drunken fumblings with Abigail Jones, I decided that Susan had the perfect right to play the field, like me. And who better to do that with than one of my closest friends?

"You've got no chance there Big Man," said Craig.

"Yes I have. And I'm after more than just a snog."

Craig looked at Shane, thinking carefully. "Well if you're going after Susan Palin I'm having another go at Big T."

"In your dreams," I laughed. "Dirty dog!"

"Not at all," said Craig. "Shane's right. I just need to tone it down a bit. Act all sophisticated and she'll be putty in my hands."

"What about you Snide?" asked Shane. "You never know. Someone might be there who takes a fancy to you." He and Craig exchanged knowing glances.

"Not bothered," I replied. "Just want to make sure the house doesn't get trashed."

Later that morning we were down the park when we spotted Eric lighting one of his famous (or infamous) bonfires.

"Hey dudes. What you been up to?" he called out, having spotted us.

We wandered over and sat down with him on his log.

"I hear you've been chasing girls," he said, pulling down the dark glasses which he wore permanently and peering at us over the top of them.

"Yeah. Might have been," said Craig.

"So which ones of you have scored then?" asked Eric, pushing his glasses back up his nose and throwing some more brushwood onto the fire.

"Scored?" I asked, shrugging my shoulders.

"Yeah, scored with a chick? Potted the pink."

We all burst out laughing at this last comment.

"What? So you're all still virgins," continued Eric. "Hell dudes. I lost my virginity at fourteen. It was to a girl I met at the Isle of Wight Festival. We'd both been taking magic mushrooms and LSD so we were well out of it. Then we just found a spot in a nearby field and did it. It was so cool."

"The Isle of Wight festival?" I said. "But that was in 1968 wasn't it? So according to that, you'd be 24 now. I thought you were older than that."

In truth, we all knew that some of Eric's stories about his earlier life were pure fiction. Normally we let it go, but on this occasion I couldn't help myself.

"Yeah. Well maybe it was an earlier festival then," muttered Eric. "Hell man, I can't remember every date exactly. I spent most of the sixties stoned you know!"

"Yeah. We understand," said Shane kindly.

160

"Anyway, you dudes take my advice," said Eric. "Get yourselves some Durex. Last thing you want at your age is to get some chick in the club."

"Which club?" asked Craig, looking confused.

"He means pregnant," said Shane.

And so it was, later that day that the three of us were stood awkwardly outside our local chemist.

"You go in Big Man," said Craig to Shane. "You look at least sixteen."

"It's not illegal to buy Durex under the age of sixteen," I said.

"Isn't it? I thought it was the same as fireworks," laughed Craig, in reply. "Cos I know one thing. There'll sure be fireworks going off once I get hold of Big T."

Shane raised his eyes to heaven. "I'll do it," he said.

We watched as he entered the shop then, seeing a young lady being served at the counter, loitered behind a display of women's hair dyes.

"Come on," laughed Craig. "Let's go in and watch."

Eventually, the customer having been dispatched, Shane walked nervously up to the counter.

"Yes," said the rather bored looking female assistant.

With his head bowed, Shane muttered something that was inaudible from where we were standing.

"Pardon?" said the assistant. "You'll have to speak up dear."

"Three packets of Durex please," repeated Shane, nervously.

"What type?" asked the assistant in a flat voice.

This obviously threw Shane and in a panic he pointed wildly at the display behind the counter. "Err those ones please," he squeaked.

The assistant picked three packets from the display and plonked them down on the counter. Hastily, Shane handed her a note, stuffed his purchases into his pocket and waited impatiently for his change. Then snatching the coins from the assistants hand, he rushed from the shop followed closely by me and Craig.

Saturday 2nd September - Summer's Final Fling

"Now promise me, you won't have anyone round the house," said Mum, standing hands on hips in the hallway.

"I won't." I said, slightly uncomfortable at telling such a blatant lie.

"And definitely no parties. I haven't forgotten what happened up at Mr Jones' house the other week," continued Mum.

"I know!"

Dad staggered downstairs carrying two huge suitcases that were fit to burst.

"You are only going away for the weekend aren't you?" I remarked, pointing at the growing pile of luggage accumulating at the front door.

"Don't blame me," said Dad. "Ninety percent of this stuff is your mum's." He raised his eyebrows at me and mouthed the word; "Women," whilst shaking his head.

I smiled.

Suddenly, the phone rang. "Hello!" barked my dad, as if attempting to communicate with someone in Australia. "Oh. Yes he is. Hold on."

He handed me the receiver. "It's Craig," he said, with his usual hint of disapproval.

"Hi Craig," I said. "What's up?"

"Alright Snide? Sorry, I thought they'd have gone by now. What time d'you want me to bring the booze round?"

"About 11," I replied hastily, fearing my parents could hear Craig's every word. "Yeah. I'll meet you down the park."

"Eh - what do you mean, meet me down the park? Oh, I see. They're listening in, are they?" Craig laughed.

"Bye then," I said and hastily put down the receiver.

Mum, eyed me suspiciously and, as she did so an old phrase sprung momentarily into my mind: 'You can fool all of the people some of the time, you can fool some of the people all of the time, but you can't fool a mother.'

Eventually she broke the silence. "We'll be back Monday afternoon. Make sure this house is immaculate."

I didn't reply. I just looked at her guiltily.

Having obviously understood my cryptic message, Craig turned up dead on time at 11 o'clock, carrying a box containing mostly beer, supplemented with a small amount of whisky and vodka.

"Jim owed me one," he said, by way of explanation.

We spent the afternoon *partifying* the house, by stowing away in the loft, anything breakable or of value. We also paid a visit to the local hardware store to buy some low wattage, coloured light bulbs which we used as replacements in virtually every light fitting in the house.

By five o'clock we were ready, so we sat down to crack open a couple of cans.

Shortly afterwards, there was a knock on the door.

It was Shane, dressed in a smart black open necked shirt and white jeans.

"Whoa! It's John Travolta!" cried Craig, laughing.

"I told you," replied Shane, calmly. "Sophistication. Tonight is the night." And in saying so, he withdrew his packet of condoms from the back pocket of his jeans and held them up as a statement of intent.

I handed him a beer which he took a sip from, grimacing slightly.

"What time did the invites say?" asked Craig.

"Six," I replied.

But six o'clock came and went without any sign of guests. By seven, we started to worry - well Shane and I did. Craig just passed the time by downing beers to the point where he neither knew nor cared what time it was anyway.

Eventually, guests started to arrive, the music was turned up and we had a party on our hands.

Most of the early guests were boys but, just as Craig and Shane were beginning to lose hope, Susan and Terri appeared on the doorstep.

In the days leading up to the party, I'd assumed that both Craig and Shane would have had an uphill struggle to make any inroads with Susan and Terri but, with apparent ease, they were accepted as chaperones for the night and soon I found myself in the familiar role of party wallflower.

However, as is often the case when alcohol flows, things began to take an unexpected turn. And it was Craig this time who suffered the brunt of it.

"Stupid cow!" he shouted, bursting into the kitchen where I was mooching. "That's it. I'm finished with her!"

"What happened?" I asked.

"I don't know!" slurred Craig, spreading his hands in disbelief. "I was acting all sophisticated, like Shane said. She was kissing me and all that stuff. Then I got the Durex out of its wrapper and dangled it in front of her face and she went mad. Called me a vile pig."

"It's not getting any better is it?" I joked.

"What do you mean?" asked Craig, breaking into another can.

"Well last week you were only a dog," I replied. "Now you're a pig."

Craig took a long swig from the can. "Where's Shane?" he asked.

"Dunno," I said. "He was with Susan last I saw."

Just then, the doorbell rang and moments later Abigail Jones appeared at the kitchen door. "Hello Snide," she cooed. "Thanks for the invite."

I looked at Craig, who shrugged his shoulders dismissively, picked up a quarter bottle of vodka, stuffed it into his back pocket and disappeared into the living room.

"Alright Abi," I said, politely.

"I thought you'd have all the girls chasing after you tonight," giggled Abigail.

"Are those new glasses you're wearing?" I asked, by way of reply.

"No," replied Abigail, nonplussed.

"Oh sorry," I said. "Just looked like the lenses had a rose tint to them."

Abigail looked at me blankly. Then, finally getting the joke, she giggled and poured herself a generous measure of vodka with a dash of lemonade.

What a great party this has turned out to be, I thought to myself. Shane had disappeared somewhere with Susan Palin, Craig was well on his way to total inebriation again and I was stuck in the kitchen valiantly trying to entertain Abigail Jones.

Abigail awkwardly nursed her glass. She looked up at me, appeared to be about to speak, then changed her mind.

"I suppose I'd better mingle," I said at last. "I'd better check on . . "

"Do you want it or not!" Abigail suddenly blurted out. "I've got a Durex, if that's what you're worried about."

I stared at her open mouthed, then got to my feet in shock and leaned back against the sink.

In response, she stood up, removed her glasses and kissed me passionately on the lips.

'Oh my God,' I said to myself. 'This really is it. It's now or never.'

I looked into her face and she smiled back. "Come on," she whispered, taking me by the hand and leading me out of the kitchen.

I can't remember how long we'd been upstairs in my room but, half dozing in an alcoholic haze, with Abigail warm and soft beside me, I was suddenly disturbed by a commotion downstairs. The quiet hubbub of a dozen or so guests had been supplemented by the raucous noise of, what appeared to be a large number of older boys.

As my panic rose, the music suddenly became louder, accompanied by a loud cheer.

Quickly, I leapt from my bed and rushed downstairs. In the living room were a group who I recognised immediately as those who had invaded Abigail's party. As I looked on, one of them came out of the kitchen, shaking a can of beer vigorously. Then opening it, he sprayed its contents all over the furniture, carpet and walls.

I sensed Abigail at my side and turned round. "I'll call the police," she said, dashing off into the hallway.

Then, as if things weren't bad enough already, Craig lurched into the room, barely able to stand and threatened to take all of them on.

I looked around in desperation as several of my guests, sensing trouble, started to make their exits leaving me and Craig alone.

Where was Shane when we needed him? I already knew the answer to that - Abigail and I had caught him and Susan making out in the spare bedroom earlier.

Then, above the din of the music, there came the unmistakeable sound of a police siren. Within seconds, the house was invaded by half a dozen policemen, one of whom marched straight over to the stereo and turned the music off.

"Right!" he shouted. "Who's in charge here?"

I raised my hand nervously, as if in the classroom.

"The neighbours have been complaining about the noise," he continued. "This party is now over. You all need to leave. Otherwise you will be arrested." Then he turned and pointed to me. "And you. Next time you think of having a house party, think again. We've got better things to do with our time than sort your problems out. Bloody kids!"

Slowly, reluctantly, the gatecrashers left, taking what little was left of the booze with them.

Having escorted them out, the police left without another word.

I turned to Abigail. "Thanks," I said. "For everything."

She smiled, coyly. "The pleasure was all mine Snide."

I wandered into the kitchen, desperate for some water and found Craig hunched over the sink, retching. Hearing me behind him, he straightened himself up and turned to face me, a dribble of vomit running down his chin. "Great party Snide!" he exclaimed.

Back in the living room, Shane had reappeared. "What happened?" he asked.

"No matter," I replied.

"Are you ready Shane?" came the familiar voice of Susan from the hall.

"I'm walking her home," explained Shane, awkwardly and he left.

The most surreal moment of the evening, however, was yet to come. And it came with a knock at the front door. Opening it, I found myself standing face to face with none other than the fearsome Mr Jones!

"Oh. Good evening," he began, pleasantly. "I've come to pick up my daughter, Abigail."

On cue, Abigail appeared, hugged her dad and thanked me politely for being a great host. Then they left.

If only he'd known what I had been up to with his daughter just minutes earlier, I thought. He probably would have gone there and then back to his car and fetched his cane.

I laughed to myself, then remembering Craig, went back to the kitchen to check on him. I needn't have worried. He was laid spark out on the kitchen floor in an alcoholic stupor, snoring loudly.

Sunday 3rd September - Are We Boys or Are We Men?

It was the final day of the summer holiday and Craig, having stopped over, had helped me to tidy the house. Considering we both had huge hangovers, we didn't do a bad job at all, although the beer stain on the wallpaper next to the kitchen door would need some explaining.

Just as we'd sat down to take a break, the doorbell rang.

It was Shane. "Morning boys," he said, crashing down into an armchair. "Good party last night wasn't it?"

I looked at him carefully. There was something different about him. I couldn't quite put my finger on it but, even by Shane's standards he was super cool, super calm, super collected.

"Might have to go down the chemist later," he crowed. "I need to replenish my stock."

"You'll be lucky," I said, aiming to burst his bubble. "They're shut. It's Sunday."

"Oh well. I'm sure my hot honey can wait another twenty four hours."

Suddenly Craig's eyes lit up as the penny dropped. "What? You mean you and Susan? You did it?"

"A gentleman never tells," replied Shane calmly.

I felt jealous at the thought of Shane and Susan together. Then I remembered with warm affection the intimacy I had shared with Abigail.

"You're not the only one to get lucky," I said.

Suddenly, Shane burst out laughing. "You mugs," he laughed. "I'm winding you up."

"Then you didn't," I surmised.

"I would have if I'd had the choice," said Shane. "But Sue's too classy a girl to go dishing it out first time. Anyway, she's underage. We would both have got arrested if we were found out."

"Would you?" gasped Craig, in surprise.

"Sure thing. My dad was talking to me about it yesterday."

Craig turned to me. "So what did you mean Snide, when you said Shane wasn't the only one to get lucky last night?"

In view of what Shane had just revealed, I thought it best to retract my partial confession. "Oh nothing much," I replied. "We just had a bit of a snog."

"And a grope?" asked Craig, hopefully.

"That's for me to know and you to find out," I replied.

"Anyway. Sue has asked me to see her again," continued Shane. "And you know what? I think I'm in love."

"Ha ha ha," laughed Craig. "Shane and Susan, sitting in a tree, K-I-S-S-I-N-G."

"Oh grow up Craig!" said Shane, slightly irritated.

And on that point, I had to agree.

It was clear that we were indeed all growing up, it was just that some of us were doing so faster than others.

As for me, my session with Abigail had provided a most satisfactory conclusion to the summer holiday. I wasn't, however, prepared for what was to follow in the ensuing weeks on our return to school. Whatever happened between me and Abigail that night (and I am not prepared here to reveal any more than I already have) it had triggered in her an emotional attachment to me that I soon realised I was not ready for.

In fact it took three long months of holding her at arms length before she finally got the message. And when she did, it left me with a feeling of guilt, the likes of which I'd never experienced before.

So maybe I wasn't so grown up after all.

We, all three of us, had a few summers left before we could truly claim to be fully fledged adults. And anyway, who wanted to grow up?

Being a teenager was pretty good fun for the time being.

Unfortunately, I didn't realise as the summer of 1978 drew to a close that storm clouds were brewing at home, the long term consequences of which would be life changing. 1979, as I was about to learn, would be a year that would remain engrained firmly on my memory for more than one reason.

1979

THE
VACATION

CONTENTS

THE VACATION

When I was younger, The West Country was always the default holiday destination for Mum, Dad and me.

It began in 1971 with a wonderful fortnight in Newquay. At the tail end of a romantic, golden age of holidaying before commerciality took a stranglehold, Newquay was the perfect family destination. With sandy beaches topped by rugged cliffs, it had everything a young boy could want. From the safe, walled paddling pool at Towan Beach, through the numerous pasty and beach shops, to the expansive beauty of Pentire Head and the surfer strewn Fistral Beach, it was a holiday paradise.

Our exploration of The West Country continued through the 1970's with holidays in Falmouth (1972), Paignton (1973), St Ives (1974) and Penzance (1975).

Then things took a turn for the worse. In 1976, Dad lost his job as a journalist - something from which he never really recovered. As a result, our annual holiday had to be put on hold. By the end of 1978, family relationships had gone past the point of no return.

Then in the spring of 1979, Dad walked out on us. It was not as if he'd found a better life somewhere else. It was more a case of him feeling that he had nowhere left to turn. So he turned his back on Mum and me.

In a desperate attempt to instil some normality into our lives, Mum booked us a holiday in the north Somerset seaside town of Watchbourne. Not the hotel based type of vacation we'd enjoyed when Dad had been with us. Instead, it was a case of self catering in a static caravan. It was all mum could afford.

But in a further attempt to cushion the blow of Dad's leaving, she made a decision that would make this holiday, probably the most memorable of my entire childhood.

"Do you want to bring Shane and Craig along?" she suddenly asked one morning, over breakfast.

Naturally, I jumped at the chance.

Within the space of a couple of days it was all organised. Shane's dad had volunteered to make a contribution towards costs. Craig, of course didn't have such support but Mum was happy to bring him along for free. "He virtually lives with us during the holidays anyway," was her only comment on the matter.

For Craig, Shane and Me, it was a chance to take our gang *on tour*. And I for one was fully prepared to make the most of it. After all, it was a perfect opportunity to forget all of the woes that home life had thrown at me and mum in the last few months.

Saturday 11th August - Departure

Luckily for us, in 1978 Mum had learned to drive and bought herself a car. So for a short time we were a two car family.

Then dad departed, taking the family car with him and we were left with Mum's runaround - a rusting, bright orange Ford Escort. By today's standards it was very basic. No computer controlled ignition systems and built in sat nav in those days. It didn't even have power steering or an automatic choke. And as for the interior! The seats were all PVC, meaning that in winter they were freezing cold and in summer, you'd emerge with the back of your trousers wringing wet with sweat. An even worse fate awaited you if you wore shorts. A combination of warm plastic on sweat ensured that your skin became stuck to the seats with the result that you had to painfully unpeel your thighs in order to extricate yourself from the car's interior.

It didn't help that the in car heater was permanently stuck in the ON position, necessitating the opening of all windows (manually of course) before embarking on even the shortest of trips.

Nevertheless we loved Mum's car. It was a car with real character. To begin with, ignition was never a foregone conclusion, especially if there was even the faintest amount of humidity in the air. A failure to start would mean dismantling the distributor, points and plugs, drying them out and trying again. Even then, by the time all of this had been done, the battery was usually flat, with the result that I spent many hours pushing it up and down the road, whilst Mum attempted to bump start the engine into action.

Fortunately for us, the morning of Saturday 11th August was a warm and dry one, perfect for the prospect of embarking on a summer holiday.

Craig was the first to arrive. He came equipped with a large, red and white Adidas bag that had undoubtedly seen better days. At one end the stitching holding the zip in place, had come away allowing the bulging contents to force it open.

He hurriedly put it into the boot, then joined me at the kitchen table.

Mum followed him in.

"You got any toast Mrs P?" asked Craig hopefully.

"Of course Craig dear. Do you want jam or marmalade?"

In order for the holiday to get off to a good start, it was obvious that she'd made the decision to be especially friendly to Craig.

"Can I have both Mrs P? I'm starving!"

Mum went off to the cupboard without reply.

Craig leaned over to me. "Hey Snide. No need to worry. I've got plenty of supplies."

"Supplies?" I repeated.

"Yeah, booze!" hissed Craig, leaning closer.

As he did so, I felt sure I could smell the sweet, sickly stench of alcohol on his breath. And it was only 9 o'clock!

Craig had started drinking at an early age and by now was a regular. Looking back, it seems obvious that even at the age of fifteen, he was already an alcoholic. But in those days, an alcoholic was someone who drank three bottles of vodka a day and lived in the gutter. As far as I was concerned, he just liked a drink.

Of course none of this would have been possible without the support of his stepdad Jim. Having initially handed out many beatings to Craig, and his mum over several years, things seemed to have improved more recently. This followed a period when Jim and Craig's mum, Joyce, split up over the physical abuse he was dishing out.

Eventually, after six months, Joyce allowed Jim back into the family home, on the strict condition that if any violence started up again, they would be finished for good.

Remarkably, Jim kept his side of the bargain. However, although the beatings had stopped, the underlying cause, Jim's alcoholism, hadn't.

This was where Craig, always a survivor and opportunist, came into his element. In order to placate Craig's mum, Jim had convinced her that he would only indulge in an occasional drink at lunch time whilst she was out at work. The reality, however was that he kept a secret stash of whisky hidden in the house which he dipped into at various points throughout the day. In the true nature of an alcoholic, he kept his intake high enough to satisfy his cravings, but not so much that it would become evident to Joyce in his behaviour. Craig, already aware of Jim's stash, latched onto this and, short of blackmailing him, persuaded Jim to let him dip into it whenever he felt like it, in return for his silence.

"I've got some fags as well," continued Craig. "Courtesy of Jim. He's always so obliging."

"No thanks Craig," I said, sighing. "I can't stand them. Neither can Shane."

As if on cue, there was a gentle knock on the door.

Mum rushed off to answer it.

"Hello Shane dear. Oh you do look smart!"

"Thank you Mrs Percival," came the unmistakeable voice of Shane.

"Let's get your things into the boot of the car," continued Mum.

"Oh allow me," said Shane, trying every inch to sound like an adult.

My mind flashed back momentarily to when the three of us first met and how close a bond we had back then. Now, we were all very different. In particular, the gulf between Shane and Craig was so great that it was difficult sometimes to understand why we still all hung out together.

It was certainly true that over the last twelve months the group dynamic had changed. Craig had once been our gang leader, a role he maintained partly through his fearful reputation as our year group's hard man. And although he still fulfilled this role (nobody ever messed with Craig at school), he found himself far more on a level with Shane and myself. We knew that he needed our friendship and, whereas in the past it was always Craig's way or no way, now we were always prepared to argue the toss with him.

Also, with the gap between Craig and Shane's respective outlooks on life widening, it was hardly surprising that in recent months they had begun to argue more. Shane, was a physical giant for his age and, as such, he was probably the only person in our year group who truly didn't fear Craig, so the arguments sometimes became quite heated.

My main hope for this holiday, therefore was that all three of us would get on.

Shane appeared in the doorway. "Morning boys," he said cheerily.

"You alright big man?" replied Craig. "You want some toast? Mrs P is just knocking some up."

"No thanks," replied Shane rubbing his belly. "Already eaten."

I breathed a sigh of relief. They both seemed in good spirits.

Craig leaned forward in an exaggerated manner and glanced furtively at Mum. "Hey Shane!" he whispered. "I've got the stash safely in the car."

In response, Shane raised his eyebrows and looked at me. In a vain attempt to keep the peace, I nodded with a vague hint of enthusiasm.

Craig rose from the table. "Just going for a slash Mrs P," he declared, leaving the room.

Making sure Craig was out of earshot first, Shane spoke softly to me. "Have you smelt his breath?"

"Yep!"

"Does your mum know?"

"No."

"Christ! Some holiday this is going to be."

Mum walked over to the table carrying a plate piled high with toast.

"Why don't you let me help you with that?" said Shane, rising from his chair.

"No, no. I'm fine," replied Mum, brushing him away. "But it's very kind of you to offer Shane."

"Oh that's quite alright Mrs Percival," said Shane, gazing adoringly at her.

"You're the perfect son she never had," I joked as she left us alone again.

Shane looked away shyly.

Breakfast over and right on time at 10 o'clock, we piled into the car and were on our way. Shane had opted to sit in the front to keep Mum company and map read, whilst Craig and I sprawled out in the back.

It was the usual journey you would expect driving down the M5 on a Saturday in August. As far as Bristol, we made good time, then inevitably the traffic became heavier and heavier. So it was something of a relief when we saw the exit for Watchbourne and turned off onto quieter roads.

With the aid of Shane reading directions and following the map studiously, it wasn't long before we turned down the final of a succession of country lanes and saw up ahead a large board with SUNNYVIEW CARAVAN PARK written on it.

"Here we are at last," said Mum, sounding relieved.

We pulled in at a small, ramshackle hut with RECEPTION painted onto the door in white paint and disembarked. Mum knocked on the door and waited. There was no reply.

"Maybe we're too early," she said at last. "They did say to arrive after two."

"Yeah," I said, glancing at my watch. "It's only half one."

As if on cue, a man of similar age to Mum appeared from the far side of the hut. With him was a girl who smiled at us.

"Just arrived?" he asked.

"Yes," replied Mum. "We were just after our key."

"Yes. They're not a lot of use here," he said. "You might have quite a wait on your hands. Just you and the boys is it?"

"Yes. We're here for two weeks."

"Why don't you let me buy you a coffee," said the man. "There's a café on site and you can see reception if you sit outside. Rachel and I don't mind waiting with you do we Rachel?"

Rachel gave a fairly non committal shrug of the shoulders.

"Oh sorry, where are my manners?" continued the man. "I'm Steve. Rachel and I are stopping here for three weeks. We arrived last Saturday."

"A coffee would be lovely," smiled Mum. "Why don't you boys go and explore. I'm sure somebody will turn up soon." She fished out a piece of paper from her pocket and, pulling her reading glasses from her handbag, consulted it, carefully. " Our caravan number is 37."

Needing no second bidding, we immediately headed off in what we hoped was the direction of the sea. In truth, we weren't sure how far away it was but we could hear the distant sound of waves and, following our ears, came across a small wooden sign in the shape of a pointing hand with the word BEACH written on it.

We followed a winding path through some sand dunes, then finally climbing to the top of one, Craig pointed triumphantly. "I win. I was first to see the sea!" he cried. We followed him up and, as we reached the top, the unmistakeable smell of iodine invaded our nostrils.

Craig plonked himself down and reached into his jeans pocket. "Gentlemen, do you wish to partake?" he asked, pulling out three whisky miniatures.

We each took one and sipped at them like wine connoisseurs. It was a perfect moment for me - the sun beating down on my back, a gentle sea breeze blowing on my face and my two best friends sitting on either side of me.

"This is going to be a brilliant fortnight," I said.

"You want to watch that Steve though," warned Craig.

"What do you mean?" I asked.

"He was hitting on your Mum back there."

"Was he?"

"Believe me," continued Craig. "I'm an expert. The number of men who hit on my mum before Jim came along. Before you know it, he'll be your new stepdad." He drained what was left of his miniature.

"No way," butted in Shane. "Your mum's got more taste than that. She can afford to pick and choose. She's a highly desirable woman."

"Shane!" I cried. "That's my mum you're talking about."

"Just saying," said Shane, smiling to himself.

"I tell you what as well," added Craig. "I don't trust him. Did you see the way that girl Rachel was? Scared to speak, she was. Yeah. He's a bully. No doubt about it. You better watch your back there Snide."

All of which put a bit of a damper on my perfect moment. However, I decided to put Craig's warnings and Shane's lusting after my mother to the back of my mind for the moment and enjoy the day.

Having finished our drink, we ran down the other side of the sand dune onto the wet sand of the beach. Here, all three of us removed our trainers and socks and walked down to the edge of the sea. The cold shock of the water around my bare feet took my breath away.

"Hey Snide!" shouted Craig.

I turned to face him just as he kicked a mixture of sea water and sand into the air, covering my clothes and soaking me.

In response I grabbed hold of him and took his feet from under him in a crude impression of a judo throw. It was effective though and Craig, completely losing his balance, fell flat on his back in the water.

What followed was a playful wrestling bout which resulted in both our clothes becoming drenched.

Then noticing that Shane had remained dry throughout, we each grabbed one of his arms and pulled him down into the sea as well.

Momentarily, Shane looked annoyed at losing his usual cool composure but, realising he wasn't going to win, he eventually joined in kicking and splashing water in every direction like a whirling dervish, much to our amusement.

Having tired ourselves out, we retired to the dry sand of the dunes and spent some time lying on our backs staring up at the sky as our clothes slowly dried out.

"We'd better find this caravan then," I said, eventually. "Mum will be wondering where we've got to."

"Don't worry about her," said Craig. "She'll be busy with Steve."

Much to my relief though, Craig was wrong. Mum was alone but not, it seemed, in the best of moods.

"Sorry we were gone so long. Were you worried?" I asked, completely misreading the situation.

"Not about that," replied Mum. "But I am worried by this." And in saying so, she delved into Craig's bag and proceeded to pull out a substantial quantity of beer, whisky and cigarettes.

"Oh Christ!" muttered Craig under his breath.

"This lot is going in the bin!" said Mum crossly.

"We didn't know," I lied, pointing at Shane and myself.

"It's not on Craig!" snapped Mum. "I'm responsible for your welfare on this holiday."

"Sorry Mrs P," said Craig, staring at the floor.

Mum made a great show of systematically emptying each can and bottle down the sink. Then she emptied what remained of the stash into a bin bag, tied it up and disappeared in the direction of what I guess was the camp refuse site.

"Thanks for stitching me up Snide," said Craig.

"He didn't stitch you up," argued Shane. "You brought that stuff with you. It was nothing to do with us. We don't even like cigarettes."

"You enjoyed my whisky though, didn't you?" countered Craig.

There was an awkward silence.

"Oh well, I'm sure we can find an off licence somewhere," said Craig, at last.

"They wouldn't serve you," said Shane. "You don't look old enough."

"Yes, but you do," replied Craig.

Whatever else happened over the next fortnight, I thought, Craig's pursuit of alcohol was certainly going to leave its mark.

Monday 13th August - We Are Not Amused

My dad always referred to the first full day of any holiday as a 'settling in day,' which roughly translated meant ' a sitting around doing nothing day.' It would be accompanied by explanations such as; "There's plenty of time to go exploring. We are here for the full fortnight you know," or "There's nowhere open on a Sunday, so we might as well just stay put until tomorrow."

Mum had continued with this policy, opting to unpack then check out the mini supermarket on site, which remarkably was open for a few hours on a Sunday, to get some essential supplies in.

Consequently, the three of us opted to make our way down to the beach again where we wasted away the morning. Then Craig, still smarting from the confiscation of his stash, made the decision to go into town alone to seek out an off licence which he intended to talk us into visiting the following day.

Shane and I returned to the caravan later in the afternoon and were surprised to see Craig had already arrived and was in considerably better spirits. In this case however, it was nothing to do with drink or cigarettes. Instead he was sitting in the children's playground talking to Rachel.

"Oh hiya!" she called, spotting us and waving.

Shane and I ambled over.

"I was telling Rach about the amusement arcade I found down the sea front," said Craig. "Thought we might go down tomorrow."

"Great," I replied. "Are you coming as well Rachel?"

"No. My dad wouldn't let me go into town without him," said Rachel, gloomily.

"Sounds like a bit of a bully to me," added Craig, giving me a knowing look. "And I found an off licence Shane. So maybe you could pick us up a few cans of beer."

Shane said nothing, but I could see from the expression on his face that he wasn't too happy.

However, the next morning, having tried to reason with Craig, Shane had finally admitted defeat and we soon found ourselves standing outside a small, seedy shop on the corner of two rather drab looking streets in a residential area of the town. Quite how Craig had found it was beyond me. It was nowhere near the caravan site or the beach.

We all trooped in, heads bowed, Craig eventually nudging Shane towards the counter where an assistant stood watching us with interest.

"Three cans of Heineken please," said Shane in as deep a voice as he could muster.

The man looked him up and down. "How old are you sonny?" he asked, knowing full well that any answer he was about to receive was surely going to be a lie.

"Eighteen?" said Shane hopefully.

The assistant walked to the end of the counter and peered out of the window, as if in search of some hidden policemen who might have his shop under observation. Then, apparently satisfied, he turned back to Shane. "Behind you," he said, pointing.

Shane picked up three cans and put them on the counter.

"One pound fifty," said the man.

"That's a bit much isn't it?" protested Craig.

"Do you want them or not!" said the man crossly.

Reluctantly Shane delved into his pocket and pulled out a pound note and a fifty pence piece.

"And don't come back," said the man snatching the money from Shane's hand and stuffing it into the till. "And don't drink it anywhere near here."

We found our way back to the sea front and, seeing a quiet spot on the beach among some rocks, sat down and enjoyed our cans. Although, enjoy was not a word I would personally have used. I found the taste of canned lager disgusting (as did Shane), but in an effort to keep up with Craig, we swigged heartily until all three cans were emptied.

"Come on then lads," cried Craig, getting to his feet and hurling his can across the beach. "Amusements are this way."

Craig led the way, Shane picking up Craig's can and putting it in a bin along with his own as we followed.

The amusement arcade was no more than five minutes walk away but, by the time we reached it, the effects of the lager were starting to take hold of all three of us.

"Penny Cascade!" shouted Craig over the noise of the various machines. "Come on."

He made off in the direction of a large, hexagonal structure, piled high with pennies on sliding shelves. The idea of the game was to drop your own pennies down a chute and, in doing so, dislodge some that were on the edge of the shelf, sending them cascading into a winnings tray at the bottom. Well that was the theory anyway.

Craig delved into his pocket and we were surprised to see him pull out a small, plastic bag full of coins.

"I came prepared," he grinned.

Shane and I rummaged in our own pockets but didn't have anything appropriate.

"Over there," said Craig, pointing. "That bloke in the booth will change your money into ones and twos."

Shane and I crossed over to the booth and each got ourselves twenty pence worth of pennies. Just as we were about to return to Craig though, we heard a commotion coming from the direction of the Penny Cascade.

"Bloody stupid thing! It's a fix!" came the unmistakeable voice of Craig.

We turned round just in time to see him give the machine an almighty kick. However, rather than have any effect on the pennies inside, it simply caused Craig to jump back clutching at his foot and shouting in pain. "Ouch, ooh, bloody hell, my toe!

Stupid bloody machine." And with that he lunged forward and administered and almighty thump to the glass cover which smashed sending a shower of glass all over the piles of pennies.

Immediately, the man was out of his booth, shouting; "Oi! What the hell do you think you're doing?"

As he ran, he was joined by another, much larger man who had emerged from an office at the back.

"Let's get out of here," I muttered to Shane.

Seeing another door at the side of the arcade we made a run for it but not before, in my slightly inebriated state, I'd run headlong into one of many one armed bandits that were scattered randomly throughout the arcade!

Eventually, safely outside, we took in our surroundings. We'd emerged onto the bottom end of the pier.

"Come on," said Shane, leading me along the decking and well away from the amusement arcade.

We weren't far gone when we heard the sound of uneven footsteps and, turning round we were confronted by the sight of Craig, half running, half limping and clutching his tightly clenched fist. His t shirt was covered in blood, as was his hand but, in true Craig fashion, he didn't seem too perturbed.

"We've been banned!" he gasped, throwing himself down on a nearby bench.

"I'm not surprised," I said. "What were you doing back there?"

"It took all my money," complained Craig. "Bloody swizz. That's what it is. A bloody swizz!"

Shane examined Craig's hand. "You'd better get Mrs Percival to have a look at this," he said. "You might have glass in it."

"Feels alright to me," replied Craig, shrugging his shoulders.

However, on this occasion, Shane and I overruled him and the decision was made to make an immediate return to the caravan park.

It wasn't the easiest journey home. Apart from having to negotiate our way past the amusement arcade in order to get off the pier, the sight of a bloodied, limping Craig also drew considerable interest from passers by.

However, we eventually made our way back to Mum, who made full use of the first aid kit she'd thoughtfully packed.

"Oh and by the way," she concluded as she tied the final knot in the bandage that now encased Craig's hand. "Let that be a lesson to you."

"What do you mean?" I asked.

"He's been drinking again," she replied, looking at Craig. "Haven't you?"

Craig looked up at Mum but said nothing.

"Sober people don't go around smashing glass screens with their bare fists," continued Mum. "And besides, I can smell it on your breath. So tell me the truth. Have you been drinking?"

Craig nodded as Shane and I nervously exchanged glances.

"This needs to stop Craig," she said. "Because if it doesn't, we will all be going home early. It's bad enough *you* drinking. But before we know where we are you'll have these two at it."

"We tried to talk him out of it Mrs Percival," pleaded Shane, innocently.

Craig looked sulkily up at both of us but, obviously deciding not to grass us up, said nothing.

Tuesday 14ᵗʰ August - Marooned

Thankfully, having slept on it, Craig had for the moment seen the error of his ways and had promised Shane and I that he would lay off the booze for the rest of the holiday.

Relieved of the burden of having to manage Craig, I suggested a trip to the beach.

"Hey, why don't we go out to that rock," said Shane.

I immediately knew what he was referring to. We had spotted the isolated, rocky outcrop the previous day whilst on the beach. It lay some distance out but, at low tide could be reached on foot.

"Yeah, I'm up for it," I said. "Providing it's low tide. I don't fancy wading through the sea to get to it."

"Let me check for you," said Mum, picking up a small pamphlet that lay on the coffee table. "Now then. What's the date?"

"Fourteenth," we all replied in unison.

"Right. Well low tide is at 10:34 today."

"Perfect," said Shane. "What about you Craig? Are you in?"

"Yeah. Count me in," replied Craig. "You got any food we could take Mrs P?"

Mum's response was to put together a small picnic for us, comprising sandwiches, crisps, scotch eggs and cans of orangeade.

"You'll need that in case you get thirsty," she said, eyeing Craig suspiciously as she packed the cans into a small rucksack.

"Don't worry Mum. We'll keep an eye on him," I said, reassuringly.

We arrived at the beach at about half past ten, just as the day was really beginning to warm up. Although we had awoken to a clear blue sky however, it had now begun to cloud over. But it was still warm enough to sit out in t shirts and shorts.

The outcrop, which only seemed a short distance from the safety of the sea front, actually turned out to be a substantial walk away. Eventually though, we were scrambling up the landward facing edge and settling ourselves down in a kind of well in the centre. From here, we felt completely cut off. We could see the sky, which was now a uniform grey, but could see neither the town nor the sea.

Hungrily, we broke into the rucksack and started to devour its contents.

Having finished, I got up and went for a wander. There were several crevices leading out from the centre of the well, some too narrow to access but others wide enough to squeeze into and explore. In one of these I found a substantial pile of rubbish. Flotsam deposited over the years, I thought to myself. Amongst the broken pieces of wood, there was also rope, netting and several pieces of plastic whose origins I could only guess at.

As I returned, Shane pulled out a transistor radio from the front pocket of the rucksack and played with the tuning knob until finally some rather distant, distorted pop music emanated from its tiny speaker.

"The reception's no good here because of these rocks," he said. "You need to place it at the highest point to pick up the best signal."

In response, I got to my feet, took the transistor from Shane and clambered up and out of the well.

Here I stopped and looked around. "Jesus Christ!" I gasped.

"What's the matter with you?" asked Craig, lazily closing his eyes.

"I can't see the town," I replied.

The rising panic in my voice alerted Shane who scrambled up to join me.

"Sea fog," he said with authority. "It's quite common on the coast. Even on a summer's day."

It was at this point that we realised that this was the least of our problems. "Hey Snide, I don't want to alarm you any further, but I think the tide's coming in faster than we thought," said Shane.

I looked down and was horrified to see small waves splashing around the base of the outcrop.

"We'd better get back before it gets too deep," said Shane. "Hey Craig. Come on. We've got to go."

Craig was soon at our side.

"Hang on," he began. "Which way is the town?"

"It's that way," I said pointing blindly into the fog.

"I don't think it is. It's that way isn't it?" countered Shane, pointing in an entirely different direction. "What do you think Craig?"

Craig stood up, hands on hips, looking one way then another, then leaned forward as if, in doing so, he would be able to see through the fog better. Finally he raised both his hands in the air. "I dunno," he said, dejectedly.

"OK. This is what we do," said Shane. "We don't panic. Sea fog often only lasts a short time. So we wait for the fog to lift. Then we get off here."

"But what if the water's too deep?" I asked.

"Then we swim," replied Shane. "It's only a couple of hundred yards."

The blood drained from my face as I felt a rising panic grip me.

"Come on Snide," continued Shane. "It's not far. We could manage that. We'd have to leave the rucksack and radio here and pick it up tomorrow at low tide."

"But I can't swim!" I interrupted.

Shane looked at me in disbelief. "What do you mean, you can't swim?"

"What I mean is I CAN'T SWIM!" I shouted.

"How come?" asked Craig.

"I still haven't learned," I confessed. "I've been trying for years, but I'm afraid of the water."

"Is that why you never used to come swimming with us?" asked Craig.

I nodded. "It was one of the reasons. You see, the thing is, when I was six I nearly drowned. I was on holiday with my mum and dad in Worthing. I went into the sea on my own and suddenly I couldn't find the bottom with my feet. I panicked and splashed about for a bit and swallowed a load of sea water. Then a wave caught me and pushed me back in and I found my footing again. Ever since then I've just been afraid to go anywhere out of my depth."

"Bloody hell!" exclaimed Craig. "So what are we going to do? I'm getting cold now."

As if on cue, the wind began to pick up.

Then the rain started. It was only a few spots at first but, within minutes, it was falling steadily. With nothing to protect us, we returned to the hollow and instinctively huddled together.

We sat for some time saying nothing. Gradually, the rain became heavier and the wind picked up further.

"I'm going to see if the fog's lifted," said Shane at length. He climbed back to the top of the outcrop and shouted down; "It's cleared a bit. I can just about see the town now."

Immediately, we joined him. Although it was fairly indistinct through the mist, we could now just about make out the beach and, beyond it, the esplanade.

"I'm going for help," said Shane, beginning to scramble down the rock face. As he reached the bottom, he carefully lowered himself into the water. Then he waded a few steps (at least he was still in his depth, I thought to myself) before throwing himself forward into the water and starting to swim towards shore.

Thankfully there were no currents along this part of the coastline and Shane was a strong swimmer. We watched as he made his way steadily towards the beach, standing up every so often before relaunching himself with renewed vigour.

At last, we saw him wade out on to the sand then make a bee line towards an indistinct group of people, promenading along the sea front.

Despite the distance and the obscuring rain, we could just about make out that, having caught their attention, he was now pointing in our direction.

Then one of the party ran to a phone box a short distance away.

"I need to get warm," moaned Craig. He slithered back down into the well, out of the wind, and started doing exercises.

I joined him. "You know what Snide," he said. "If we could find something to burn, we could start a fire."

"What would we light it with?" I asked.

Craig pulled a box of matches out of his pocket. "The only thing your mum didn't confiscate," he said, smiling grimly.

"Hang on a minute," I said. "I found a load of old wood and stuff earlier. We could burn that."

I led him to the crevice and we hauled anything we considered flammable back to the centre of the well.

"We need kindling to get it going," said Craig, expertly.

He rummaged in the rucksack and pulled out a pile of paper napkins my mum had thoughtfully included in the picnic. Screwing them up, he made a neat pile, then laid the driest wood over the top.He lit a match and the pile of napkins burst into flames.

However, just as it was producing enough heat to ignite the wood, the flames started to die down again.

"We need more," said Craig.

In response I ran back to the crevice. Here I picked up anything I could find that was sheltered enough from the rain to still be dry. Quickly, I returned with a coil rope, netting and some dry seaweed I'd found clinging to the rock.

"Quickly!" shouted Craig. "Before it dies!"

Without hesitation, I hurled my collection of kindling onto the now smouldering remains of the napkins.

At first, nothing happened. "It's no use," I said, dejectedly.

"No hold on!" cried Craig. "Look."

As he did so, we saw a small flame run along the edge of the dried seaweed. Then slowly, miraculously, it began to take hold, spreading first to the netting, which burnt out almost immediately, then to the rope, which burned with far more intensity.

"Pile some kindling onto that," said Craig pointing.

Immediately, I picked some small pieces of dry wood and expertly stacked them over the burning rope, still allowing enough air for the fire to breathe.

Slowly but surely the fire increased in intensity. Soon there was enough heat to pile on some larger pieces of wood. Then, with the damper pieces being dried out nicely by the heat of the blaze, these too were placed on top.

"We've got Eric to thank for teaching us this!" cried Craig.

"Nice one Eric!" I shouted into the air.

As the fire continued to increase in intensity, we sat down, warming and drying ourselves.

In fact, we were so enthralled by our survival skills that we didn't at first hear the distant drone of an outboard motor engine. As it got louder, it was Craig who first took heed.

"What's that noise !" he said, standing up.

We made our way back up to the top to see a bright orange boat of the RNLI making its way across the bay towards us.

As it pulled in close, we carefully made our way down onto the lowest rocks.

"Which one of you is the non swimmer?" shouted a man dressed in a bright yellow oilskin. I raised my hand sheepishly.

"Right, stay there. I'll come to you."

Having both been kitted out in life jackets, Craig and I were safely loaded onto the boat which immediately headed for dry land.

"And in future," said the man. "Stay away from that rock. The tide comes in really fast in these parts. Do you understand?"

"Yes," I said.

"Yeah, soz," added Craig.

As we reached the beach, we could make out the figure of Shane, wrapped up in a blanket, drinking a steaming mug of tea.

Having been given permission to disembark, we waded ashore and Craig started to sing at the top of his voice:

Oh Shaney is our hero,
Oh Shaney is our hero,
Trala, la, la, trala, la, la

In response, Shane clasped his hands above his head in the style of a champion boxer.

"It's a shame really," said Craig, turning to me. "But I'm about to wipe that smile of his face."

"What do you mean?" I asked.

"I just realised," replied Craig. "We've left his bloody transistor radio behind!"

Saturday 18th August - Happy Families

Mum decided to keep a closer eye on us after the lifeboat incident.

This wasn't too difficult though as the weather closed in on Tuesday evening and we were confined to the caravan for the next couple of days by rain.

Mum had suggested we go to the amusement arcade but Shane managed to talk her out of that idea without revealing the real reason why we couldn't set foot on the premises.

Eventually, following two days of unbroken rainfall, Mum announced that she was taking us out for an evening meal at a local steak house.

The evening passed very much as expected. Craig ate everything that was put in front of him, including an entire bowl of salad! Shane seemed more interested in ingratiating himself to my Mum than eating anything.

From my point of view, I felt relieved that the whole evening was passing without incident.

That was until Steve turned up late on in the evening with Rachel.

As soon as they entered the restaurant, they spotted us and came over.

My heart sank.

"Well, hello. Fancy seeing you all here," said Steve smiling at Mum. Rachel said nothing.

"Hi Steve. Hello Rachel," replied Mum. "How lovely to see you both. What brings you here?"

"Hmmm. I wonder," muttered Craig under his breath.

Spotting two empty seats at the end of our table, Steve sat himself and Rachel down. "We just fancied a late supper, didn't we Rachel?"

Rachel nodded gloomily.

"How are you enjoying your holiday?" asked Mum. "The weather's been awful the last couple of day's hasn't it?"

"Yes but the forecast for tomorrow is good," replied Steve, beckoning to a waiter. "Rachel and I were thinking of going down to the beach."

"Well, best make the most of it whilst the weather's good," said Mum.

"Hey!" cried Steve clapping his hands together. "Why don't you join us? We could all go down together."

"What a lovely idea," replied Mum. "What do you think boys?"

Shane looked disapprovingly at Steve. Craig looked at me and raised his eyebrows.

"Yeah OK," I said unenthusiastically.

"What do you think Rachel?" asked Steve.

Rachel smiled weakly but said nothing.

Our respective reactions, however, seemed entirely lost on Mum. "Right then. It's a date," she said firmly.

"You need to keep an eye on him Snide," hissed Craig, pulling me to one side. "Did you see Rachel's smile then. That was out of fear. The mouth may have been smiling, but the eyes weren't. I told you, he's a bully. You wait and see. He'll have your mum under his spell before you know it. Then you'll be out of the picture. I can promise you that."

Overhearing Craig, Shane interrupted. "Craig's right. He's far too smarmy for my liking. Your mum deserves better than that."

I felt quite helpless as, for the remainder of the evening, I watched Mum hang on to Steve's every word, lapping up his compliments and laughing at his feeble jokes. I immediately felt resentful. A far as I was concerned, there was no way he was going to worm his way into our lives.

However, what I could really do about it, I wasn't at all sure.

In the short term, I had to negotiate my way through a day on the beach in his fatuous company. Still, at least Rachel would be with us. Maybe, I thought, if she felt the same way, she might be able to help me ensure that this holiday dalliance went no further.

The next morning, Mum was all of a flap.

"Hurry up boys!" she urged. "Steve and Rachel will be here soon and you're nowhere near ready."

Her comment couldn't have been better timed as there was a knock on the caravan door. Mum rushed over to open it.

"Hello Steve," she beamed. "We're nearly ready. Hello Rachel dear. Come on then boys. Hurry up! Hurry up!"

Having finally got ourselves sorted out, we followed behind at a distance as Mum and Steve led the way to the beach. After a while, Rachel, dropped back to join us.

"Alright Rach," said Craig cheerfully. "Should be a good laugh today. You coming in the sea?"

"Well I wasn't planning on swimming," replied Rachel, eyeing him suspiciously.

"Why's that then? Are you like Snide - can't swim?" enquired Craig, mockingly.

"What the lady means," interrupted Shane. "Is that she doesn't want to go swimming. She's got better things to do with her time. Isn't that right Rachel?"

"Hmm, something like that," replied Rachel, dismissively. "What about you Snide? What do you fancy doing?"

"Dunno," I said.

As we walked on, making casual conversation, I couldn't help but notice that some sort of competition appeared now to be taking place between Craig and Shane. The aim seemed to be to win the attention of Rachel although, in reality, both were failing dismally.

As we reached the beach, Steve made a big issue of selecting the best spot for us to sit.

"Over here, the sand is driest, plus it's close to the café and ice cream parlour," he said. "Also, we have the benefit of a wind break in the shape of these rocks."

"Well I don't mind," said Mum.

"What about you?" Said Steve, suddenly turning to face me. "Do you like it here?" He paused. "I'm sorry but I'm not really happy calling you Snide. What's your real name?"

"Oh sorry Steve," laughed Mum. "He doesn't like using his real name, but I'm sure he won't mind me telling you will you C..."

"Yes, here is fine," I interrupted. "Don't you think so Shane?" I continued, my voice taking on a ludicrously, exaggerated manner. "I mean to say. It's out of the wind, close to the ice cream parlour and the pier. An excellent choice all round. I couldn't have come up with a better place myself."

Mum, picking up on the sarcasm in my voice, shot me a withering glance.

"Well that's splendid then," said Steve. And as he did so, I couldn't help recalling Craig's words from the night before. Although he was smiling, something in his face told me that his friendliness wasn't at all genuine. It was simply a case of him doing the right thing to please Mum.

Nevertheless, we busied ourselves, staking a claim to our small piece of territory on the beach. Shane, seemingly having given up on Mum, rushed to help Rachel put out her towel, much to Craig's annoyance.

"Here. What's your game?" hissed Craig.

"What do you mean?" answered Shane. I'm just helping the lady with her towel.

"The lady?" snarled Craig. "God you're so up your own backside sometimes."

"Oh grow up!" snapped Shane.

Ignoring the pair of them, Rachel turned to me. "Fancy going down to the sea?" she asked.

I nodded.

"Er, hold on there," interrupted Steve. "How about you boys coming with me to get an ice cream. Now what does everybody want?"

Rachel pulled a face then plonked herself down on the towel.

Having taken everyone's orders, we obediently followed Steve on to the promenade where the ice cream parlour was located.

As we joined the queue, he turned to face the three of us. "You boys like my daughter don't you," he said.

"Yeah, she's cool," replied Craig.

"Hmm, and the rest," continued Steve. "I couldn't help noticing you buzzing round her like bees around a honey pot."

We could have taken this comment quite lightly, but there was something about the manner in which he spoke and his body language that made us all feel uncomfortable.

Nothing more was said and, having bought our ice creams, we walked back to the beach in silence.

Mum looked first at me, then at Craig and Shane. "Is everything OK?" she asked, frowning.

I nodded meekly. "Yeah, we're fine," I muttered.

Mum took one last enquiring look at me then turned her attention back to Steve.

"Are you coming down to the sea then?" Rachel asked me hopefully.

"Maybe in a bit," I replied, looking carefully at the two adults, who were now deep in conversation. "Let's just have our ice creams first."

And so the tone was set for the rest of the day. Rachel, obviously feeling she'd been rebuffed by me, kept herself to herself whilst Craig, Shane and I went off together for a while, returning only when we got hungry.

As for Mum and Steve, they made the decision to go for lunch together, leaving the four of us behind on the beach.

"Here's a pound," said Steve, handing Rachel a crumpled note. "Get yourself and the boys something to eat. But stay together. Don't go wandering off anywhere. Do you understand?"

"Yes dad," replied Rachel, sighing.

As we watched the retreating figures of Mum and Steve, Craig looked at me. "I told you," he said. "You won't get a look in now."

As it turned out, Mum and Steve were gone far longer than any of us had expected. And with Craig, Shane and I now roped into babysitting Rachel, it made for a boring afternoon. To make matters worse, it clouded over during the afternoon and, as the wind picked up, it began to rain again.

We had just made the decision to return to the caravan park and face the consequences when Mum and Steve reappeared. It was obvious from Mum's manner that she'd had more than just food.

"Hiya boys!" she cried, waving her arms in the air. I would have been more embarrassed but, by this point the beach was virtually deserted.

"We're going back to the caravan," I announced, moodily packing up the towels and shoving them into our brightly coloured beach bag.

"Yes, well it is starting to rain," added Steve, dismissively. "Rachel, did you have some change from that pound?"

Rachel delved into the small pocket at the front of her rucksack and produced the twenty pence we had left over from our four cones of chips. Steve examined the small pile of coins closely then pocketed it.

Back at the camp site we waved goodbye to Steve and Rachel and I finally had Mum to myself.

"Mum?"

"Yes dear?"

"You know Steve?"

"Oh don't worry about him darling, he's just a friend. Nothing more than that. Well, how could it be? He lives up the other end of the country."

I felt a surge of relief. It all made sense. Even if Mum really liked him, it couldn't go anywhere. Not with him living so far away.

"Of course, we could go up and visit from time to time," continued Mum, dreamily.

My heart sank. "But Mum, he's a bully!" I argued. "He controls Rachel."

"Whassat?" asked Mum. "What nonsense. Of course he doesn't. He's just concerned for her safety. You know he's a widower. He's already lost one person he loves. He just worries about losing another."

Realising I wasn't going to make any headway with her, I fell in with Craig and Shane.

"She's already under his spell," said Craig. "You need to make her see him as he really is before this holiday is out."

And I couldn't help feeling that he was right.

Monday 20th August - Time on Our Own

Sunday was another wet day but it gave me the chance to reflect on the holiday so far. Mum had organised it as a chance for me to have a good time to help get over my dad leaving.

In reality though, it was turning out to be a case of me fighting a rear guard action against someone who seemed hellbent on replacing him.

True, if we did keep in touch after the holiday, it would give me more of a chance to get to know Rachel, who I genuinely liked. But the pay off would be Steve worming his way into our lives and I couldn't stand for that.

I thought long and hard about what Craig had said, but couldn't come up with any satisfactory way of getting mum to see Steve as he really was. As Craig had put it "Your mum thinks the sun shines out of his backside."

However, the next morning an opportunity arose totally out of the blue.

I'd wandered down to the camp site store on my own for no particular reason, when I bumped into Rachel.

"Hi Snide," she said, obviously pleased to see me.

"What you up to?" I asked.

"Nothing much. Just wanted to get some fresh air," she replied.

"Yeah, your dad can be a bit overpowering," I said.

Rachel laughed. "You don't know the half of it. He's so possessive."

"You know he warned us off on Saturday," I continued.

"When?"

"When we went to buy ice creams."

Rachel sighed. "That's not the first time, I can tell you. I'm fed up with it to be honest. A boy only has to look at me and he comes barging in. And he can be quite scary sometimes."

"I tell you what, do you fancy a walk down the beach?" I suggested, a germ of an idea forming in my head.

"What now?" replied Rachel, looking rather surprised.

"Yeah now."

"Do you know what?" said Rachel, emphatically. "I think I do!"

We wandered down to the beach through the sand dunes. It was a perfect morning - probably the best weather we'd had so far on the holiday. A warming sun beamed down from a cloudless sky, drying the rain soaked sand beneath our feet.

"So you've never had a boyfriend?" I asked.

"Never. I've had a few boys I get on well with at school but I've never dared bring them home cos of Dad. What about you?"

"I had a brief fling last summer with a girl called Abigail. She wasn't much to look at though. Anyway, we got off at a party and . . "

"Got off?" interrupted Rachel. "What do you mean, kissing and stuff?"

I hesitated. "Yeah, that sort of thing," I replied. "But she got really heavy and I couldn't handle it. I mean I didn't even fancy her."

"So why did you get off with her then?"

"Cos she wanted me to. And the thing was, I used to have really bad acne, so she was like the first girl ever to show any interest in me."

"You had acne?" cried Rachel, in surprise. "I don't believe it!" She stopped and studied my face closely. "How did you get rid of it?"

"I'm on this medication," I answered. "I think they're like mild antibiotics. I have to take one a day. They've worked a treat though."

"They sure have," said Rachel, still studying my face.

I felt myself blush. "Shall we sit in the sand dunes out of the wind?" I suggested.

In reply Rachel threw herself face down in the sand and rolled onto her back. I knelt down next to her, feeling a surge of adrenaline coursing through my veins.

We looked at each other and for a moment, I felt an overwhelming urge to kiss her. Then, picking up on my body language, Rachel suddenly sat up and turned away.

I wasn't sure whether it was through fear of her dad or that I had totally misread her intentions but, sensing she had become ill at ease, I changed the subject.

"Nice here isn't it?"

"Snide," began Rachel. "I really like you but . . . well, you know. With your mum getting on so well with my dad, well it's all a bit complicated isn't it? I mean to say, if they ended up getting married, we'd be step brother and sister wouldn't we?"

"Married?" I cried out, my voice rising in panic.

Rachel turned back to face me and seeing my expression, burst out laughing. Then, realising the absurdity of my reaction I did the same.

We spent what seemed like ages sitting there amongst the marram grass, just talking and I guess it must have been getting on for lunch time when we returned to our caravan.

"Where the hell have you been!" snapped Craig as we walked in.

"Just went for a walk," I answered.

"Yeah and left me here on my own."

"Well you had Shane with you."

"No I didn't, he went shopping with your Mum. Bloody do-gooder."

"Yes and very helpful he was too," shouted Mum from the kitchen.

We were interrupted by a sudden hammering on our caravan door. Then without waiting for a reply, it was thrown open and there stood Steve.

"Rachel, where have you been?" he shouted, spotting his daughter.

Rachel's demeanour changed immediately. "I just went for a walk down the sand dunes. It's OK, I was with Snide."

"It is not OK!" shouted Steve angrily. "I didn't know where you were. I've been looking everywhere for you. I even came round here but nobody was in."

I looked over at Craig who half smiled at me and shrugged his shoulders.

"Sorry Steve but we were out shopping," said Mum, calmly.

"Well he obviously wasn't!" snapped Steve, pointing an accusatory finger at me. "He was out, romping in the sand dunes, trying to seduce my little girl."

"Now hold on a minute," said Mum, her voice taking on a harder edge. "If my son wants to go for an innocent walk with your daughter then that's perfectly acceptable to me. After all they are fifteen years old."

"Innocent walk?" snorted Steve. "My God you're bloody naïve."

"What do you mean?" retorted Mum, angrily.

"Well, I should have expected it really," continued Steve. "I mean look at the company your son keeps. One looks like he's been dragged up in the back streets and as for him!" Here he pointed at Shane. "Whatever were you thinking taking the likes of him on holiday with you?"

"Are you referring to the fact that he is black?" asked Mum, incredulously. "Because if you are then I think . . "

"Come on Rachel, we're leaving," said Steve, ignoring Mum and grabbing his daughters hand, pulling her towards the door.

"Sorry Rachel," I muttered as she was led out.

Mum shut the door firmly.

"Well!" she exclaimed. "Fancy behaving like that. Who on earth does he think he is? I can't believe it!"

"I can," said Craig, under his breath.

Mum, obviously shellshocked by the whole incident, returned to the kitchenette, followed closely by the ever helpful Shane.

"Job done?" said Craig, smirking at me.

"Mission accomplished," I confirmed.

And we high fived.

Tuesday 21st August - Revelations

The next morning, with the fine weather looking to continue, Craig, Shane and I had returned to the sand dunes with the intention of spending some time lazily soaking up the sunshine.

"You got lucky there," said Craig, referring to the incident the previous day with Steve.

"Yeah. I don't think Mum wants anything to do with him any more," I said.

"I'm telling you," continued Craig. "You really dodged a bullet with that one. He's just like Jim was when he met my mum."

"Really?"

"Yeah. The first time Mum brought him home, he was all over her - compliments and all that stuff. Then he started buying her gifts. He even bought me stuff. He got me that ghetto blaster. I thought he was great. I was too young to understand then what he was really like.

"The drinking was the first thing I noticed. That's when I started to feel uncomfortable. Cos it wasn't only him drinking - it was Mum as well. They used to get totally wrecked and left me to my own devices. Sometimes they'd go down the pub and leave me on my own. Other times it was booze bought in from the off licence. It always ended the same way though. I might as well have not been there.

"Then came the arguments. They always started after a long drinking session. Usually it was after I'd gone to bed. They'd wake me up, screaming at each other. I used to lie there thinking, why do they drink if this is how it always ends up? And they'd be arguing about the most stupid things. Like one of them had made a comment in passing and the other one had blown it out of all proportion. Then they'd both fight to the death over it. It was like they were different people.

"Then one night, everything changed." Here Craig paused, deep in thought.

By now Shane and I were fully focused on his story. We had never heard Craig talk like this and, although we had always suspected much about his home life, he'd never told us about it in any detail.

"Jim had had a real skinful down the pub with his mates. I was still up when he got in and Mum was dead angry with him. Anyway, she started on him and he just blew up in her face. Next thing i knew, she'd lashed out at him and scratched his face with her fingernails."

He paused again, collecting his thoughts.

"Go on," said Shane, softly.

"Well he exploded," said Craig, his voice quivering now. "Beat her up. Right in front of my eyes. Punched her in the face, knocked her to the floor . . . kicked her in the stomach." He sniffled and allowed a tear to run down his cheek.

"Then he turned on me. He didn't hit me. Not that time anyway. Just told me to go to my room.

"I didn't sleep that night. I felt sure that Mum would get rid of him, like she'd done with all the others who'd turned nasty. But she didn't. The next morning, they'd made up. Mum said it was just the drink talking. So they carried on."

"Jesus Christ!" I muttered.

"Then a few days later," said Craig. "It happened again. This time I tried to protect her and got a black eye for my troubles. But again they made up."

"But your mum threw him out in the end didn't she?" said Shane.

"Yeah, but not until after he'd given both of us a good few beatings," replied Craig. "She threw him out three times in all, but each time, after a few weeks they'd make up again and be all lovey dovey."

"But it's stopped now," I said. "Hasn't it?"

"Yeah. Mum gave him a final ultimatum. If he touched us ever again, that would be it."

"And he's stuck to it?" asked Shane.

"So far," replied Craig. "But I still don't trust him. And he's still drinking. It's only a matter of time."

"But they're getting married aren't they?" I said.

"They said they were. But there's no date yet. Hopefully, she'll throw him out first."

We sat in silence taking all of this in.

"So if you've seen what drink does to those two, why do you drink?" asked Shane.

Craig dried his eyes on his t shirt. "I don't know why. I just do. Everything feels better after a drink."

"I feel sorry for Rachel though," I said. "It's not fair the way *he* controls her."

"She'll be alright," said Shane. "She's tough. I can recognise that in her."

"Oh and what makes you such an expert with your privileged life," snapped Craig. "You've never suffered."

"Really?" replied Shane, sharply. "So having to put up with irrational abuse and prejudice every day just because of the colour of my skin is okay is it? You heard what Steve said yesterday about you all hanging out with *the likes of me*. I get crap like that all the time.

" What about last year when I got sacked from my job at the shoe shop because someone falsely accused me of stealing money from the till? And I've lost count of the number of times that, when us three have got into trouble, it's always *me* they tell off, as if you two weren't even a part of it.

"But you have to be tough and learn to live with it. And hope that one day, people's attitudes will change."

"Soz Big Man," said Craig, looking awkwardly away.

"I'm not belittling what you've just told us Craig, but we've all got baggage to carry round with us. Even Snide. I mean it must be tough on you losing your dad, eh Snide?"

"It was certainly a shock," I answered truthfully. "And with Steve, I don't think it was so much that I was worried about him being a bad person. It was more to do with me not wanting anybody to replace my dad. I don't want anybody to do that. Not yet anyway."

"At least you know who your dad is," said Craig. "I've never even met mine."

We sat in silence for some time, watching the waves roll in.

"Come on boys," said Shane, eventually. "Let's get back to the caravan."

"Yeah I'm starving," added Craig. "Shane. Can I ask you a favour?"

"Certainly Craig."

"Can we go back to that off licence tomorrow?"

"But you promised not to drink again this holiday," I protested.

"I know, but talking about it just now. . . Just one can. Your mum wouldn't know Snide. We could have one each, take them down the beach. What do you say?"

Shane and I looked at each other.

"Just the one?" said Shane, warily.

"Just the one," confirmed Craig.

"Maybe," said Shane. "We'll see how it goes tomorrow."

Wednesday 22nd August - The Accident

On our return to the caravan, Craig had managed to persuade Shane to buy some beer for the beach but, the following morning it didn't seem to be quite such a wise idea. Craig's recount of his home life, rather than helping him come to terms with it seemed, in the short term at least, to have destabilised him even further.

I recognised the symptoms as soon as we got up. He was very loud and hyperactive. So much so that at one point Mum even pulled me to one side to ask if he was OK.

Shane and I, concerned how the day might unfold, held an emergency conflab on the grass in front of the caravan.

"Is it really wise giving him beer, the mood he's in today?" I asked.

"Yeah, but I already promised him," replied Shane. "If I say no now, it might make him worse. Besides a couple of cans of beer might quieten him down."

We couldn't have been more wrong!

Having told Mum we were off to the beach for the day, we made a bee line for the off licence and bought a four pack, giving two to Craig and keeping one each back for ourselves for the beach.

Rather than wait, though Craig broke into his first can immediately on leaving the shop - much to the annoyance of the assistant who gesticulated through the window for us to clear off.

We hadn't reached the bottom of the street before Craig had finished it and was opening his second.

By the time we got to the sea front, this had also been consumed and the empty can dispatched into the gutter.

"Come on boys," shouted Craig, manically. "Let's get to the beach and pull some birds!"

Alarmed by the volume of his voice, several passers by had begun to turn around and stare at him. In response, Shane and I pushed on ahead, pretending we weren't with him.

"I've got the whole world in my hands!" sang Craig, loudly, spreading his arms in the air like the wings of a soaring eagle.

I looked at Shane in embarrassment.

In response, Shane buried his head in his chest and began to walk even faster in order to put some distance between himself and the drunken lout that was now pursuing him.

What happened next only took a few seconds but has remained firmly etched into my memory ever since. I once read that what we perceive as long term memories are in fact re-remembered every time they are revisited. In doing so we actually remember our most recent memory of the event, not the original event itself. In this way, most memories become modified over the years.

This is not true however, in the case of traumatic events. And it was a traumatic event that was about to unfold in front of my eyes right at that moment. Quite why I turned back to face Craig , I don't know. Maybe it was premonition. But, having done so, I was just in time to see him catch his shoe on the raised edge of an uneven paving slab.

If he had been sober, I feel quite sure he would have recovered his balance. But in his inebriated state he fell. However, rather than fall forward, for some inexplicable reason, he lurched sideways and staggered into the road.

There was a screech of brakes followed by a sickening thud. Then Craig lay sprawled on the tarmac. The driver leapt from the car and ran to his aid. "I couldn't do anything!" he cried. "He just appeared in front of me. I couldn't stop in time."

Shane and I ran over and knelt down beside Craig. He lay immobile, his legs twisted in one direction, his head in the other. A small trickle of blood ran from his mouth.

"Craig? Craig!" shouted Shane. "Snide. Go and fetch your Mum."

"But the caravan park's miles away," I protested.

"Then run!" shouted Shane.

Confused, I tried to find my bearings then ran blindly in the direction of the caravan park.

It's amazing how, under the influence of adrenaline, the body can perform extraordinary feats. And so it was that within the space of a few minutes minutes, I'd run the full mile or so back to the caravan and was banging on he door, screaming at Mum for help.

Fortunately the owner of the site overheard the rumpus and offered to drive us back down to the scene of the accident. As we tried to pull out of the gates, we were stopped in our tracks by an ambulance, its blue lights flashing, hurtling down the country lane in the direction of the sea front. Tucking in behind it, we followed it all the way to what was now a scene of confusion.

A large crowd had gathered around and were being moved back by two policemen. Shane had also been moved away but, spotting us, pushed his way through to meet us.

"He's still alive," he said. "He stopped breathing at one point. We all thought he was dead, but a policeman gave him the kiss of life."

I stared at Shane dumbfounded, hardly able to take in what was happening.

In front of us, the police had pushed the crowd apart to allow the ambulance to get nearer to Craig. Two men jumped out and pulled out a stretcher. Then carefully moving Craig onto it they carried him round to the back where a lady had opened the doors.

Mum immediately pushed her way through.

"He's with me," she blurted out.

"Are you his mother?" asked the lady, frowning.

"No, but he's on holiday with me, my son and his friend."

"So you're responsible for him then."

"Yes."

The lady made sure the stretcher was secure then paused, leaning over and sniffing the air in front of Craig's face. Then she turned her attention back to Mum. "How old is this boy?" she asked, sternly.

"Fifteen," answered Mum.

"Did you know he'd been drinking?"

A look of horror swept across Mum's face. Then she turned to me.

"It was my fault, Mrs Percival," said Shane. "I bought him the beer. We just wanted to cheer him up."

By now, we had been joined by one of the policeman.

"Did you say you bought him beer?" he asked.

"Yes," replied Shane, guiltily.

"And how old are you, son?"

"Fifteen," said Shane, staring at the floor.

"Well if you don't mind madam," the policeman said to Mum. "I think we will need to continue this conversation down at the station."

Mum was about to reply when the policeman held his hand up. "Not now of course. I'm sure you'll all want to be accompanying this boy to the hospital. But if you wouldn't mind dropping by at the police station before you return home." He handed Mum an official looking piece of paper with some details on.

"Thank you officer," said the ambulancewoman, giving him a knowing look. "You three had better come in the back with us."

We all climbed aboard and soon we were off.

Once at the hospital, Craig, still unconscious, was carried into the casualty unit and put onto a trolley. After a short wait, a doctor appeared and gave him a thorough examination.

Having satisfied himself that he had seen all he needed to, he had a few quiet words with a nurse, who wheeled Craig away.

"Mrs err . . Percival," he began. "Craig has suffered a nasty blow to his head. He almost certainly has concussion. We're taking him down to the x-ray department now to check if he has any broken bones. More concerningly, he stopped breathing for several minutes after the accident. It was only the quick thinking of one of the policemen on duty that saved his life. Nevertheless, the length of time he spent without oxygen is worrying. It may have resulted in brain damage. There's no way of knowing until he comes round . . if he comes round at all. In the meantime, I suggest you go back to your holiday home and wait. We have the phone number of the site so we can call if there are any developments. Visiting hour is seven o'clock. If you ask at reception, they will tell you which ward he is in."

"Can't we stop with him until he comes round?" asked Mum.

"I'm afraid it's not hospital policy," replied the doctor dismissively. "After all, you're not actually his mother. We'll let you know if there's any news." And with that he tucked his clipboard under his arm and marched off.

The rest of the morning was spent dealing with the fallout from Craig's accident. First we paid a visit to the police station where Shane and I were made to give the address of the off licence who sold us the beer. Shane himself was cautioned for buying beer whilst under the age of eighteen but, much to our relief, the policemen informed us that the matter wouldn't be taken any further. Then, having got Craig's home address from us, arrangements were made for a local policeman in Streetside to inform Craig's mother.

We hung around the caravan for the rest of the day, waiting for news. And when it did come, we were relieved that it was all good. Craig had regained consciousness without any apparent brain damage - although tests were still being carried out. Otherwise he'd received no broken bones, only a badly bruised hip and thigh at the point where the car had struck him.

So it was with some relief that we took a taxi back to the hospital in time for visiting hour.

Watchbourne Hospital was only small, what would be described as a cottage hospital. So having spoken with reception, we didn't have too much difficulty in locating Craig's bed.

When we got there however, we were surprised to see a bespectacled man wearing a dog collar sitting beside the bed, deep in conversation with Craig.

Spotting us, Craig waved weekly. "Snidey!" he cried out. "I survived."

The man got to his feet and shook Mum warmly by the hand.

"My name is John Childs," he said. "I'm the hospital chaplain. I've just been chatting to Craig."

"Is he alright?" asked Mum. "They were worried about brain damage because he stopped breathing for so long."

"That's what I wanted to talk to you about actually," said the chaplain. He paused, as if collecting his thoughts. "Mrs Percival. It would appear that Craig has had some form of near death experience."

"Near death . . . experience?" repeated Mum, slowly. "What do you mean?"

"Maybe I should allow Craig to explain," replied the chaplain. "I'll come back to visit you tomorrow Craig, good night for now. May God bless you all. And with that, he left.

"What did he mean by a near death experience?" asked Mum.

"It's all true Mrs Percival," said Craig, beaming seraphically at her. "I've seen the light." Here he stopped to laugh. "What I mean is, I have literally seen the light."

Mum, Shane and I all looked at him perplexed.

"It was the most amazing thing," continued Craig. "The moment I hit the road, it was as though I'd been thrown clear out of my body. I was looking down on myself. I saw you two kneeling down beside me but I felt no pain. Only warmth, like someone had wrapped me up in a blanket.

"That was when I saw the light. It was like a long tunnel, with a bright light at the end of it. I've never felt so at peace in my whole life. Then I heard His voice!"

"Whose voice dear?" asked Mum.

"God!" laughed Craig. "God spoke to me. He told me not to worry, that my time hadn't come yet. He said that I still had much work to do here."

A voice interrupted us. "Mrs Percival?"

We turned to see a doctor examining the clipboard at the end of Craig's bed.

"We're going to need to keep the boy in for a couple more days for observation. He's quite heavily sedated at the moment."

"He said that God spoke to him," said Mum.

"Ah yes," replied the doctor. "Probably a side effect of the drugs. I wouldn't worry about it. I'm sure he'll be back to normal in a couple of days."

But, as we were about to find out in the fullness of time, that couldn't have been further from the truth. The old Craig we'd known and grown to love, had gone.

Forever!

Friday 24th August - Homeward Bound

We'd all heard about near death experiences before but never met someone who had claimed to have actually had one.

Shane, who it turned out had had a far more Christian influenced upbringing than we ever realised, bought into it totally and was thrilled for Craig. Mum, being an adult was cynical and fully expected the old Craig to return once he'd recovered, as the doctor had intimated.

My view of the whole matter lay somewhere in the middle. I have always been (and still am) an agnostic and so found the whole thing fascinating.

Much more difficult for all of us though was coming to terms with the new Craig.

We returned to visit on Thursday evening to learn that Craig's mum had spoken to him on the phone. She had told him she loved him but couldn't make it to Watchbourne because it was too expensive and took too long to reach.

Before the accident, Craig would have been upset by this but, uncharacteristically he took it all in his stride. "She's right," he said. "It's a long way to come and I'm sure she trusts Mrs Percival to get me home safely."

"I feel like all of this is my fault," said Shane. "If I hadn't bought you that beer, none of this would have happened."

In response, Craig grabbed hold of Shane's wrist and squeezed it. "No worry big man. It was my fault. I pushed you into it. You only bought the beer. I didn't have to drink it, did I?"

It was the next day that the message came through via the camp site owner, that Craig had been given the all clear to go home. He was still weak, we'd been informed, but had made enough progress to be discharged.

Mum made the decision to go home straight from the hospital so we spent Friday morning packing and loading up the car before making the short journey there.

"He must take it easy for the next couple of weeks," said the doctor administering his release. "No strenuous exercise or stress. Just calm convalescence."

"No problem," said Mum, emphatically. "He'll be staying with us for the rest of the summer holiday."

I knew Mum had taken exception to the fact that Craig's mother hadn't visited, but was surprised by this.

"He's staying with us?" I echoed.

"Yes," said Mum. "Poor lad needs looking after."

So that was that. Craig did indeed spend the rest of the summer with us. For Shane and I, it gave us a chance to reboot our relationship with the 'New Improved Craig Mark II.'

For Craig, it was a whole new start. The term 'born again' could have been written specifically for him.

As 1979 merged into 1980, more and more of Craig's life centred around our local church and its associated youth group. Whatever his mum and Jim made of that, we never found out - Craig rarely mentioned them.

In the meantime, we were embarking on the most important year of our lives so far. Next summer we would be taking our exams and making decisions which would affect our entire futures.

And, as I was to find out, someone was about to enter my life who would further weaken the bonds that had held our gang together for so many years.

1980

THEN LIFE BECAME
COMPLICATED

CONTENTS

THEN LIFE BECAME COMPLICATED

When Craig had regained consciousness the previous summer, following his road accident, he had given a vivid description of having undergone some sort of near death experience, something that caught those of us present at his bedside by surprise.

I guess we all felt though that the 'Hard Man' Craig that we knew so well would resurface in the fullness of time.

But it didn't. Craig's insistence that he had briefly come face to face with his maker during the short time that his heart had stopped, remained undiminished.

Not that this was in any way a bad thing. It was just that it brought about such a huge turnaround in Craig's whole attitude to life that he became barely recognisable.

Before the accident, he had been on a downward spiral of dependency on alcohol with all of the traits of erratic behaviour and irrational emotions that accompanied it.

Shortly after leaving hospital however, Craig announced that he would never touch another drop and was instead going to treat his body with the respect that it deserved. After all, as he put it, it was God's creation.

On returning home from Watchbourne, he quickly sought out and linked up with the vicar of Streetside All Saints Church, The Reverend Tim Eastlake and became a regular churchgoer.

None of this mattered to me. He wasn't the kind of born again Christian who rammed his views down everybody's throats. He just dedicated more and more of his time to doing good deeds. Consequently, much of it revolved around the Streetside Youth Centre, which Rev Eastlake, was himself heavily involved in.

Craig's explanation for this was simple - he hadn't been given much of a start in life, as Shane and I were painfully aware. He had been neglected to a greater or lesser extent by his mother and her string of partners over the years. So he wanted to reach out to boys in similar situations and give them a place where they could come if they ever needed any form of help or support.

And it had to be said, Craig was damn good at what he did. His natural empathy for others which had suddenly emerged following his accident was instantly applied to his new charges and blossomed under the guidance of Rev Eastlake, making Craig a highly respected member of the youth team.

Not only that but in himself, he became a much calmer, happier person. The constant need for drink induced highs had gone - seemingly forever. And relieved of the burden of looking after him, Shane and I found that our friendship with the new Craig deepened.

In short, after a period of a couple of years where our gang had begun to drift apart, we now all valued each other's friendships with a new found maturity and the bond between us was as tight as ever.

Well, for a short time at least.

But of course, nothing ever stands still and developments in the spring and summer of 1980 meant that, once again the three of us found ourselves pulling off in different directions. Two of these, inevitably, involved Craig and Shane moving on to pastures new (more of which later).

The other was Amanda.

So who was Amanda?

You may well ask!

Looking back now forty years on, memories of my first proper girlfriend are remarkably sketchy.

So let me deal with the who, how, where and why details first.

Amanda was a girl in the year group below me at Streetside Comprehensive who I recognised but knew nothing of, other than that she lived two doors down from Shane. So when we bumped into each other in town it was Shane who stopped to say hello. And, after we'd all spent some time chatting, it was Shane who persuaded me to ask her out.

Why he did this, I was never quite sure. But it was undoubtedly true that we immediately hit it off.

When I finally asked Amanda out, it was a classic case of teenage angst complicating a very simple request.

Rumours had been going around school about me and Amanda for some weeks, mainly because we were spending an increasing amount of our break and lunch times in each others' exclusive company. It was true that I fancied her. I just didn't have enough confidence to think that she would reciprocate my advances. So I held my peace and convinced myself that friends was good enough . . . for the moment anyway.

Then, I guess you could say that fate threw us together. I had been held back after school by my French teacher to discuss my disappointing 'mock O level' result. Having promised to revise hard over the coming months, I walked out of a near deserted school to see Amanda. I have no recollection of why she was so late leaving but, having spotted me, she immediately fell in with me as I exited through the main gates.

"Hiya Snide!" she called.

"Hi Amanda."

I blushed, then cursed myself for doing so.

"You know there's rumours going around about us," she said, smiling sweetly at me.

"Yeah. Stupid aren't they?" I responded.

Amanda looked a little disappointed.

"I mean we do enjoy hanging out together a lot," I continued, trying desperately now to backtrack. "But, well, you know. People like to make things up."

Amanda stopped and grabbed me by the arm, pulling me into her. I looked briefly into her eyes, then nervously away.

"Come on Snide," she said softly. "Don't be shy. Tell me how you really feel."

"About what?" I asked, desperately trying to buy time to find the right words.

Amanda sighed in frustration, let go of my arm and started to walk away.

My immediate reaction was that I'd blown it. But then, something inside me snapped and I heard the words; "You know how I feel!" coming from my lips.

Amanda stopped in her tracks but didn't turn round. I chased after her and playfully grabbed her around the waist.

"So what are we going to do then?" asked Amanda, still refusing to face me.

"Dunno," I replied, dumbly. "Go out somewhere?"

That is about as much as I can remember. Except that we did start seeing each other outside school and, inevitably we became more than just friends.

As I grew to know her better though, I discovered that, although I was very attracted to her, Amanda had one fault - she was a terrible snob.

When I say snob, I don't mean, like many people did at that time, that she talked in a posh voice. I mean that she thought that people, who didn't come up to her exacting standards, were beneath her and deserving of contempt. This became something of a problem for me for two reasons. Firstly, it clashed with my ethic of treating everyone equally (my mother had brought me up never to look up to anyone or down on anyone). Secondly, and of more immediate concern, it lead to a clash of interests over Craig.

Amanda was well aware of Craig's history and background and disliked him for those very reasons. That in itself was difficult for me but, what made it a whole lot worse was that her attitude to him turning to religion was one of ridicule. "Oh no, here comes the God Squad!" was her favourite saying whenever their paths crossed.

Not only that but she was so open in her disdain for Craig even though she knew full well that he was one of my closest friends. Looking back now it almost seems as though her motive for such behaviour was jealousy. It was as if she felt that I should be basing my whole life around her, not taking time out to talk to someone who she considered to be beneath both of us.

The situation was made all the more frustrating by the fact that, whilst the old Craig would have briskly told her where to get off, the new compassionate Craig, took it all on the chin, never saying anything in retaliation.

Ultimately, Amanda's snobbery was a principle part of our break up later that year. But during those early days, I was too besotted with having a real girlfriend on my arm to do anything other than tolerate her intolerance!

Friday 25th April - The Last Day

Eleven years of education and today was going to be the very last time that all three of us would have to go to school. Well, that wasn't exactly true. I would be returning to the sixth form in September and we all still had our exams looming in front of us like an immovable obstacle. But as far as Craig, Shane and I turning up for registration at nine o'clock in the morning, this was definitely our last time.

Of course, it wasn't to be like any ordinary day. Lessons still took place, although by this stage these were mostly final pep talks from our subject teachers on revision and exam technique.

However, a Streetside Comprehensive tradition that went back to the founding of the school in 1961 decreed that on leavers day, pupils were allowed to turn up out of their usual school uniform. In the early days of the school this would no doubt have been a welcome opportunity for both boys and girls to dress down in casual clothes but, in recent years there had been a definite trend towards wearing fancy dress. And this year, we were determined to be the most outrageous year group to date.

Underhand plans had been afoot since February, although as far as we knew, the teachers were still unaware of what they were going to be confronted with at that final registration.

As luck would have it, despite being in different academic groups, Craig, Shane and myself were all in the same registration group, and had been since we started the school back in the autumn of 1975. Consequently, every morning we met up at the bottom of Shane's road, to walk to school together. This was one of the few rituals that survived even the appearance of Amanda on the scene. Despite living two doors down from Shane, she opted to continue to walk to school with friends from her own year group, although we did sometimes bump into each other at some point on the journey.

As far as today went, the three of us had decided early on to keep our fancy dress under wraps from each other. That way, we thought, it would be more fun.

I was first to arrive and felt quite pleased with my own personal get up consisting of a Tiswas t shirt, very brief running shorts (as was the fashion at the time) and a huge Mexican sombrero hat that I'd borrowed from Amanda.

Craig had opted to turn back the clock to 1977, turning up in his full punk gear, consisting of; ripped combat trousers, fluorescent green t shirt and donkey jacket with HATE written on the back. He'd even spiked up his hair. Unfortunately, Craig had grown somewhat in the last three years and his combat trousers now finished somewhere short of his ankles, although thankfully his donkey jacket now fitted him perfectly!

"What do you think Snide?" he beamed. "Have I still got it or what?"

"I'll tell you what," I laughed. "If you'd turned up last year dressed like that, they would have expelled you. But not now."

"What do you mean?" asked Craig.

"Because you're the golden boy of the fifth form now aren't you?" I said. "The reformed sinner. Beyond reproach."

Craig laughed.

"I bet Shane goes for the sophisticated look," said Craig.

"You know what," I replied. "You're probably right."

And he was! We didn't have to wait long before we saw the distant figure of Shane emerging from his house and striding down the pavement. Even from a distance we could see he was dressed in white. As he got closer we began to pick out more details.

"White jacket, black shirt and white tie with a white carnation," Craig summarised.

"And if I'm not mistaken, crisply ironed cream linen trousers," I added. "And look at his shoes. He's wearing black and white spats."

"Good morning boys," said Shane in as suave a voice as he could muster. "The name's Bond, James Bond, licensed to kill." And with that he removed his jacket and threw it over his shoulder with a flourish.

Then he looked at the two of us and his jaw dropped. "Bloody hell it's Sid Vicious and the Cisco Kid!" he exclaimed. "Aren't you cold in those shorts Snide?"

"No!" I replied, although in actual fact it was a bit chilly round my thighs.

Registration was a riot but, for once, our normally dour form master seemed to enter into the spirit of things - he was probably relieved to be getting rid of us!

As we all went off in different directions to lessons, we arranged to meet at the front gates at lunch time. As a show of trust in us as we moved towards independence, the school had allowed fifth form pupils off the premises during lunch times in the final term and that usually meant a mass exodus to the local chip shop.

Today however, we had different plans. We were going to try our luck at the local pub, The Priest and Scripture - or as it was better known locally, The Streetside Youth Club, due to its relaxed attitude to underage drinking.

I guess they didn't realise that it was our last day as the bar staff looked horrified when thirty or so sixteen year olds all in various types of fancy dress burst in through the doors.

And for once, the manager, probably worried about losing his licence, decided to clamp down on the over 18s only rule and ushered us all outside.

Temporarily at a loss, we gravitated to the beer garden and, as general confusion reigned, one boy climbed up onto a table and addressed us all. I recognised him as David Colquhoun, a boy in my maths set who I'd spoken to a few times over the years but didn't know terribly well.

"Ladies and gentlemen," he shouted. "Owing to the rather antisocial behaviour of our local landlord on this momentous day, it would seem that we are to be denied our favourite tipple. I am pleased to inform you however that this is not to be the case. Thankfully, my friends and I anticipated such a situation and have stocked up with beer and cider at my house. For those of you who don't know, I live just two doors down the road in that direction. Donations to my good self of just two pounds will buy each of you unlimited booze. That is until it runs out!"

This announcement was met by a loud cheer and soon we were all milling around in the front garden of his rather grand house, supping on cans of beer and bottles of cider. As the lunch hour wore on, small groups began to drift down towards the chip shop where the crowd eventually reformed itself on the narrow pavement outside its frontage. By now, some amongst us were getting rowdy and passers by were beginning to take notice.

It came as little surprise then, when two police cars pulled up and four angry looking policemen piled out.

"How old are you lot?" shouted one, who by way of the three stripes on the arm of his tunic, I recognised as the sergeant in charge.

Craig, who was the only one of us notably not drinking, stepped forward. "We're from Streetside Comp officer. It's our last day. We're just having a bit of fun."

The officer didn't seem to take this comment in the right spirit.

"Right you lot!" he hollered. "You're causing a nuisance. You need to go back to school now or you will be arrested for a breach of the peace."

This seemed to suddenly sober most of our peers up and, in dribs and drabs, we started to turn back towards school.

"Hold on!" shouted the policeman. "First things first. Cans in the bin. Now!"

Taking a few last desperate swigs from half empty cans and bottles, we began depositing our litter into the tiny bin provided by the chip shop.

"Right. Now, we will be escorting you straight back to the school gates," continued the policeman.

As it was, by the time we finally got back into school it was half past one and we'd all missed registration. From that point onwards, the day slowly disintegrated. Rather than attend scheduled lessons, some pupils opted to sit around in groups outside or in the cloakroom talking. One or two disappeared into the toilets, looking rather ill. Others, who hadn't left school at dinner time, took the opportunity to talk to the teachers who had been freed up, about the forthcoming exams.

Eventually, at ten to three, Mr Evans, our year group leader, rounded us all up and ushered us into the assembly hall for our final ever assembly.

This was traditionally led by the head teacher, Mr Brentworth as a sort of send off into the adult world.

We first realised that there was trouble brewing when we saw the police car parked outside the main entrance as we filed into the hall. Then when Mr Brentworth swept in, wearing his headmaster's gown, he didn't look best pleased!

What followed was a prolonged telling off about how we'd brought shame on the school with our drunken behaviour. Unfortunately, one or two of us, still feeling the effects of the beer and cider, began to giggle. This did nothing to improve the situation.

The assembly ended with a warning for all of us to go straight home and to avoid the shops. This was no doubt due to the fact that the previous fifth form, on leavers day had taken part in a huge egg and flour fight outside the local convenience store.

Unfortunately, his warning fell on deaf ears. Anticipating a backlash from last years fight and a consequent refusal by the store to sell eggs or flour to school aged children, several of our peers had stocked up beforehand and were sitting right there in the hall with their school bags stuffed with ammunition.

If only he'd known!

Consequently, as the final bell rang and Mr Brentworth ordered us to leave in an orderly manner, there was a mass rush for the exit.

Within minutes, the mother of all food fights had broken out right outside the school gates. Unfortunately, children and parents of other year groups got caught in the crossfire as cars, clothing and even passers by got covered in flour, eggs and milk!

"Could've made pancakes with all this lot," commented Craig, cryptically.

Although we knew full well about the food fight, Craig, Shane and I had made the decision to keep out of it; Craig because he disapproved of wasting food, me because I was staying on at the school's sixth form in September and feared retribution and Shane because he didn't want to get his suit dirty!

As it turned out though, it was difficult not to get involved because the school gates formed a natural bottleneck and there was no other way of getting home other than by passing through them.

Having hung back, with a number of other pupils, we were just about to risk going for it when, for the second time that day, two police cars screeched to a halt.

I recognised the first policeman to get out as the sergeant who'd escorted us back to school earlier.

With the help of his colleagues, he soon had the area clear, allowing us to exit through the gates safely.

"Well," said Craig, smirking as we made our way home. "They won't forget our year group in a hurry, will they?"

"You're not wrong there," I replied.

Saturday 10th May - A Day Out

Amanda was a bit of a culture vulture. Her favourite subject at school was English Literature. Whereas I was always primarily a writer, Amanda was a reader. And she loved to read highbrow stuff. I could never quite make out whether she gained genuine pleasure and insight from it or whether she just enjoyed the intellectual prestige of having such an in depth knowledge of classic literature.

Personally, I couldn't see anything in it. I have lost count of the number of times I have tried to revisit the works of Dickens or the Bronte sisters, only to be left cold and disappointed.

As for Shakespeare, I couldn't make head nor tail of it. I literally didn't know what the characters were talking about half the time, although I could appreciate a kind off poetic beauty in the flow of the words.

Amanda on the other hand was a Shakespeare aficionado. Even by the age of fifteen, she had read half a dozen plays and knew the basic storylines of many others. Not only that, but she was always eager to impress her love of the Bard onto anyone who might show willing and that included me.

If it had been anyone else, I'm sure I would have declined any offer of an education in Shakespeare but, because I fancied Amanda like crazy and wanted to impress her, I was a willing recipient for her tutorial advances.

Try as much as I could, I never really got past Romeo and Juliet (the text that we had studied for English literature 'O' level at school) and invariably, if the subject of Shakespeare cropped up with Amanda, I would always try to bring it back to the one and only play I had any knowledge about.

Then, quite out of the blue, Amanda produced two tickets to a production of Romeo and Juliet at The Royal Shakespeare Theatre, Stratford-Upon-Avon. It was for a matinee performance so she thought it might make the basis for a cultural day out.

Stratford-Upon-Avon was only an hour away from where we lived by train so it certainly seemed possible. Also, having been there before, I thought that it would be a lovely place to visit with Amanda, particularly with the opportunity for romantic walks along the banks of the River Avon.

My big mistake however came the following evening, when I met up with Craig and Shane down the local park.

Eric was just locking up the pavilion by the bowling green when he spotted us.

"Hey dudes," he called. "What are you up to?"

"Nothing much," shouted Craig. "Just hanging out."

"Are you still working down the Youth Centre, Craig?"

"Yeah, most nights. But it's closed Mondays."

"And what about you Snidey? Still in love with . . . err what's her name?"

"Amanda. Yeah. As a matter of fact she's taking me to the theatre on Saturday."

"Theatre?" echoed Shane and Craig, in surprise.

"I didn't know you were into all that stuff," said Shane, smirking at me. "Where are you going? The Grand in town?"

"No," I replied. "If you must know, we're going to the RSC in Stratford."

"Stratford?" repeated Craig. "That's a long way to go to see a play isn't it?"

"Yeah well we're making a day out of it," I said.

"A day out in Stratford," said Shane. "Hey Craig, what are you up to Saturday?"

"No!" I said, firmly. "It's just me and Amanda."

"Yeah I know that," said Shane. "But we could meet up for a bit. Do they still hire out rowing boats on the river?"

"I don't know. I don't think so," I lied. "Why do you want to come anyway? You'd just be in the way. And you know Amanda doesn't like Craig." As soon as I said it, even though I knew it was true, I felt ashamed.

"Snide's right," said Craig. "If they want to go alone, let's just leave it."

"OK. Well how about just me and you then," suggested Shane. "We could have a right laugh down by the river. And it's dead easy to get to on the train."

"Well it's up to you," I mumbled, sulkily.

Nothing more was said on the matter and, by the time Saturday came, I assumed they'd dropped the idea.

I arrived at Amanda's early and we walked down to the railway station. Here we caught the train into Birmingham. Then, after a short wait, we found ourselves on the slow, stopping train to Stratford.

"Well this is nice isn't it?" said Amanda, reclining in her seat and stretching out her legs.

"Hmm," I replied, looking her up and down and fancying her.

"Time better spent than hanging round with those two idiots," she added.

"What, Shane and Craig?" I asked.

"Of course, Shane and Craig!" she exclaimed. "Mr Cool and The God Squad! Honestly, I don't know how you choose your friends."

"They're alright," I protested, half heartedly.

I turned to look out of the train window at the countryside flashing past. In a way it seemed to mirror my own life. Everything was changing and here I was sitting back in my seat as a mere spectator, allowing it all to happen. Whatever the circumstances though, I was happy right in the here and now with Amanda opposite me. If this was the future, then I was fully prepared to buy into it.

We talked , joked and flirted, enjoying every moment of each other's company.

Then, the connecting door to the next carriage opened and I heard a familiar voice.

"Don't worry about money Craig. I've got plenty of cash on me. You just say what you want to do and I'll . . . " Shane stopped in mid sentence as he spotted me and Amanda.

"Snide!" he declared. "And Amanda. Fancy seeing you two here. Don't tell me you're going to Stratford too."

"Hello Shane," said Amanda politely, looking him and Craig up and down with some annoyance.

She leaned over to me and whispered; "What's *he* doing here? Seeing Shane's bad enough but did he have to bring *The God Squad* with him?"

Immediately I felt annoyed. Annoyed with Amanda for being so rude about my friend and annoyed with Shane for putting us all in this situation.

Shane and Craig sat down on the seats facing us.

"You Ok Snide?" asked Craig looking slightly embarrassed.

"Yes thanks Craig. It's good to see you man," I replied, more to make a point to Amanda than anything.

"You're looking good Amanda," said Shane, trying his best to turn on the charm.

"Thank you," said Amanda rather coldly, pulling her dress down firmly to cover her knees.

The rest of the journey, which up to that point had flown by, seemed to take forever. All four of us sat, mostly in silence with Shane trying unsuccessfully to strike up a conversation.

Finally we pulled into the station and people began to disembark.

"Well it was very nice seeing you two," said Amanda, primly as she got up. "But we have tickets to the theatre."

"Matinee doesn't start until two," said Shane. "And it's only half eleven. How about I treat you all to some lunch. I can pay. I've got plenty of cash."

"Yes, you already told everyone on the train that earlier," I remarked, giving Shane a withering look.

"OK well the offer was there," he said, sounding a little disappointed. "Do you want to go down to the river Craig?"

"Yeah, great," replied Craig, obviously relieved to get away.

Any thoughts of splitting up though, were soon quashed when we realised that both the theatre and the river were in the same direction from the station.

Shane fell in with Amanda so I took the opportunity to apologise to Craig about Amanda's behaviour towards him.

"That's OK," said Craig, amiably. "It's water off a duck's back to me. I've had far worse."

"So why was Shane so keen to come here today?" I asked.

"I really don't know," replied Craig. "He's been acting really strange recently. Haven't you noticed?"

234

"What do you mean, strange?" I asked.

"Well, sort of clingy really," answered Craig. "I can't quite put my finger on it. I mean we all like to hang out, but at the moment he seems obsessed with us all doing stuff together."

I thought about Craig's words and realised that there was some truth in what he was saying.

"So why do you think he's acting like that?" I asked.

"I don't know," replied Craig. "But something's going on in his world that he's not telling us about."

"Maybe it's because we're finishing school," I suggested. "Actually, now I come to think about it, there was something odd the other day. Do you remember when I was talking to him about having a laugh when we started sixth form in September."

"Not really," said Craig. "What about it?"

"Well, he didn't reply. He just looked away. He looked, sort of sad. I don't know. I can't explain it either, but you're right. There is something. Maybe he'll tell us when he's ready."

I looked across at the Shane and Amanda, deep in conversation. A twinge of jealousy hit me.

"Oh look Amanda," I interrupted. "Here on the left. It's Shakespeare's birthplace. Do you want to go inside and look around?"

"Ooh yes please!" replied Amanda.

"Right, well maybe we'll see you two later," I said to Shane and Craig.

Once they were out of earshot, I decided to ask Amanda if she knew anything.

"Nothing I'm aware of," she replied. "Maybe he's going to do his 'A' levels at college. After all, he was talking about going on to study law at university. So he'd have to get an 'A' level in that first, surely. And I don't think they do law at Streetside."

"Yes. You're probably right," I said.

With Shakespeare's birthplace done, we still had an hour to go until the start of the performance, so Amanda and I found ourselves wandering down to the river to buy ourselves ice creams. The sun was quite strong now and, having finished my '99 with a flake' I lay down on the grass with my head on Amanda's lap.

It was nice to see Craig and Shane but I really wanted today to be about just me and her. And now that we were alone again, it felt like a perfect moment. It was as if we were enclosed in a bubble, isolating us from the rest of the world - a bubble so strong that nothing or nobody could penetrate it.

I sighed contentedly and closed my eyes.

"Oh my God," said Amanda suddenly pointing. "Look!"

Sitting up I followed her gaze. At first I couldn't see anything out of the ordinary. It was a normal, busy summer scene - families and small groups of friends spread out on the grass, picnicking, playing or just talking, and beyond them, the river, full of rowing boats all moving in various directions.

Then I saw it.

One boat, going frantically round and round in circles. Eventually it stopped and drifted slowly downstream, its two occupants apparently having some kind of a disagreement. Then the frantic rowing began again. Even from this distance, I recognised its two man crew. It was Shane and Craig.

"Oh my God!" I cried out. "What are they doing?"

Amanda cracked up, laughing. "Shane wanted us all to go out as a foursome, you know," she laughed. "Good job we didn't. Not with those two rowing anyway. We could maybe hire a boat, after we've seen the play though. What do you think?"

"No thanks!" I said, abruptly.

"Oh, OK," said Amanda, in surprise. "I just thought it might be fun."

"It's not that," I said, nervously. "It's just that I can't . . . well . . . I can't swim, actually."

"You can't swim!" repeated Amanda in disbelief. "How come?"

I went on to tell her about my near drowning experience at the age of six and how it had given me such a fear of water that I'd found it impossible to learn.

"Oh Snide!" cried Amanda, hugging me. "You poor thing." She stopped, deep in thought for a moment. "You know what? I'm going to teach you."

"No but."

"No buts," said Amanda, putting her finger to my lips. "I'm going to teach you."

I kissed her outstretched finger, more in relief than anything - relief that she hadn't ridiculed me.

"OK," I said , softy. "It's a deal."

We got up and walked over to the edge of the water. By this point, Craig and Shane had apparently regained control of their boat and were gradually making their way upstream towards the bank.

"Hey Craig. Shane!" I bellowed.

I saw Shane point in our direction, then Craig, who had his back to me, turned and gradually their boat changed direction and started, still rather erratically, to make its way towards us.

After what seemed an age, they pulled up alongside the bank a little downstream from us.

"How long have we got?" I asked.

"Curtain's up in thirty minutes," answered Amanda. "Come on, let's just go and say a polite hello to them then we'd better go."

The sun was beginning to set when, tired and hungry, we trudged out onto the platform of Stratford-Upon-Avon station. Amongst a handful of passengers, two familiar figures were sitting on a bench already waiting for the train.

"Be nice to Craig, please," I said quietly.

Amanda looked at me and nodded.

I sat down next to them whilst Amanda went to study the timetable on the wall of the waiting room.

"So how was Shakespeare?" asked Shane in a slightly mocking tone.

"Really good actually," I answered. "So much easier to understand when you've got an expert sitting next to you."

"Oh Romeo, Romeo, wherefore art thou Romeo?" cried Craig throwing his arms out to Shane.

"I'm over here my lover," shouted Shane in reply, laughing.

"Shows how much you know," I said. "Wherefore means why actually. She was asking him why did he have to belong to that family."

"Oooh quite the expert yourself now," laughed Shane.

"Yeah," I said. "I'm almost looking forward to my English Literature exam now. I think I'll answer just the Romeo and Juliet questions and leave the rest.

"No Dickens?" asked Shane.

"No."

"Keats?"

"No."

Amanda rejoined us.

"Snide here reckons he's an expert on Shakespeare now," said Shane.

"Not yet," replied Amanda, putting her arm firmly around my shoulder, pulling me towards her and away from Shane. "But he will be, once I've finished with him."

Monday 23rd June - Final Exams

It was a strange feeling, walking back into school after the shenanigans of leavers day. But the school seemed to have come out of it all unscathed. The teachers were okay about it as well. It was as if nothing had ever happened.

However, there was something new and very different about examinations. We were left in no doubt about that. This was serious. Even the most laid back of our teachers were remarkably formal during the process of invigilation. Looking back now on those days, I guess the teachers had as much invested in our success as we did. Poor exam results reflected badly on the school and its teachers and there could be no doubt, given the outlandish behaviour of some fifth form pupils in the last few weeks, that there was a certain nervousness amongst the staff about how this particular year group would perform as a whole.

They needn't have worried. We were all to learn later, on results day, that the overall grades in both 'O' levels and CSEs were the highest the school had ever achieved. How difficult that must have been for our headmaster to swallow!

As far as the three of us were concerned, Shane and I met several times in school over the exam period - after all we were both doing 'O' levels. We didn't however, cross paths with Craig at all. Being in the lower sets, Craig was put in for less prestigious CSEs in all subjects.

Forty or so years later, I can remember very little of this time. I knew I was blessed with an ability to excel in examinations and so, can remember walking into each one with my head held high and full of confident expectation.

Shane, on the other hand, was more of a worrier. This was undoubtedly due in no small part to the increasing pressure his parents were putting him under. As the first exams approached, Craig and I saw very little of him. He later told me harrowing tales of being forced to revise for several hours every day and of his various devious methods for relieving the pressure.

Amongst these was his brand new Sony Walkman which he had bought earlier in the year and stashed away in his bedroom. It allowed him to listen to music during his long, lonely hours spent in confinement.

Craig was a different case altogether. His mum and stepdad had no aspirations for him at all. Instead, he'd been told quite bluntly by Jim that, as soon as the last exam was over, he was to go down the job centre and get a job so that he could start contributing towards his keep. It seemed ironic to me that this came from a man who had avoided paid work in all the time that he had been a part of Craig's life.

As luck would have it, I found myself sitting in a desk alongside Shane for what was to be our final exam. I can clearly remember that it was a very easy maths paper. So much so that, despite being given two hours, Shane and I (and several other pupils) finished it within an hour.

This left us with a major problem - what were we to do with the final hour. Some schools allowed pupils to leave early if they felt they'd finished their exam. Streetside Comprehensive was not one of them. Instead, we were expected to go over our answers again and again to 'check, double check, triple check,' as our maths teacher had kept reminding us in our final few lessons with him.

To make matters worse, on this particular day, the teacher in charge was one whose real name eludes me to this day but, who we all referred to as Dr Death! With huge staring eyes, a receding hairline accompanied by a vast unkempt beard and a great, hulking body, he was a perfect teacher for ridicule.

And with nothing better to do, it was only a matter of time before someone started to mimic him. That someone in this case turned out to be Shane. With his head laid on the desk, in order not to be seen he opened his eyes really widely and frowned at me. My immediate reaction was to laugh but, of course under exam conditions, we were all expected to sit in absolute silence.

I stifled a giggle, triggering Shane off in the process. Hearing our sniggers, another boy from our maths set who was sat in front of Shane, turned round.

Shane checked the coast was clear before pulling the face at him too. At first we thought the boy didn't get it, but then his lip began to tremble and he threw his head down on to his desk to bury his laughing.

Gradually, the giggling, sniggering and guffawing spread throughout the exam hall, like ripples on a pond, eventually drawing the attention of Dr Death himself.

"Err silence," he ordered, getting slowly to his feet, his bulging eyes nervously surveying the room. This only served to make matters worse. At the time it seemed hilarious but I guess the poor man must have been frightened to death of losing control of the situation.

With half an hour remaining, Dr Death was replaced by another teacher but by this point, it was too late. We were now laughing for the sake of laughing. Fortunately it appeared that nearly everyone in the room had now finished and shortly after taking over, the replacement teacher took the unusual step of saying that any of us who wanted to leave could hold our completed papers in the air. Then, having collected them all in, he told us we were free to go.

As soon as we were outside, Shane again pulled the Dr Death face at me and this time we both collapsed in a heap laughing until tears ran down our faces.

We walked home slowly that day, revelling in our new found freedom.

"Well that's it until September," I said. "Then we'll be sixth formers."

"Yes," said Shane, quietly. "Snide, are you hurrying off home? I just thought we might call for Craig. He finished two days ago you know."

"Yeah, OK," I said, in surprise.

We carried on walking in silence to Craig's house, Shane seemingly lost in his own thoughts, a strange turn of events it seemed considering we'd had such a laugh that afternoon.

Craig let us in and took us upstairs to his room. We told him about Dr Death, then sat around chatting for a while.

Then Shane, who had been rather quiet, suddenly butted into the conversation. "Boys, there's something I need to tell you."

We both stopped and looked at him. Whatever it was, it was obviously serious.

"I'm moving away," he said.

Neither Craig nor I said a word.

"My dad is starting his own business on the south side of Birmingham so we're moving to a new house in Solihull."

"When are you going?" I asked.

"The end of next week," said Shane. "I was going to tell you sooner but exams got in the way and I wasn't quite sure how to break it to you both. I mean, we've been best mates for nearly six years now."

"Jesus," I muttered. "I'll miss you Shane."

"Me too Big Man," added Craig, patting Shane on the shoulder.

By way of reply, Shane said nothing.

He didn't need to.

Friday 27ᵗʰ June - New Perspectives

Amanda and I had gone for a long walk in the countryside to mark the start of the summer holidays. Pausing at a field of ripening wheat, we both clambered up onto the padlocked gate and sat with our legs dangling just above the thick bed of nettles that grew around its base.

"I know you've been such good friends for years," she said on hearing of Shane's news. "You must be pretty gutted." She put her arm around me and hugged as best she could without either of us losing our balance.

"What I don't understand," I began. "Is why you didn't see the for sale sign outside his house."

"Oh, I know why that is," replied Amanda. "They're renting it out. My dad told me last night."

"Renting it out?" I said. "That's a bit odd isn't it?"

"Not really," replied Amanda. "They've rented the house in Solihull for twelve months to see how things go. If they're not happy, they're going to move back here. I think it was Shane's mum who pushed for the move to a posher area. You know what she's like."

I nodded in reply.

"It still all seems so strange though," I said. "It feels like everything is changing. Me, Shane and Craig have been so close for so many years. I still can't get my head round it."

"Yes. Well you've got me know," said Amanda, kissing me gently on the cheek. "We all have to grow up and move on."

"I suppose so," I muttered, avoiding her loving gaze. "I think Craig took it pretty badly. He didn't say much at the time, but I could tell by the look on his face. He's always admired Shane you know."

"Hmm," replied Amanda, pulling a slightly disapproving face. "Well, I'm sure he will be fine with all his friends in The God Squad to support him."

"And me!" I added.

Amanda looked at me patiently. "And you," she finally replied. "But you know what I think?"

"What?"

"I think it was Shane that kept you three together. I mean to say, what have you and Craig really got in common?"

"We have a history. Six years of friendship. And we've been in a few scrapes during those years."

"Yes, but you can't keep hanging on to the past. What's gone is gone.Craig's a different person now. You've said so yourself. He's got a new group of friends, new interests. It's time for you to start looking forward. To the future. Our future!"

I continued to stare down into the nettles. I couldn't help feeling that, despite her sympathetic words, Amanda was quite pleased that Shane was leaving. It gave her the perfect excuse to drive a wedge between me and Craig so she could have her all to myself.

I reflected on the reality of my new situation. Whilst it was a good thing that Craig, Shane and myself had had such a tight friendship, the downside was that outside of our gang, we had very few friends at all. I felt sure that Amanda was right about Craig. He would no doubt now throw himself much more into his work with the church and local youth club.

For me however, it was a different case entirely. I was not a naturally gregarious person and had difficulty making friends. The outlook on that particular front was now bleak. And whilst Amanda was correct in her assertion that my future lay with her, I did feel rather stifled, even trapped by the developing situation.

"You're very quiet," said Amanda, interrupting my thoughts. "Are you OK?"

"Yes, fine," I replied, swinging my legs back over the gate and jumping down.

Amanda brought one leg over then held her arms outstretched to enable me to help her down. I allowed her to grasp the back of my neck then grabbed her waist as she lowered herself to the ground. As she did so, she fell forwards into my arms and I briefly smelt her warm femininity.

I immediately felt aroused, but at the same time confused. Did I really feel the same emotionally about Amanda as she did about me? Or was my attraction to her purely physical? Momentarily a wave of guilt swept over me. Then, feeling her nuzzling my neck, I responded with a long, passionate kiss.

Yes. Maybe it was physical. But it was too damn good to throw away.

For the moment anyway.

Monday 30th June - Parting of The Ways . . .

Craig and I had come to an understanding with Shane fairly early on in our friendship with regards to his mother. Mrs Small, he told us in no uncertain terms, was very house proud and didn't want horrible children dirtying her carpets and furniture.

Consequently, in the six or so years we'd known each other, we had never been to Shane's house. If we arranged to meet, it would always be at the bottom of his road. That was the way it was and we never questioned it.

However, the news that Shane would be moving away in a few days, changed all that.

It was me that suggested the bold step of actually knocking on Shane's door unannounced. Craig was a bit uncertain. He didn't want to feel that we were compromising our friendship with Shane just before he moved away. However, after a bit of gentle persuasion, he went along with it.

Shane's road was one of the poshest in Streetside and only the wealthiest lived there. You could tell it was a bit special because, unlike where Craig and I lived, each house had it's own individual design. I guess they were built around the early twentieth century, most of them having mock Tudor gables and leaded windows.

As we approached, we passed Amanda's house, then stood at the bottom of the drive. I could feel a knot in my stomach at the prospect of coming face to face with Shane's mum and I could see that Craig was equally hesitant.

"Come on," I said, nervously. "We're doing no harm."

We walked slowly and purposefully up the long drive then stopped at the large, oak panelled door. To the left of the door was a metal pull with a triangular handle at the bottom.

"Is that to ring the bell or flush the toilet?" I asked, stifling a giggle.

Craig bit his lip.

Grabbing the handle I gave it a firm tug and a distant bell rang from somewhere within the house. Just as it seemed as though our call was going to go unanswered, we heard footsteps. Then the door opened and there stood Mrs Small. Unlike Shane and his dad, who were both large and heavily built, his mum was slight and quite short - nothing like I'd imagined her.

"Oh!" she said in surprise as she looked us up and down. "I suppose you've come calling for Shane."

"Yes please, thank you Mrs Small," replied Craig getting his words jumbled up in his nervousness.

Again, I stifled a giggle. This time it was over the aptness of her name!

She cast me a suspicious look and said; "Yes, yes, I know, small by name, small by nature." This time I couldn't help myself and laughed out loud, then checked myself.

"It's alright boy," she said, half a smile flickering across her face. "I do have a sense of humour."

I breathed a sigh of relief. At least she seemed to like me.

"Well. Come in then," she began. I stepped forward but was rewarded with Mrs Small's outstretched hand blocking my path. "After you have taken your shoes off!" she ordered.

"Oh gosh, sorry!" I blurted out.

"Yes sorry Mrs Small. Thank you, " echoed Craig.

We tiptoed into the hall and took in our surroundings. It was a vast, high ceilinged affair, with a balcony running all the way around the top.

My attention was caught however by Mrs Small staring quizzically at Craig's feet. Following her eyes down, I could quite clearly see her concern. It was Craig's socks or what was left of them between the many holes through which stuck various toes.

"My mum can't afford any new ones yet," mumbled Craig.

"Take them off," barked Mrs Small in a brisk, but not aggressive way.

Craig did as he was told and Mrs Small whipped them from his hands and dropped them in a bin which was positioned at the bottom of the staircase.

"Shane," she shouted up the stairs. "There's two friends here to see you." She paused to look once again at Craig. "And bring a fresh pair of socks down with you, will you."

After a short pause, one of the bedroom doors opened and a confused looking Shane appeared at the balcony clutching a pair of black socks.

"What are you doing here?" he gasped looking first at us, then at the retreating figure of his mother.

"We've come to call for you," said Craig. "And your mum just threw my socks in the bin."

Quickly, Shane descended the staircase and handed Craig the socks.

"They're a bit big for you," he said, slightly embarrassed. "I'm size eleven. What size are you?"

"Six," said Craig. "But tell your mum thanks anyway. I can't remember the last time I had socks without holes in."

Shane led us into the dining room and sat us down around the table.

"Well?" said Mrs Small, brusquely as she entered the room. "You haven't introduced us Shane."

"Oh, this is Craig and this is err . . Snide."

"Snide?" said Mrs Small. "That's a funny name."

"It's just my nickname," I replied.

"Yes, we always call him Snide," interrupted Shane.

"Hmmph" said Mrs Small. "Snide by name, Snide by nature is it?"

I laughed at her joke.

"Well I don't need you boys cluttering my house any longer than necessary," said Mrs Small firmly.

"Ok mum," said Shane. "We'll go out then."

"Back by five!" shouted Mrs Small as we headed for the front door.

Once outside, Shane was the first to laugh. "So you finally met my mum," he said.

"She's alright," I replied.

"Very generous," added Craig as he inspected his new socks for one last time before slipping them into his battered old corduroy trainers.

"What do you want to do then?" asked Shane.

"Something special," I announced. "This could be the last time we ever do anything together."

"I think it will be," replied Shane, sadly. "I've got all my stuff to pack tomorrow. Then Wednesday we're off to Solihull."

"Let's go the den!" said Craig suddenly.

"The den?" I exclaimed, in surprise. "Christ, we haven't been there since last summer."

"It would certainly be a trip down memory lane," added Shane.

"So let's do it then!" cried Craig.

We were surprised as we approached, that the pathway leading up to the doorway of the den was clear.

"Someone else must have been using it," said Craig, leading the way.

We followed Craig in and took in the musty damp smell.

It's funny how smell evokes memories far more clearly than any other of the senses.

"Remember what it smelt like when Viktor was living here?" I said.

"Stunk of piss," replied Shane.

"We never did know what became of him," added Craig. "Never saw sight nor sound of him, ever again."

"He saved our lives you know, when we got trapped in here by that fire" I said, looking up at the hole in the roof through which he'd pulled us.

"How stupid was I then?" remarked Craig. "Making you set fire to his belongings to prove your loyalty to the gang. Poor man."

"I don't think he ever knew," said Shane. "That we set fire to his things deliberately, I mean. I think he thought it was just a grass fire that got out of hand."

"It certainly was a dry summer," I added. "Do you remember the thunder storms that broke the drought?"

"How could I forget," replied Craig. "One of the houses on our road got struck by lightning. The whole roof went up in flames. Do you know, I actually stood outside when the fire brigade came, pointing and laughing. I can't believe I was such a nasty little so and so."

"We were just kids," said Shane reassuringly. "You're a better person now man."

"Well, I just hope I'm forgiven," said Craig, gloomily. "By him upstairs."

"I'm sure you are," replied Shane.

"I'll tell you what else I remember about the summer of 1976," I said, grinning. "Eric's bonfires!"

"Wow yeah!" cried Craig. "How he never set fire to the whole woods sometimes, I'll never know."

"Well, we used to help clear around the edges when the flames got too hot," I said. "Do you remember?"

"I think we should go down and see him now," suggested Shane. "It's been some time."

We all agreed and, having scrambled down one side of the cutting, we made our way towards the park.

"I hope he's there," said Shane. "It would be a shame to leave without saying goodbye."

As we emerged from the woods into the park itself, we could see no sign of Eric.

"Let's try the pavilion," said Shane.

We walked around to the front of the building where it faced onto the bowling green and could see that the door was slightly ajar.

I poked my head in. "Anyone around?" I called.

There was no reply, just the sound of what appeared to be something heavy being dragged around in the next room.

We all three ventured inside to investigate. Suddenly Eric appeared in the doorway.

Although so much had happened in our lives over the last four years, Eric was the one constant which, reassuringly, never changed. It may have been 1980 but he was still wearing his familiar flared trousers and dark glasses and reeked of petula oil.

"Dudes!" he cried, opening his arms in an exaggerated gesture of welcome. "Where have you been these last few weeks?"

"We've been busy," I explained. "Taking exams."

"Huh, you don't need exams. I didn't have to take no 'O' levels in fire starting or park keeping for my job, did I?"

We all laughed.

"I'm with you there," said Craig. "You don't need no qualifications to love your fellow man either."

"I need them though, if I'm going to follow my dad and become a solicitor," said Shane.

"Anyway," said Eric, suddenly serious. "You dudes won't be seeing much of me any more."

"Why not?" I asked.

"I've lost my job. Been made redundant."

"What? Seriously?" gasped Craig. "But who's going to hire out he bowls and all that stuff?"

"Nobody," replied Eric. "The pavilion is being decommissioned. The council can't afford to run it any more. It's the cut backs."

"What will you do?" I asked.

"Probably go back to being a roadie. I've still got plenty of contacts in the music business."

We stood dumbly, taking all of this in. So much for Eric being the one constant in our lives.

"You won't be seeing me either," said Shane, after a long pause. "I'm moving to Solihull the day after tomorrow."

"Actually, I've got some news as well," said Craig, awkwardly. "Tomorrow, I'm finally entering the adult world."

"What do you mean?" I asked.

"I've got a job," replied Craig.

"Where?" asked Shane.

"Working as a labourer on a building site. You know I told you Jim said I had to get a job. Well I went down the Job Centre on Friday. And that's where I got it. I had to go into town on Saturday and buy the special boots and everything."

"So it looks like we're all moving on," concluded Shane.

"Except me," I said. "I'll still be living in boring Streetside, going to Streetside School Sixth Form."

"We can still meet up some weekends," said Craig. "You could come and help out at the youth club. We always need extra hands."

I didn't reply.

"I tell you what dudes," said Eric. "I've got some cider out the back. Let's drink a toast to moving on."

We followed Eric into the back room where all of his work gear and bowls paraphernalia had been neatly packed into boxes.

He rummaged around in one of the boxes and pulled out a large bottle of Woodpecker cider and three chipped mugs.

"Not for me," said Craig, firmly. "I don't touch that stuff any more."

"How long's it been now?" asked Eric.

"Ten months, eight days since my accident," answered Craig. "And I haven't touched a drop since."

"Well done man," said Eric, patting him on the shoulder. "But if you don't mind us mere mortals having a cupful."

"Of course not," said Craig.

We sat and sipped at our cider.

"Remember when you were all punks?" said Eric, laughing.

"Yeah and Shane had that hair brained scheme to start a car washing business," I added.

"On someone else's patch, mind you," said Shane, smiling.

"Tweedledum and Tweedledee!" I cried, remembering the overweight twins who ran the rival business.

"Oh, and the man whose car aerial we broke," laughed Craig.

"And the time you ate that man's fertiliser cos you thought it was cocaine," I said.

We sat for a while reflecting on our happy memories.

"And which summer was it that you dudes had all those parties?" asked Eric.

"1978," I answered. "Do you remember Craig? You kept trying to cop off with Terri Donnerly."

"I don't remember much about any of those parties, I was too drunk," answered Craig. "But what about you Snide? You and Abigail Jones. You never did tell us what you got up to at that party of yours."

"Didn't I?" I replied, obtusely.

"No you didn't," grinned Shane.

All three of them look at me expectantly.

"You really want to know?" I asked.

"Yes!" they chorused.

I hesitated for a moment then shook my head. "Not a lot really. Just a bit of a snog and a grope."

We finished our cider and said our goodbyes to Eric.

Then, a few short minutes later, it was time to say goodbye to Shane.

"Stay in touch Big Man," I said.

"Sure thing man," replied Shane. "I'll give you a call just as soon as we're settled in." And with that he turned and sauntered off up his driveway, turning just once to wave goodbye.

I walked with Craig back to his house but he had a long list of things to do before starting his new job so he also said his goodbyes.

Which left me to walk home alone with my memories.

But what memories!

. . . . AND FINALLY

I never did get that phone call from Shane. At first, I assumed he was busy, but as days turned into weeks, it became obvious that he had moved on and I wasn't going to hear from him.

I did meet him once more though. It was several months later. I was in town when I saw him with a large group of friends. I was unsure whether to say hello but, spotting me he came over and high fived me. He was soon giving it big in front of his new mates, not at all the quiet, reserved Shane I'd grown up with but, as we parted, I noticed a familiar glint of affection in his eyes as he lowered his voice.

"Hey Colin, take care man," he said, gripping my hand in an all too familiar vice like grip.

"You too Big Man," I replied, smiling.

It felt something of a shock hearing my real name coming from someone who'd always referred to me as Snide. I suppose it was a signal that we'd both finally grown up and moved on.

I never saw Shane again, although I heard on the grapevine that he went on to graduate in law and opened up his own legal practice specialising in compensation, somewhere up north.

And what of Craig, you may ask?

Well, we saw each other from time to time, but he was often busy helping out with church initiatives, or down the youth club. And, of course he was holding down a full time job. We still had some laughs though, catching up over a pint down the local pub every so often (well, I had a pint - Craig never touched alcohol for the rest of his life).

Then, quite suddenly, he was gone.

I can still clearly remember first reading about it in the local newspaper. 'Young builder falls to death from scaffolding,' was the headline - or something like that. I later found out that his employer had been sued by Craig's Mum and Jim for an insecure handrail that had given way under Craig's weight as he leant on it.

It seemed such a cruel twist of fate for a young man who had finally sorted out his demons and had his whole life in front of him. He'd even just began to settle into a long term relationship with a girl he'd met at church. He was just nineteen years old.

And what about me - Colin?

Well, my great romance fizzled out soon after the summer of 1980. It turned out that I was right about my feelings towards Amanda. Despite our strong physical attraction, it soon became clear that we had very little in common.

All of which left me quite isolated for a time. But slowly, I met new friends in sixth form, then ditched them for more new friends at university.

Then, having graduated, I walked into a job I hated and spent the next thirty five years in it.

Finally, having taken early retirement, I decided at the age of fifty six to try turning my hand to becoming an author.

But that's another story entirely . . . . .

CPSIA information can be obtained
at www.ICGtesting.com
Printed in the USA
LVHW100731271022
731694LV00014B/287/J